HEAT LIGHTNING

HEAT
LIGHTNING

John Lantigua

G. P. PUTNAM'S SONS
New York

G. P. Putnam's Sons
Publishers Since 1838
200 Madison Avenue
New York, NY 10016

Library of Congress Cataloging-in-Publication Data

Lantigua, John.
Heat lightning.

I. Title.
PS3562.A57H43   1987   813'.54   87-10744
ISBN 0-399-13300-3

Printed in the United States of America
1   2   3   4   5   6   7   8   9   10

Many thanks to the men and women of Mission Station, San Francisco Police Department, to Inspector Prentice Sanders of the Homicide Detail and to Paul Goepfert for his friendship and counsel during the writing of this book.

This book is for Maria.

CHAPTER 1

Homicide Inspector David Cruz arrived at the empty lot on Twenty-first Street at 4:15 on a Saturday afternoon that had San Francisco as hot as the Mojave Desert. The fog that usually rolls off the Pacific to cool the coast in August was taking its sweet time offshore, and the city was sweating its way through a killer heat wave. Still, it was clear the young woman lying on the cracked, dry earth hadn't died of heat prostration. In Cruz's experience young Latin women didn't die from the heat, which meant there had to be another cause of death. From the look on her terrified face, at least, it appeared someone had scared her to death.

A priest had beaten Cruz to the scene. In his black robes and bright purple stole he leaned over the girl, his hands moving in the air like a magician's. A Latina girl would almost certainly want to deal with a priest before a cop, Cruz figured. He walked away and waited his turn.

In the street a large and noisy crowd had gathered and a ghetto blaster sounded. Santana was being seduced by a black magic woman: "Tryin' to make a devil out of me."

The block was mostly Latin, but in the audience there was a bit of everything you found in the barrio these days, all the races of the earth. Oriental women, distracted from their Saturday shopping, watched the proceedings from under brightly colored parasols. White folks squinted in the glaring sunlight. In the very front row, a black kid in a baseball hat licked a pink ice-cream cone. As far as he was concerned, he was at a Saturday matinee, this time with a real live corpse.

The sun pulsed in a high blue sky. Cruz mopped his neck and licked his dry lips. You cursed the fog, but once it cleared, the sun cooked your senses. Before the call had come from Communications, he had been holed up in his Bartlett Street flat, sipping a cold Dos Equis, watching the temperature rise in the thermometer and just waiting for it to happen. If any-thing, Cruz knew he had wanted something to happen. If you told somebody that, it wouldn't sound right—like you wanted people to get blown away. That wasn't it. But if you had to choose between sitting around an empty apartment that still smelled of "her," who had just walked out on you, or going to a murder scene, it was no contest. There were days when a stiff was better company than no company at all.

"She's a fox, isn't she?" someone said behind him.

Cruz turned, but the ambulance jockeys were talking about the dead girl, not about his wife. The priest was still painting crosses on the girl.

Cruz scuffed the dirt with his white shoe. He was short and wiry, with thick black hair, bronze skin and a face chiseled by his years growing up on the streets of the city's Mission District. From those years, he had inherited a nose that was slightly crooked and the nervous energy that came from always being small, but never giving ground. When he questioned the witnesses and suspects, he was in constant motion, like a bantamweight boxer, bobbing and nodding in agreement, wincing in consolation. Until someone tried to jive him. Then he froze, his head tilted cynically and the gaze in his jet-black eyes sharpened, like a shiv used in a street fight.

Now his crooked nose twitched. The smell of fried pork

rinds, *chicharrón,* drifted out of a nearby kitchen. Wonderful on the tastebuds, but murder on the arteries. He looked at the surrounding houses, old, rambling Victorians that never dreamed they would be inhabited by this mixture of humanity that now crowded the Mission—the odors, the strange languages, the foreign faces. The melting pot, they called it, a slowly cooking stew of Latins, assorted Orientals and Arabs, blacks and whites, with some Bombay Indians, Hmong tribesmen and other spices thrown in for flavor. The place was a zoo. It was on this very street that, during his days on the beat, Cruz had answered a complaint and found a Cambodian man in a third-floor walkup tending a half dozen goats. It had come as a great surprise to the man that he was breaking the law.

And sometimes the law was broken in more serious ways. In the rhetoric of the local politicians, the district was "a model for multiracial understanding," "a mosaic of ethnic diversity and tolerance." But that was only until the heat hit. Then the juice began to flow, the beer and the Caribbean rum, the rice wine and the rotgut. The melting pot boiled over, and pieces of the mosaic came unglued.

One of them had come unglued—from the looks of her, very unglued—and had fallen on Twenty-first Street.

The priest stood up now, made one last pass over the girl and moved away. His face was covered in sweat. When Cruz was very small, growing up in the Mission, he had believed that priests were extraterrestrials, that they didn't sweat, that they didn't sin, that they didn't die. But back then he had also believed he would find a wife, a one true love, and live happily ever after.

The white-coated ambulance men and uniformed patrolmen began to close in on her.

"Give 'er some air," Cruz said, squeezing through, and he crouched next to the body.

"She's one of yours." That's what Communications had told him over the phone. It was true she looked like she might be Mexican, but maybe from farther south too. These days a lot were coming from farther south, particularly El Salvador and Guatemala. She was around twenty and, as they said, a fox. In other circumstances, at least, she had been beautiful. But now she had been dead a while: long enough so the pallor of death had already mixed with her clear mahogany skin and had drained the color from her full lips. Her mouth was open in a cry and her dark brown eyes were fixed on the sky straight above, as full of fear as dead eyes could be. A good scary face for the black boy and the rest of the matinee audience. Any actress could have duplicated the look of fear, but not that deadness at the bottom of her eyes. That was for real.

"Christ, it looks like they scared her to death, doesn't it?" he said. The ambulance men grunted.

Cruz exhaled through his nose to expel the odor. He took out his notebook, wrote down a description of the woman and then checked out her clothes. Her get-up was strange; you might call it schizo. She wore a gauzy, see-through black blouse unbuttoned to mid-chest and you saw a black lace bra and the tops of dark brown breasts. Strapped to her feet were gaudy spike heels, designed to add four inches to her small stature. But she also wore a long, modest, old-fashioned red skirt, like peasant women still wore down south, and around her throat hung a thin gold choker and a small gold cross just like a good Catholic Latin girl would wear. Between the see-through blouse and the gold cross she was sending a mixed message: You can have my body, but you can't have my soul, she was saying.

Cruz wrote a description of the clothes and shifted position. The wound—he could see evidence of only one—was at the back of her head and that also was as real as could be, not the work of any makeup artist. It had left a small puddle of coagulated blood beneath her. It was a clean job of killing, not like some of the bloody messes Cruz had to wade through. He craned over to get a close look and saw the girl's hands pulled around behind her back in an awkward position. They were tied together, not at the wrists as you might expect, but by the thumbs. They were tied with black waxed string, so tightly it had broken the skin on both thumbs, leaving the flesh there more swollen and discolored than the other fingers. The girl had not been tied anywhere else and he saw no other wounds.

He looked up at the big blond uniformed cop named Wyman who had answered the original call.

"This is the position she was in? Right in this spot?"

"Uh-huh, right there," Wyman said.

"Nobody touched her?"

"Not that we know."

Cruz looked back at the dead woman and frowned, as if she had said something that made no sense. You tied the thumbs so she couldn't fight you off, did what you wanted, threw her face-down, put the gun to the base of the skull and popped her. Then you disposed of the body and walked away with a nice clean job done.

That's what made sense. Except that's not what the guy had done. Carved into the dirt next to the body was the other detail Communications had told him about over the telephone. It was a drawing: a rough outline of an animal that looked like a bull. It had four legs, a thick body and two long horns that curved in the dirt right toward the girl's head. It was a signature and it reminded Cruz of the drawings made on cave walls in primitive times by hunters.

"Some sort of caveman must have been here, whaddya think?" he said.

"Could be," Wyman said, but you could tell he didn't know what Cruz was talking about.

Cruz rocked on his haunches and stared at the drawing in the dirt and the tied thumbs, as if they were mistakes of some kind. He wondered if she was illegal. If she was, did anybody even know her? There was that case where the coyote, the people smuggler, had taken money from illegals to sneak them across the border and left them in the desert to die of thirst. Cruz had read about it in the paper. This girl had made it farther. In her case, it was too far.

He stood up, walked away, cleared his nose of the smell, stared at the crowd, and mopped his neck.

On the street, death was exercising its fascination. There were kids everywhere, screeching like monkeys, climbing porches and lightpoles, trying to see the corpse. The sidewalks were lined with men in T-shirts on their day off and women in Saturday-afternoon hair curlers, with their arms crossed under their breasts, shaking their heads and muttering in a way that meant trouble. If you wanted proof that there were big problems in the world, all you had to do was talk to some of these people who had come to the Mission the past ten years—the Cambodians, the Salvadorans, Palestinians and others. Cruz had dealt with all of them. They could tell you stories to make your hair stand up. This girl lying dead, for that matter, she looked like she had one to tell.

Santana sang, "You got to change your evil ways, baby."

A siren approached and died up the block and the crowd stirred.

Then a short, balding black man with a goatee, carrying a doctor's satchel, came across the lot. He and Cruz exchanged greetings and the other man looked down and made a face.

"Jeez, look at that puss," he said.

He opened his satchel, took out a pair of plastic, disposable gloves. When he put them on you could see his sweaty black hands through them. Cruz looked away. The sight of plastic gloves always made him feel clammy.

"It's a nice face, if it wasn't all scared like that. Nice body, too," said the coroner's man.

"Don't fall in love on me," Cruz said crouching again next to the corpse. "Not in this heat."

"I'm saying, why would anybody kill all that?"

Cruz shook his head. Before they had split up, his wife had told him he spent too much time with the dead. "Maybe you understand corpses or killers, but you can't relate to real people. You have no belief in anybody," she'd told him. She was an artist, a painter with her head in the clouds. She never had to smell the dead. "Art and murder aren't compatible," he had told her over and over, until she had finally gone. That was over two months ago.

In the distance he heard the muddled crackle of a loud-speaker, another political demonstration on Twenty-fourth Street. She was probably there, chanting with the others, U.S. out of Central America, U.S. out of one place or another. She had always tried to drag him to the meetings and the speeches by the visiting guerrillas fresh from one jungle or another. He never went. They were going to tell him the world was messed up, violent and bloody. Given his job, that was something he already had down.

Cruz mopped his face.

"She was shot," he said to the black man. "You get close, you can see powder burns on her neck."

The other man leaned over to get a look at the wound. "Uh-huh. From the looks, the gun was right up against the skin." He pointed at the thumbs. "Strange way to tie someone, isn't it? Why not tie the wrists?"

"That would be easier and stronger, wouldn't it?" Cruz said.

"Maybe he didn't have enough cord," the black man said.

"Maybe," Cruz said. "Or maybe he was just being economical."

The black man nodded.

"He was economical, all right. One bullet right in the head." He exhaled out of his nose, frowned and pointed at the drawing. "What's this about? Some kinda art work?"

Cruz shrugged. "God knows," he said.

He got up and turned to Wyman, the patrolman. Wyman was broad-shouldered, with a drooping blond mustache and a way of standing with his thumbs hooked in his gunbelt, his feet far apart, that made him look like a Western marshal ready for a shootout. He was the image of Old West justice, while Cruz, in his Hawaiian shirt with the blue cresting waves and his white loafers, was the image of New West justice, he supposed.

"Whaddya have?" Cruz asked.

Wyman pulled a leather-covered notebook from his pocket. "She was found right around four," he said. "An old guy from Twenty-second Street walking his dog. The mutt wandered in here and started howling. The old guy said it almost gave him a heart attack, but he says he didn't touch anything."

"Any ID?"

"No wallet or purse," Wyman said. He removed a card from the notebook. "This was in her shirt pocket."

At the top of the card was printed "Mission Mental Health Clinic," a public facility just a few blocks away. The card said the bearer, G. Soto of 1797 Shotwell Street, was scheduled for an appointment Monday at 3:00 P.M.

"Rizzo went to the address to see if anybody can identify her," Wyman said, referring to another patrolman from Mission Station. "She does look a little crazy," he said.

"Scared out of her wits is more like it," Cruz said. "Recognize her?"

Wyman shrugged his big football shoulders. "Looks like she might be a hooker, but I don't recall her. Maybe she's new."

"Ya think so?" Cruz didn't take his eyes from the dead girl.

"The new ones are more likely to make mistakes, go off with some psycho," Wyman said. "Or maybe she was just out for the night, needed drug money or milk for the baby. That kind could go off with anybody."

"Maybe," Cruz said. But he didn't like Wyman jumping to conclusions, not about a nice Catholic Latin girl. A white girl dressed like that, he wouldn't think that about. "And maybe she's not a hooker at all," he said. "Sexy shoes, but lots of girls wear sexy shoes."

"It's the thumbs that made me think," Wyman said. "Looks like a sex thing, bondage." He shrugged.

"Could be," Cruz said without enthusiasm. "We want to ask the neighbors if they heard anything out here last night."

Wyman said something about shots, but Cruz shook him off.

"She wasn't shot here. Not enough blood around. She was killed somewhere else and dumped here. We want to ask if they heard someone dumping a body, a car door slamming, a trunk lid or someone walking out here. Try the neighbors. Hit the bars too for a few blocks around.

"Baby you gotta change," Santana sang.

His wife had told him, "You're trying to prove you don't know how to love. That there is no love. Well, you've proved it." Cruz was good at proving things.

Pigeons had landed on the eaves of the adjoining house, looking down on the body like vultures waiting for their pickings. Cruz grabbed a small rock out of the dirt, threw it and flushed them.

Out in the street the crowd had grown and the murmuring was louder. Some people had gone, others had arrived for the second seating. At the very front, in place of the black kid, Cruz spotted Joe the Actor, a grizzled local drunk who claimed he had once been a big star in the New York theater, a leading man who had made women swoon. He had a mane of white hair and deepset eyes and could be seen on the street delivering garbled soliloquies to passersby and to lightpoles. Like many drunks in San Francisco, he lived in the Mission because it was the warmest part of town. He slept in alleyways and doorways, with an empty wine bottle always standing guard. He was worthless, but he was harmless.

Now he stood on rocky feet, a grief-stricken face staring across the lot toward the dead girl, as if a director had instructed him to look as sad and miserable as could be. His lips were moving, but Cruz couldn't hear him.

Joe watched as the black man from the coroner's office finished his examination and stood up. Beads of sweat had formed on his bald black head.

"Last night," he said to Cruz, stripping off the plastic gloves. "Offhand, I'd say twelve to eighteen hours. No more than that, not in this heat."

"The one shot killed her?"

"Looks like it. One shot right up into the brain. We'll recover the slug when we get her on the table. I don't see any other wound and no sign of intravenous drug use. I can't tell about sexual molestation, but I don't see the usual superficial indications."

"No sign she put up a fight," Cruz said.

The coroner's man shook his head. "Her nails are nice and long and freshly painted. No breaks, no chips, no sign of skin or hair under them. Then again, if you have them tied behind your back, it's tough to defend yourself. I guess that was the idea."

"I guess," Cruz said.

Somewhere in the crowd another ghetto blaster sounded, somebody singing in Spanish:

It's your cunning, honey, that made you play and lose
It's your cunning, honey, that made you leave without paying

"We got a regular circus here," Cruz said to no one in particular. In the center ring was the girl with her frozen stare, as if the sky were shattering and falling on top of her.

A patrolman brought Cruz a can of soda and he popped it, drained half in a swallow and looked through the crowd. Only two blocks away on Twenty-third Street his mother lived and he half expected to see her with her shopping bag. She always waited until late Saturday to do her shopping, knowing at the end of the day she could haggle the produce sellers for better prices. "It will be rotten by the time you open Monday," she warned them. The next day was a feast day, something to do with the Virgin, and she was planning a family dinner. Right that moment she was probably extorting vegetables from some grocer on Mission Street.

Cruz sipped his soda, scanned the crowd and then looked again at the girl. He stared a long time at the tied thumbs and the drawing in the dirt as if they were related, symbols that would become clear through meditation.

Then there was a commotion in the crowd and a patrolman came across the lot. It was Rizzo, a barrel-chested cop with a sparse, black mustache. Following him was a short, middle-aged man wearing a loud red shirt on which were emblazoned bright green parrots. Cruz went to meet them.

Rizzo introduced him to the man. "This is Mr. Victor Soto of 1797 Shotwell," he said. "His niece, Gloria, didn't come home last night. He didn't know about it until now. Her mother, Maria Soto, didn't report it because she and her daughter are from Central America, from El Salvador, and they're illegal. She thought there would be trouble." Rizzo looked toward the body and then back at Cruz. "The description of the clothing is a match. I guess he just has to look at her."

Victor Soto looked very nervous. He was smoking and the

cigarette trembled between his fingers. His jaundiced eyes looked as dry as the dead girl's.

"Do you mind, Mr. Soto?"

The man nodded bleakly.

Rizzo led him to the body. Soto stepped forward and looked down at the girl's terrified face. Then he closed his eyes, pressed his lips together as if he were in pain and nodded. "Yes, that is my niece," he said.

Cruz studied Soto's face carefully. You never knew when you might have a killer right in front of you. When Soto opened his eyes again, they were full of grief. He looked down again and then his glance fell on the girl's hands. It was only for a split second and then his eyes flinched away again, as if he had touched something hot. For that split second, however, his eyes had widened and there was fear in them like a flash of heat lightning. If there was a resemblance between him and his dead niece, it was that fear in the eyes, Cruz thought. Soto brought the cigarette to his mouth, trembling even more now. He turned to Cruz.

"I better go and tell her mother," he said.

"Does any of this mean anything to you, Mr. Soto?" Cruz asked. "This drawing here or the way your niece is tied?"

The man looked bleakly at Cruz and his head made small, nervous shakes, like a twitch. "No, what could it mean to me?" he said. "I have to go to her mother now, I should tell her before she hears it from someone else."

It was as if the girl had died of some plague and he was anxious to get away. Cruz tried to meet the man's gaze, but Soto pulled at the trembling cigarette and looked away. Cruz squinted, studying the man carefully.

"Okay, Mr. Soto," he said finally. "You go back and tell her."

He pulled Rizzo aside and told him to go back to the house and stay with Soto and the girl's mother until he arrived, not to let Soto out of his sight. Rizzo said he'd do that. Cruz watched them walk away until the crowd swallowed them.

Then he scanned the crowd. On television they told you killers returned to the scene of the crime, to lose themselves in multitudes like this one and observe. But in the Mission you had too many foreigners and the killers hadn't watched enough television. They had the sense to go off and hide.

He crouched next to the dead girl again, shaking pebbles in his hand like dice. His wife had told him, "You have no deep feelings, no illusions." She'd told him that one night, after he'd returned from a two-day extradition trip to New Orleans, to bring back a Filipino who had shot and killed a guy over a parking place. How could you expect someone to have illusions when people killed each other over parking spaces or when beautiful girls got shot in the head and dumped like garbage in empty lots?

In the street, the crowd began to disperse. People drifted away, crawling back into the woodwork of the Mission District. One who stayed was Joe the Actor, his ravaged eyes still full of sadness, his mouth moving, but nobody bothering to listen.

CHAPTER 2

Cruz drove south on Mission Street under a late afternoon sky that pulsed with heat. On the car radio, Ray Barreto had his congas rolling, the sound of the jungle.

Mission Street around Twenty-fourth Street was palm trees, renovated Victorian buildings as big as riverboats, electric buses and their tangle of overhead wires spanning the street, like enormous tropical spider webs. Cruz crawled through traffic, past Ramona's Bakery, Lucky Pork, Sang Sang Market, the Tico Nica Bar. The sidewalks were crowded with shoppers. At the corner market, the bins were piled high with oranges and grapefruits, cantaloupe and honeydew, looking ripe and delicious. Then there were brooding, bobbing boys on the street corners, and the young girls who stripped down to narrow halter tops to beat the heat and made the boys' blood boil.

He turned off Mission down to Shotwell and found Rizzo's patrol car parked in front of a weathered stucco house.

That stretch of Shotwell, Cruz knew from his days on patrol, was mostly Central American. Some of them had been there since the forties and fifties. Many more, especially Salvadorans and Guatemalans, had come in the past ten years after the bad troubles had begun in those countries. The neighborhood had formed in the classic way: When there was an apartment vacant, the tenant next door always had a brother, a brother-in-law, a cousin or a friend from his old country who wanted it. Often, a few families were crammed into one flat, and instead of moving to another street, they waited for an opening in the same building or neighborhood. The noise made in the overcrowded apartment was usually a factor in driving out a neighbor or two. During his years on patrol Cruz had answered the complaints. In time, you came to have stretches that were just like provinces or towns back home, complete with the local slang, cuisine and, sometimes, feuds.

A Latina woman was walking down the block now, a grocery bag balanced on her head, two small kids hanging off her bright skirts. In a side yard a palm tree arched gracefully, and an old mongrel lay on the sidewalk, sleeping, not bothering to snap at the flies. The air buzzed with heat.

On the front landing a very old man in a chewed-up straw hat sat in a rocking chair. He must have been at least ninety, and his skin was lined and blotched from too much sun, too much rum, too much of just about everything at that age. His mouth was open in a silent roar, a handful of yellow teeth visible. In his eyes, although he was looking into nothing, there was a ferocious pleasure. Cruz climbed the front steps and said hello, but it didn't register at all. The old fellow rocked furiously and didn't respond. He was long gone.

It was Rizzo who answered the door. He led Cruz into a shabby foyer. The smell of fried bananas was in the air. Next to the door, on a table, was a makeshift religious shrine: a statue of the Virgin, several prayer cards picturing sad-eyed saints and two fluted vases full of dried-out flowers that reminded Cruz of death. From the back of the house came the muffled sobbing of a woman.

"That's the girl's mother," Rizzo said. "She's broken up pretty bad. She hasn't stopped crying. Soto's shook up too. He says now he knows who did the killing."

Cruz raised his eyebrows.

Rizzo said to him: "He got back here, told the girl's mother, called another relative and then he tells me he knows who killed his niece. He said the same guy killed somebody else in the family and he's afraid he'll kill him too. He's real worried."

"Why didn't he tell us that to begin with?"

Rizzo shrugged. "He said he was too scared. He didn't know what to do."

He led Cruz into the living room. It was a room painted a bright shade of pink. The furniture was covered in flowered slip covers and those were covered in clear plastic. The walls were decorated with supermarket art: clown faces, a fluorescent Chinese junk painted on black velvet. In addition, on the wall over the couch hung a large painting of Jesus Christ, his chest laid open and his heart engulfed in red and yellow flames. On the other side of the room, above the old mantel, hung a poster-sized black-and-white photograph of a young Latin man. It was a handsome face with a mischievous look in the eye. Cruz didn't recognize him, but hanging across from Christ and with that look in his eye, he had the air of the devil.

Cigarette smoke hung suspended in the light that slanted through the window. Soto was pacing and puffing away as if he were trying to fill the room with smoke. If it were possible he looked even more nervous than before.

"You have to give me protection," he said excitedly, as Cruz approached. "My life is in danger."

Cruz asked him to calm down and got him to sit on the couch. Next to each other, Soto in his parrot shirt and Cruz with the waves on his, they looked like the coastline of some tropical island. Cruz took out his notebook. There were Latins who looked at Cruz's face, heard his name and trusted him to understand them more than they would a white cop. There were others who reacted just the opposite, as if the bronze skin was just a disguise and underneath it there was the soul of a white man, who in the end would screw them around. In either case, Cruz was "some kind of hybrid," as his wife had called him, who didn't belong to one tribe or the other.

He mopped his neck and talked to the man in soothing tones.

"Now just who is it you think killed your niece, Mr. Soto?"

"Think nothing! I know who it was. It was Eric Hernandez." Soto balled his right hand into a fist, kissed the back of the thumb and shook it over his head. "I swear to God it was him. He followed Gloria here and killed her and he will kill me too. Death is following me everywhere I go. I can feel it."

Soto's nose had a bend to it, like the parrots on his shirt. He looked to be in his mid-fifties, and had a few strands of tinted black hair, which he combed over his skull to try to cover his baldness. He wore his shirt open to mid-chest and a jade shark's tooth hung in his springy white chest hairs. He was a Latin lover about twenty pounds overweight and twenty years too late.

"And who is this Eric Hernandez?" Cruz asked.

"He is a guerrilla fighter, a trained killer," Soto said. The man's eyes were wild with fear. "You don't know about any of this," he insisted. "But he will kill you too if you are not careful."

Cruz bobbed.

"Thanks for warning me, Mr. Soto." He opened his notebook and began to write. "What makes you so sure this Eric Hernandez killed your niece?"

But Soto didn't hear him. He was staring into a cloud of his own cigarette smoke, as if he were reading a crystal ball.

"My brother is turning over in his grave now," he said. "I didn't protect his daughter, the only child he had left." He shook a trembling finger at some invisible being. "But I warned him. Years ago I told him we should get that whole Hernandez family off the farm. They all worked there on the plantation down in our country, the whole family. The father was a bitter, jealous man, and the son is just like him. The sister too. They were all jealous of our prosperity. I told my brother, 'These people are going to cause us trouble someday.' And I was right. They killed him too. May he rest in peace."

He blessed himself, touching parrots on his chest and shoulders.

Cruz was squinting at him.

"You're saying this Eric Hernandez also killed your brother?"

"That's right. Gloria's father. And he killed my nephew too, Gloria's brother. Ramon was his name." Soto pointed at the photo poster over the mantel of the young Latin man. "Everyone knows that. That's why we had to bring Gloria and her mother out of there right away. All the killing had driven Gloria crazy. She was seeing visions, hearing voices. Ghosts."

The man in the parrot shirt looked earnestly at Cruz.

"There are more ghosts in my country all the time," he said, as if he were stating an acknowledged fact. "Soon there will be more ghosts than there are people. Then the whole country will be completely crazy. My late wife used to say such things and I thought it was foolish. Now I believe her. I believe our people are all cursed."

Cruz nodded and stared at the panicked man. He tried to decide just how sane he was, if he could be believed at all.

"Was any other member of your family killed?"

"Three is enough," Soto said. "And it will be four soon, if you don't protect me."

He emitted smoke, which turned milky in the sunlight. Soto stared at it, as if it contained a significant message, and then turned on Cruz. "Do you know what the real problem is?" he asked.

Cruz just shook his head. Questioning someone as wired as Soto was like landing a big fish in the open sea, you had to let him run a bit, and then you could start reeling him in.

"The problem is God," Soto said. "The gun is God now.

The gunrunners, the guerrillas, the killers, they are the saints now. People who weren't born from natural mothers. Who knows where they came from? You don't realize because you haven't been in my country. You don't know this kind of people, these guerrillas. They dig tunnels under the earth, right under your feet and they reach up and drag you into your grave. Sometimes they drop out of trees. Maybe the person right next to you is one of them, and you don't know until he kills you. You don't know until you're dead."

Cruz's face was suddenly full of understanding, as if he had put on a mask.

"I know there's a war in your country, Mr. Soto," he said. "I'm sure it's a terrible thing for your people, but right now I have to investigate the death of your niece."

"It's all part of the same thing, part of the same violence," Soto said. He held out a liver-spotted hand that trembled like a leaf in a windstorm. "Look at how I'm shaking. I can't be involved in this violence. Already I have enough problems. My health is bad. My business is going to hell."

He reached into his shirt pocket and handed Cruz a business card. It said "Central America Travelrama, Victor Soto, proprietor," with a Mission Street address and phone numbers, and was embossed with a globe in one corner and the names of the Central American countries in another.

"Yes, I know where this is. It's a good location," Cruz said encouragingly.

"Yes, everyone knows where it is, and no one walks in anymore," Soto said bitterly. "The funeral homes they get more regular customers than me. Since the war started down in El Salvador, it has gotten worse and worse. People are afraid to visit their families like before, there is too much war. Now the relatives they are running and coming here."

"People like your niece and your sister-in-law," Cruz said, trying to get back on the subject.

The other man nodded sheepishly.

"I'm a good citizen," he pleaded. "I'm respected here. Many people know me and my business, but I had to help my family."

"I understand, Mr. Soto," Cruz said, mopping his neck. He knew in that situation he would have done the same as Soto. If you didn't look out for family, then you were probably no use to anybody at all. In the Cruz house, that had been the first commandment. His own people, both his mother and his father's families, had come from Mexico in the twenties. They'd worked their way north, picking oranges and grapefruit and whatever else the growers would pay them for, finally making it to San Francisco. They'd become law-abiding citizens. But later, when other relatives came, some of them illegal, Cruz's parents had helped them. Within the family, they were all equal, no matter how they crossed the border.

From the back of the house came the sound of the woman's sobbing. Soto lit a new cigarette from the old one. A pall of smoke already lay in the darkened room like a mist falling over the jungle at nightfall. Soto was staring into it with soulful eyes.

"Our plantation was a beautiful place," he said sadly, "the most beautiful in the world. The fields were flat and clean. The house was protected by tall shade trees and we had beautiful gardens." Soto shook his head. "But then Eric Hernandez irrigated those fields with the blood of my family. All we have harvested ever since is pain and more death."

Cruz's eyes were sad with commiseration.

"Why did he kill your nephew and brother?"

"Because they told him to stay away from Gloria. That's why," Soto said angrily. "Everyone knows that. He was crazy for her. From the time he was a boy and came to work on our plantation in my country, he was after Gloria. For years and years he was her shadow."

"Did your niece have a relationship with this Eric?" Cruz asked.

Soto's face twisted in disgust.

"Relationship, nothing," he said, showing his yellow teeth and blue gums. "When they were children they played together on the plantation. Later, as he grew up he always worked on the farm, but he was good for nothing." Soto sucked on the cigarette and spat out the smoke. "We never let him drive the trucks or work the cotton gins or even pack the bales. He was worthless. All he did was pick cotton and hang around Gloria, talking to her, reading to her from poetry books and politics, filling her head with ideas, telling her he was in love with her, like the stupid farm boy he was. He told everyone that Gloria would marry him some day. And him with nothing, just the rags on his back."

"So he killed her for love," Cruz said. In his voice, although he hadn't intended it, he heard a note of cynicism. His wife had said: "You don't believe in anything." But in his experience it was rare that people killed for love. People killed for sex. More often drugs and money. Many times just out of the frustration of living. But love—you didn't see it.

Soto agreed.

"Love nothing," he said angrily. "He is just crazy."

Cruz nodded.

"And when your brother and nephew told him to stay away, he killed them?"

Soto had drifted across the room and was staring at the large photo poster on the wall.

"Eric Hernandez killed my nephew Ramon four years ago. They found Ramon lying in a field, the machete sticking from the back of his neck, blood still flowing, and the vultures turning circles over him." Soto made slow spirals in the air with his finger as if he could see the birds hovering overhead, coming for him this time. "That's when Eric ran away. They said he went to join the guerrillas because he believed in their cause, but we knew he was just running to save his skin because he had murdered Ramon. Later he killed my brother, too, for the same reason—he told him to stay away from Gloria."

"Did Hernandez ever admit to those murders?"

Soto made a sound of disgust in his phlegmy throat.

"Of course not. He lied, as he had always lied to Gloria."

"Did anyone see him kill these people?"

The other man threw his hands in the air. "Nobody had to see anything," he said, getting redder in the face. "Everyone knew it was him. He was the only one with reason to kill them. He was the only one who ran away. It was because he was crazy for Gloria. A dumb peasant boy. Now he has killed her too."

Cruz jotted notes and then looked up from his notebook.

"But if he loved her so much, why did he kill her, Mr. Soto?"

Soto waved a fat finger in the air.

"Because she didn't want him anymore, not even to see him," he said. "We brought her here six months ago after her father was killed. Then two months ago he came looking for her. She had seen her brother murdered and her father. She knew now that we were right all along. That Eric Hernandez was no good, a killer. The ghosts of her brother and her father were telling her, 'That son of a bitch killed us.' And that's why he drew the bull in the dirt." Soto raised his eyebrows suggestively. "Do you understand what that means?"

Cruz nodded and said he did. When he had first seen the drawing, the same explanation had occurred to him, because the horns of the bull had the same meaning for Mexicans. They symbolized the jilted lover, the man who has been made to look like a fool. In this case, maybe Eric Hernandez. Maybe Gloria Soto had "put the horns on him."

Cruz jotted more notes and gave Soto a chance to calm down. The killings down in El Salvador, whether this kid Hernandez had committed them or not, were too old and too far away for Cruz to get a handle on. As for the death of Gloria Soto, it was starting to sound like a familiar tale. It was the story of a man and a woman, lovers, who came to the United States separately. Somewhere on the voyage one of them saw the love between them get lost, like luggage lost in an airport. It happened all the time. When the second one arrived in San Francisco, he found the relationship was over and there was big trouble. This time, maybe it had ended in murder. Cruz looked up from his notes.

"So he came here to be with her, she rejected him, he got mad and he killed her," Cruz said. "That's what happened."

"He murdered her," Soto said.

"And then he left his signature in the dirt," Cruz said. "Why would he do something stupid like that?"

"Because he's crazy," Soto said, jabbing the side of his own bald head. "I told you that. In the last week he dressed up like a guerrilla. He showed the little boys here about being a rebel, making up stories of battle. He began to follow Gloria around, to hide so that she wouldn't see him. And Eric had a gun too," he said.

Cruz's arched eyebrows went up.

"You saw him with a gun?"

"No, but he told Gloria he had one and she told me," Soto said. He bore down on Cruz with his bloodshot eyes. "Eric said to her, 'I am a guerrilla and a guerrilla is never without his gun.' "

"When did he say that to her?"

"Two days ago," Soto said. "Thursday. I saw him right outside and he was talking to her. She came in and told me. But I thought he was just talking."

Cruz nodded.

"You think Eric really did have a gun?"

Soto's face twisted and his hands flew into the smoky air.

"Look at my niece with that bullet in her head," he said.

He shook a finger again at Cruz. "And I know he has friends, demons like him, where he could get a gun." He pointed somewhere to the north. "There's one called Miranda, Dennis Miranda. He lives on Twenty-fourth Street. He was a real guerrilla. He is known in our country. He can probably tell you where Eric is if he is hiding. He's another criminal."

Cruz jotted it all down. Soto was wheezing like an old radiator and Cruz gave him another chance to cool off. He asked to see the dead girl's room and Soto led him up a flight of stairs.

At first glance, Gloria Soto's bedroom was not much different from the rooms of many teenage girls. The walls were covered with posters and photographs cut out of magazines. They betrayed the normal interests of a girl her age; rock and movie stars, lovers running hand in hand through ideally lighted meadows, lanky models in new fashions. There were also photos from housekeeping magazines of elegantly decorated homes. There were sun-splashed skyscrapers and shiny new cars that you might expect to fascinate an immigrant girl. On the walls there was a beautiful dream about the United States, a sea of white faces all smiling at her with dazzling teeth. There wasn't one face that looked anything like the one Gloria Soto had worn at her death.

Cruz searched the room. Under a church missal in a drawer, he found a color photograph of a young Latino man, dressed in a dark T-shirt and green fatigue pants and holding an M-16 automatic rifle across his chest.

"That's him," Soto said excitedly. "That's the killer."

In the photograph, Eric Hernandez looked to be about twenty-five, with a lean, dark, handsome face and large, dark, deepset eyes filled with a youthful seriousness. Cruz studied the face. If he had done what Soto was accusing him of having done, then he had good reason to look serious.

Cruz asked if he could have the photograph.

"Keep it forever," Soto sneered. "I hope you kill him and I don't have to see him again."

Cruz continued his search, but found nothing else of interest.

"Where did Gloria go last night?" he asked, gazing around at the white faces and the brilliant teeth.

Soto shook his bald, pink head where the few strings of hair had stuck to the scalp.

"I don't know," he said, "I couldn't keep an eye on her all the time. I told you she wasn't well, she still had mental problems from when her father was killed and sometimes she just took off. But maybe she went to see Miss Stoner, the social worker who was helping her."

Cruz nodded in recognition and jotted the name down. Stacy Stoner was a psychiatric social worker based at Mission Mental Health and Cruz had worked on cases with her in the past. He took out the card found in Gloria Soto's pocket and showed it to Soto.

"That's Miss Stoner's clinic," Soto said. "She was helping Gloria with her nightmares. Gloria couldn't work or study. Sometimes she couldn't even sleep. It was terrible."

They went downstairs again into the foyer. As they did, another man emerged from the back of the house from the direction of the sobbing. He was a husky young man who, despite being indoors, was wearing dark glasses. He was dressed in a kind of military uniform. His pants were dark green with a bright red stripe down the leg, the shirt was khaki, with officers' bars in the lapels and, on the chest, merit ribbons and a badge. What most attracted Cruz's attention was the holstered gun strapped to his hip, a .38.

"This is my son, Robert," Soto said. "He can tell you all about Eric Hernandez."

The uniformed man in the sunglasses came up to Cruz, straightened his back, clicked his heels and saluted with precision. Cruz was close enough to read the badge. It said, "AAA Security Patrols, Battalion Commander." The spit-and-polish soldier before him was really a fancy rent-a-cop.

"You don't have to salute me," Cruz said. "You're a commander and you outrank me."

"We're always at the service of the police," Robert Soto said. Then he smiled for some reason. He had small, very white teeth that looked like milk teeth. He was in his early twenties, but his face was beardless and chubby like a boy's. There was something soft, fatty about Robert Soto, but also something menacing.

"Your father says you can tell me about this Eric Hernandez who may have killed Gloria."

"There's no maybe about it, Inspector," he said. "We have known Hernandez all his life. He was always no good, a killer from the start. That's why he joined the guerrillas. They are a band of criminals and up here they are no different. They smuggle their friends into the country. That's how Hernandez got here. They smuggle guns the other way, down to our country. Medical supplies. Everything. And they kill. Gloria probably knew those things and that's why they had to kill her. They are just ordinary criminals. And they should be shot down like ordinary criminals."

He finished speaking his piece and flashed the same incongruous smile. Then he took the gun out of the holster, ejected the clip, checked to make sure it was full, and jammed it back, ready for firing. You could see he had watched lots of gunslinger movies. He was very taken with himself.

"You're not thinking of going hunting for him yourself, are you?" Cruz asked.

"If you would take me with you, I would go gladly," he said. "I'd like to shoot him down like a dog, the same way he has shot down my relatives. If not, I'll stay here and make sure he doesn't shoot anyone else in my family."

"Do you mind showing me your gun?"

Robert Soto smiled at Cruz. He took out the pistol, twirled it and handed it to Cruz, butt first. Cruz ejected the clip, checked and saw it was full, reinserted it, smelled the barrel, made sure the safety was on and gave it back. Soto holstered the pistol again with a snappy flick of the wrist. Cruz could see this dude trying to impress a beautiful girl like Gloria Soto with his gunplay and maybe getting mad if she didn't melt.

Cruz didn't pretend to act friendly.

"You do have a license for that, I hope."

"Of course," Robert Soto said. "I am licensed and experienced."

"And can you tell me where you were last night, between six P.M. and dawn."

Robert Soto smiled more broadly this time.

"I was on commander duty all night for my company, checking the different posts all over the city. It's all on record, Inspector."

"That's good," Cruz said. Commander duty. Cruz could just see it: drinking coffee and kibitzing with the men guards and making passes at the women in the middle of the night, hoping they would fall into bed with him just from fatigue.

From the back of the house, the sobbing could be heard again. Robert Soto excused himself, saying he had to care for his aunt.

"You don't have to worry about providing protection for us, Inspector," he said, slapping the holster. "I have this place covered. You just track down that animal."

Then he clicked his heels, saluted precisely and left. As he opened a door the sobbing was louder.

"That poor woman, her heart is breaking," Soto said, gazing through his own smoke to the back of the house. "She says her womb is cursed. Maybe it is. Only two children and now both of them dead. Her husband too. All killed by the same devil."

Cruz commiserated with Soto and said he would talk to the

woman later, when she had calmed down. In time, Cruz had learned as much as possible to spare himself other people's grief. Blood and guts was one thing. Cruz could deal with that. But grief was something else. Case after case, it weighed on you. If you let it, it got inside you, ate you up. He asked Soto where he might find Eric Hernandez and was told the "guerrilla" lived with his sister four blocks away on Alabama Street.

Soto made another face as if he had bitten into a lemon.

"The sister she is just like her brother," he said. "Ungrateful and no good. When she was a girl we brought her from the plantation to this country to work in the house here. That was twelve years ago. It was the only chance she would ever have to come. As soon as she could, she left us. She works now for the Pan-American Import-Export Company. I see her on the street and she doesn't speak to me. That's what they are like, the whole family. No respect, no gratitude."

Cruz led Soto onto the porch. The old man sat in exactly the same position, rocking in his chair, roaring soundlessly at the sunlight.

"This is my father," Soto said sadly. "He was a great man. He built our plantation. Now he understands nothing." He shook his head. "That's just as well because of what is happening to us."

Cruz nodded.

"I understand you've already started contacting your other relatives," Cruz said. Soto looked up perplexed, as if he didn't know what Cruz was talking about. Then he nodded nervously and said much too eagerly: "Yes, I have. They are very upset."

"That's too bad," Cruz said.

He looked into Soto's bloodshot eyes. It was also too bad that Soto was lying about the phone call. But he was. It was written all over his puffy face. What reason he had to lie, Cruz didn't know, but people always had secrets from a cop.

Cruz was always being lied to. Possibly nothing to do with the killing—maybe Soto booked bets or had a woman on the side. People did all sorts of bad things that weren't murder. But at least some of the sweat beaded on the man's brow and lip were there because he had something to hide.

"You knew the meaning of the bull drawn in the dirt," Cruz said. "And what about the thumbs being tied? Why would he tie her thumbs, Mr. Soto? What does it mean?"

The man's eyes jittered in their sockets, the same way they had when he had looked down at the body of his niece and seen the thumbs.

"It's a sign, a warning. It means he will kill again." His voice was hoarse with fear and his breath stale with tobacco. He grabbed Cruz's arm hard. "You don't know what it is when everyone around you is being killed, Inspector. When God is harvesting your family like so much corn. It makes you afraid. I'm telling you, death is following me everywhere I go. I must have protection."

Cruz told the man he would leave a patrol car to guard the house temporarily. From the looks of Victor Soto, death wouldn't have to follow him long. He was scared enough to drop dead at any moment. Cruz wondered if Soto would have to make a phone call before he could drop dead, just as he had had to make a call before he could say who was trying to kill him. He didn't ask. The whole Soto family was a piece of work as far as he could see.

Cruz found Rizzo in the patrol car and told him to stay outside the house until further notice. Then he went looking for Eric Hernandez.

CHAPTER 3

The house on Alabama was an ocher-colored Victorian, an elaborate old structure that had fallen into neglect. The door and bay windows were bordered by wooden pillars and the lintels over them were carved with scrolls and fine fretwork. The cornice was carved with laurel wreaths. It had been a very classy place in its time, but now the paint had been allowed to bubble and peel. A windowpane on the second floor had broken and was covered with cardboard. More than anything the wood itself seemed to be rotting. It was probably the idea of some absentee landlord, to soak the place for rent and let it decay slowly. A brilliant scheme!

In the dusty yard, bare-chested brown kids were playing soldier, running with broom handles and sticks, shooting at one another. Some of them hid behind a rust-eaten old yellow Chevy that looked to be rotting like the house. One of the kids wore a camouflage shirt that came down to his knees. As Cruz got out of the car, the kid was talking into an old cigarette box as if it was a walkie-talkie and calling for a mortar to zero in on the house. Then he made a noise as if a bomb had exploded.

As he made for the door, Cruz raised his hands and asked for a ceasefire. The kid pointed a finger and machine-gunned him.

The front stairs were splintered, as if at least one round had found its target. The front door was standing open and kids went in and out. Cruz read the name on the mailbox: "Elvira Hernandez." No mention of Eric Hernandez, but then guerrillas didn't usually put their names on mailboxes.

Cruz rang the bell. It sounded and then someone or something answered it; he heard a screeching, like that of a large bird. Then a woman's voice called out.

"Come in. I'm in the back."

Just inside the front door, a tall potted palm stood guard. Cruz walked by it and peered into the living room. The room was so glutted with plants and vines, it appeared that nature had taken it back. Potted palms were everywhere, along with rubber plants, their leaves long, thick and glossy. Hanging at the center of the room was a spiral fern the size of a ceiling fan. Vines grew from the planters on the walls and the old fireplace mantel was almost hidden under vegetation. Over the couch was a painting of a tropical volcano spewing a cloud of steam. The windows were closed, the room was hot and airless and smelled like a forest just after a rain.

There was no one in it, but from the back of the house Cruz again heard the loud screeching sound. He followed it and walked into a kitchen that was also crowded with plants. A hook hanging from the ceiling held a big bunch of green cooking bananas. On the stove, red beans were soaking in a pot of water. The back door was open.

Cruz looked into the backyard. Apart from a small patch of lawn, it was completely overgrown with giant sunflowers, various kinds of cactus, large spiraling ferns, more young palms and other plants. Vines had grown wild and wrapped themselves around the cactuses, creating an impenetrable tangle. It was a compact, private jungle hidden from the street.

Elvira Hernandez was lying in a hammock in the last of the daylight watching butterflies feed on the flowers. Her face had an Indian cast to it, like her brother's in the photograph.

It was light brown and wide at the cheekbones, tapering over hollowed cheeks to a strong chin. Her mouth was wide, too, but her lips thin. The eyes were almond-shaped, far apart and almost black. She was probably in her late twenties, a few years older than her brother. She was wearing a brightly patterned dress of some Latin American Indian design. Her knee was doubled, and her dress had crawled up exposing a smooth bronze thigh.

Next to her stood a bird cage hanging from its stand and in it was a large, bright-red bird, its feathers picking up the last of the sunset light, so that it appeared to have caught fire. It screeched as it was consumed by the flames.

At first she didn't appear to notice Cruz standing at the top of the stairs. When she did look at him, it was more as if she had caught his scent in the air. Her nose twitched, her eyes narrowed and she turned.

"Can I help you?"

Cruz introduced himself, holding up his badge like someone trying to dazzle a creature with a shiny object. She didn't dazzle easily. Her almond eyes narrowed further and she watched him warily, trying to decide if he were part of a friendly species or an enemy.

"I'm looking for Eric Hernandez," Cruz said. "I assume you're his sister."

She didn't answer that either way.

"Eric isn't here," she said.

"Do you know where I can find him?"

She looked away into the tangle.

"No, I'm sorry. He's been out of town since Tuesday. I don't know exactly where he is."

"Is that right?"

"Yes," she said, "that's right."

Cruz climbed down the stairs. As he approached the cage, the bird cocked its head to one side and watched him with a perfectly round, unlidded eye. When he put his finger up to the wire, the bird groped its way across the wooden bar on black claws and lunged at him with its can opener of a beak.

"What kind of bird is this?" Cruz asked.

She had picked up a cut crimson rose and was twirling it slowly before her eyes. Outside, the children were making machine-gun noises.

"It's a macaw," she said, "but I don't believe you came here to talk about exotic birds. You're from immigration, I take it."

"No, I'm not, Miss Hernandez," Cruz said. "I'm from homicide."

That got her attention. Her eyes fixed on him and the distance between them was suddenly closed.

"What do you mean, homicide?"

"I mean a young woman was killed last night. Her name was Gloria Soto and I'm told your brother knew her."

She was staring at the words that had come out of his mouth in disbelief.

"Gloria's dead?"

"That's right," Cruz said. "Didn't your brother tell you?"

She looked at Cruz now and her face stormed over.

"No, my brother didn't tell me," she said angrily. "I told you he isn't here. He isn't even in San Francisco. In fact, he has gone back to our country, he left three days ago and couldn't have had anything to do with it. And he isn't coming back here at all."

Cruz laid his head against one shoulder and squinted.

"I thought you said it was Tuesday, four days ago."

She glared at him. "Four days ago, then."

Cruz drifted across the yard and plucked a leaf off one of the vines. The butterflies took off in erratic flight.

"That's strange," he said. "I talked to someone who said they saw him just two days ago near Gloria Soto's house."

She looked at him with claws in her eyes. "Who told you that?"

"That doesn't matter now," Cruz said.

"It was Soto, wasn't it? Victor Soto."

Cruz mopped his neck and said nothing.

"Nobody who knows Soto would believe anything he says. Soto is a snake, an insect."

Cruz nodded. When there was bad blood between families, he knew, whole clans were demoted on the evolutionary scale.

"When did your brother leave here, Miss Hernandez?"

She hesitated, glanced at him and then away. "Tuesday," she said.

"So he hasn't come home the last four nights and he wasn't home last night either."

She started to answer and held back. Her eyes were moving as if she could sense or smell something sneaking up on her through the jungle.

"When was Gloria killed?" she asked.

"Last night. She was found today on Twenty-first Street, a bullet in her head."

"Eric wasn't here, but that doesn't mean he killed her."

"Maybe not."

"You don't know why he didn't come home," she said. "Or why he decided to go away in the first place."

"You're right, I don't," Cruz said. "Why was that?"

She looked away from him again. Her foot tapped nervously.

"Because his life was threatened," she said.

Cruz's eyebrows twitched. "Who threatened him?"

"The vultures," she said. "They threatened him."

"The vultures. Is that a new street gang, or what?"

"These aren't boys," she said. "They are men and they are killers, paramilitary assassins who work for the army in my country, who have followed him here. We call them *esquadrones de la muerte.*"

"Death squads," Cruz said. "Like in the newspaper."

"That's right."

Cruz bobbed and wrinkled his nose.

"And these death squads, these vultures, they came all the way up here to threaten your brother?"

"To kill him if they can," she said. "My brother is a hero in my country, a person of strong beliefs and courage. He's also too good a guerrilla for them to catch him."

"Is he?"

"That's right. And they killed Gloria instead."

"I see," Cruz said. "And why would these paramilitary death squads want to kill Gloria Soto?"

"Maybe because she loved Eric," she said. "Maybe for some other reason. But they did threaten Eric. They threatened to murder him and that's why he isn't here."

"I see," Cruz said.

She glared at him. "You don't believe me, do you?"

Cruz looked at her and shrugged.

"You want proof?" she said.

She reached into the pocket of her dress and thrust toward him a folded white envelope. Cruz crossed the yard. He unfolded it and found on the front three typed words: "Comrade Eric Hernandez." The envelope bore no address, stamp or postmark. Inside was a leaf of white paper and on it a note typed in Spanish that Cruz translated.

Comrade Hernandez,

We have learned of your arrival in San Francisco. We know you are living with your sister and her small daughter.

We know your whole history as a guerrilla, as a terrorist. You must know by now that our people do not want you in El Salvador. We don't want you here, either. Our forces almost killed you back home, and we promise you we will finish the job here.

You are a dead man already. You will not survive this weekend.

This jungle is our jungle.

The note was signed with a large smudged X in a reddish substance that appeared to be dried blood. Cruz read it through twice, his face twisted in disbelief. It reminded him of something kids might send each other if they were playing pirates.

"When did your brother get this?"

"Tuesday morning."

"There's no postmark on this envelope and no stamp."

"We found it stuffed in the mailbox," she said. "Just left there during the night. That's the way these people do things, like animals who only move at night. This came with it." She was holding in the palm of her hand a copper-colored bullet that appeared to be a nine-millimeter round. Cruz took it from her.

"That's why my brother isn't here to talk to you," she said. "Before the envelope came, we received telephone calls in the middle of the night. Every night this past week, at three or four o'clock in the morning, some guy speaking in Spanish. He was saying that Eric was going to die. They were trying to scare him, but he wouldn't run. Then the note came and the bullet, and he got worried. Not for himself, but for me and my daughter. He was afraid they might come after him and we would get hurt. So he went into hiding. And that's just what they wanted so that you would blame him for Gloria's death."

"You mean someone got your brother to go into hiding and then murdered Gloria Soto so it would appear that he killed her. That was clever of them."

"They are like wolves, wolves are smart," she said.

"I thought you said they were vultures."

But she didn't catch the sarcasm. "They are that, too," she said.

"Just where did your brother go, Miss Hernandez?"

She shook her head. "I don't know. He didn't want to tell me. He said it would be safer for me if I didn't know."

Cruz bobbed.

"Of course," he said.

He studied the bullet the same way he had read the letter, as if it weren't a real bullet at all.

"Do these vultures, these death squad members who have come up here, have names?"

"I don't know them for sure," she said. "That's something you should ask Victor Soto or his son, Robert Soto. Those are the kind of people he might know. People like Julio Saenz, too."

"Who is Julio Saenz?"

"He's a mule," she said.

Cruz nodded. "A mule. That's interesting."

"That's right. After the coyotes sneak people across the Mexican border they hand them over to mules, like Julio Saenz, who transport them up here. That's what he does for a living. He takes people who are afraid for their lives and squeezes their last money out of them. That's how he knew Gloria. He brought her up here. Later he went out with her. He was her new boyfriend, driving around with her in his red Firebird, which he bought with his vulture money. Victor Soto didn't tell you about him, did he?"

"No, he didn't," Cruz said jotting the name down. "The vultures, the snakes and the coyotes and now a mule. That's quite an operation."

The bird picked that moment to screech. Beyond that there was silence. Even the kids were quiet, maybe lying in ambush. Cruz flipped the bullet in the air, caught it and said nothing.

"You still think I'm lying," she said.

Cruz shrugged his shoulders.

"It's not exactly that I think you're lying," he said. "I think you're trying to protect your brother. You're a good Latin girl and that's precisely what I'd expect you to do."

Her eyes narrowed like those of a large cat, a lioness.

"You're right about one thing," she said. "If Eric had killed Gloria, I would lie to protect him. I would lie as much as I had to. In fact, I would do anything necessary to protect him." She spun the rose before her eyes and fixed him with a meaningful look. "That's if he had killed her, but he didn't kill her. Eric couldn't have killed Gloria no matter what she said to him or did to him. He's twenty-three years old and all his life he has been in love with her. Her family put him through hell for it, and she has rejected him before. The truth is he had reason to kill them all because of what they put him through, but he didn't."

"You're sure?"

When she looked up at him, he could tell she wasn't sure at all. It was the one true moment in her performance. But there was a code to be adhered to. You covered up for your own, you protected your own blood.

"It is against his nature to hurt Gloria," she said. "My brother is like one of those insects that die after they make love. He would kill himself before he hurt Gloria."

Cruz flipped the bullet. "But it's the girl who's dead, isn't it?" he said. "Your brother came all this way to be with her and she told him 'no.' You tell me she had a new boyfriend, this Saenz character. Next to the body there was a drawing of a bull with horns. The horns are the sign of a man who has been cheated on by a woman, who has been made a fool. Now she's dead and he's on the run and you're trying to tell me somebody else did it."

"My brother is a hero," she said. "He has risked his life for our people. He doesn't murder women."

Cruz mopped his face and neck. She looked away, staring into the tangle of vines.

"The problem is you don't know what people can do to each other, what people have done to each other in our country," she said. "You don't know how bad people can be. You're a policeman and you think you know a lot about evil, but you don't know much at all. We know, Eric and I and many of our people. My brother and I are the only two left in our family. The others were killed down in our village by the same vultures who you don't believe in. Tell my family that they aren't real. Tell it to Gloria. She knows who killed her. If she were here, she would tell you. But you know too much to listen. When there are more killings here and the blood gets deeper, then you will listen."

She looked away then and Cruz stood bobbing the way he always did and always had when someone tried to lecture him.

Far away a siren sounded and next to him the bird screeched. The sun had dipped below the eaves of the houses, leaving the garden in shadow, and the insects hidden in that small jungle were pulsing. The last of the orange light brought out the bronze in her face and along that smooth stretch of thigh. She met his gaze.

"The problem with you is you have been in the city too long," she said. "You have lost your instincts. You don't sense danger anymore."

Cruz's wife had said, "You don't feel. You've spent too much time with the dead. You're like a dead man yourself."

Elvira Hernandez twirled the rose and challenged him with her eyes, full of instincts of her own: preservation of the family, the protection of her young, and sex too. They were there in those black eyes.

I haven't lost all my instincts, Cruz thought of saying to her. *I have at least one left.* He met her gaze, a smile twitching at the corners of his mouth. She glared at him and for a moment he felt like a fifteen-year-old again, hanging out on the street corner, making halfass passes at women going by. Then she turned away.

Cruz squinted at the setting sun and mopped his neck.

"So your brother used his instincts and went into hiding," he said.

"That's right."

"With the help of Dennis Miranda?"

Her eyebrows lifted just a bit with surprise, but she recovered. "Dennis is a good friend, a loyal friend, but Eric can take care of himself. My brother is a guerrilla, Inspector. He's like a chameleon. With all the Latins, all the illegals here in this city, he won't be found. Not by them, not by you."

"They all say that," Cruz said.

He ran his finger over the spines of a cactus growing next to the porch. "Is he carrying a gun?"

She was staring blankly. Behind her eyes, the wheels were turning.

"Is he?" Cruz asked.

"I don't know."

"He told Gloria he had a gun."

"I never saw him with one," she said carefully, "but I don't know where he went from here. I know one thing, Inspector, if you corner an animal, he will turn and defend himself any way he can."

Cruz flipped the bullet. "Wild animals don't survive in the city, Miss Hernandez," he said. "You think you're protecting him, helping him hide because he's your family, but you could get him killed instead."

Her face was blank now, like faces he had seen so many times before when he had tried to squeeze information out of a relative of a suspect. An element in the blood caused the eyes to go empty and the mouth to clamp shut. It was a natural process called protecting your own. He knew trying to budge her would do no good. He asked to see Eric Hernandez's room.

She led him into the house, across the junglish living room

and up the stairs. Through an open door to the left he saw a child's room, dolls and clothes scattered.

She opened the door on the other side of the hall. Except for tangled sheets on the bed, the room appeared as if no one were living in it or had lived in it for some time. Unlike Gloria Soto's room, there was nothing on the walls. Not one sign of decoration. The bed was against one wall and right next to it was a rudimentary bookcase made of planks and bricks. On it there was only one book, a text, in Spanish, on guerrilla warfare. That was all that was visible in the entire room. The thought that someone had been living in it was stark. But there was also a twinge of recognition because it reminded him of his own empty walls.

In the dresser drawers he found only one stray pair of socks. Nothing hung in the closet. On the floor beneath the empty hangers was a pile of newspapers.

"Your brother lived a pretty spare existence here," Cruz said.

"That's how he lived in the mountains," she said, "and that's how he lived here, ready to run."

He kneeled to look through the papers and magazines. As he moved the pile he saw something wedged against the wall. He reached down and brought out two small boxes. One was white cardboard and was marked "Ammo .38 caliber." The other was metal and said "U.S. Army surplus ammunition M-16 automatic rifle." Also wedged back there he found a can of U.S. Army surplus gun oil.

He shook the boxes and found they were empty. Then he held them up before the woman like an offering at a mass. She just stared at them wordlessly, like a psychic trying to divine how they had gotten into the room, where the bullets might be now and, looking into the future, where they might end up. For the first time, there was fear in her eyes.

Believe in people, his wife had told him. These were the

kind of people she would have believed in. Eric Hernandez was just her kind of hero. Trust him and then when your back was turned he would use one of these bullets to put a hole in you.

He took out the photograph he had found in Gloria Soto's room, Eric Hernandez holding a rifle across his chest. An M-16.

"An M-16 is an assault rifle used by the armed forces," Cruz said. "It fires just like a machine gun. Is that what your brother is carrying around?"

Cruz gave her time to answer, but the woman stared at the boxes and said nothing. Then he crossed the hall and looked through the child's room and entered the woman's bedroom, another hothouse full of plants. After checking the closets, he looked under the bed and found a typewriter, a Corona portable in a blue plastic case. He took a piece of paper, typed the word "jungle" and compared it with the note. The type was the same.

She had come up silently and was standing next to the bed watching him.

"You type very well," Cruz said. He looked at her. "Two hours ago, the body was found. In that time everybody in the barrio has found out about it. You heard Gloria was dead and got to work on your little typewriter. Or did your brother tell you before that? Right after he killed her?"

When she looked up at him, her eyes were pained and desperate.

"He didn't tell me and he didn't kill her," she said. "I made up the note because I was afraid you wouldn't listen to us about the calls, the threats. You have to believe me that they are hunting him. They want to kill him."

"If you tell me where your brother is, maybe I'll believe it," Cruz said.

She looked him deep in the eyes again. "I told you I really

don't know," she said. There was vulnerability in her now, a plea for help. "Really I don't."

Cruz held her gaze. His tongue played with the inside of his cheek and he suppressed a smile. "When someone looks me in the eyes that way, full of sincerity, and talks with that throb in the throat, I always figure they're lying for sure."

He had meant to provoke her and he did. Just as quickly as her vulnerability had come, it disappeared. She showed her teeth, a growl escaped her and for a moment he thought she would go for his throat. Her hands formed claws and nails came out and her eyes filled with an animal rage. At the last second she made a noise like an angry cat, turned and stalked out of the room.

CHAPTER 4

A young red-haired policewoman studied Cruz suspiciously from behind the bullet-proof glass of the communications room at Mission Station and then buzzed him in. It was still early on this Saturday night and the squad room was empty. The long tables under the fluorescent lights and the old standup typewriters were waiting for the drunks, the dopers, the peace disturbers, the domestic disputers and possibly an assaulter or two. That was the usual clientele; murderers, they were special. Their faces stared from the wanted posters on the glass-encased bulletin board. They were like movie stars pictured on the coming attraction posters. The stars of crime.

As Cruz crossed the room to the water cooler next to the locker room, they tracked him with their murderous eyes. It was just fine the squad room was empty. Cruz had worked there seven years before making Homicide. Too many people there knew him and a few had known his wife as well. He didn't need the third degree.

Cruz dripped sweat, like a nervous suspect. He mopped his neck and drank water. It was in that room, when he was twenty years old, that he had started impersonating an officer, as he called it now. Growing up, Cruz had acquired all the knowledge he needed to be a cop, or, for that matter, a criminal. He had cased the Mission District and figured out the equations by which it worked: money, times smarts, times connections, divided by skin color, equaled your final take. He learned who ran what, and whose interests lay where. He knew to play his cards close to the vest. He had also learned that some people paid for their sins, but others didn't, and who not to mess with. He knew how to cover up what he really felt because that was the only way to get by. He learned not to back down, but more, how to avoid being outnumbered. One time he took a wrong turn down the white boys' street and got his nose bent. He didn't miscalculate again.

By the time he finished high school, Cruz had a fix on life. It was one of those mazes you had to figure out or you got zapped, like a dumb rat. The cops could zap you bad if you made a wrong turn and got caught. The women you bumped into in the maze were also dangerous if you let them lead you around in circles.

Three years out of high school he was still bouncing from job to job—factories, freight yards, warehouses. Make a few bucks and not get tied down, that was his modus operandi. Then he said, Screw it! He had a high draft number, but he would go into the army anyway and raffle his cookies in Vietnam. He would do his time, see the world—if he lived.

He told an uncle of his, a smart cookie who knew his way around. His uncle just shook his head and said "wrong." If Cruz was going to risk getting his ass shot off, the cops paid you better for it and they were looking for "Hispanics." The cops had become an equal opportunity employer; they were even hiring the enemy.

Crooked-nosed Cruz, who had always been smart when he had to be, passed the test. A red-faced, red-necked cop in a business suit told him they wanted him. They offered him $10,000 a year back then to drive around the Mission in a car, which was what he did a good part of the time anyway. Cruz just nodded, kept from laughing, and said "sure." It was like picking the city's pocket.

Then he started to impersonate an officer, although some people didn't like his impersonation. He always put in his time and did the job better than they expected so they wouldn't have an excuse to screw him around. But he was a Mexican from off the street and part of him was still on the street corner with the brooding and bobbing homeboys who got into trouble. Among some of the Anglo cops, there was muttering about whose side he was on. He spent time with the wrong kind. He was a Mexican who would go easy on his compadres in a way that was dangerous.

Then one night, driving the number-five car with an old beer-bellied white cop named Reiser, they got into deep trouble. Checking a disorderly complaint in a public housing unit, they bumped into a drug transaction on a dark landing and a strung-out Latino went for his gun. Reiser, out of breath from the stairs and just plain slow, was dead meat. Cruz screamed to draw the dealer's attention and the dude shifted the barrel of his gun away from Reiser and right at Cruz. The dealer got a shot off that breezed by Cruz's head, and then Cruz put two slugs into the guy and dropped him.

That won Cruz his first commendation and ended the muttering. He'd never had any trouble again with any cop. In general, they were cooler than the people on the street. Still, with a few exceptions, there was distance between Cruz and his colleagues that had never closed. Cruz was a loner who worked on his own. And it was like his mother had told him, "Your blood don't come from here."

Now he ducked into the shift commander's office and found Sergeant Phil Donnelly behind a desk. Donnelly was a friend. In the early days, he and Cruz had shared a squad car on night shifts. Donnelly was a good, smart cop who had made patrol sergeant about the same time Cruz had gone to Homicide. He was a black-haired Irishman with an understated manner and shrewd eyes. He had a fan going and was using a billy club as a paperweight to hold down reports flapping on his blotter. On the radio, a baseball announcer was doing the play-by-play. Cruz dragged a chair into the path of the fan and fell into it. He sat there a minute not saying anything, kneading his brow as if he were trying to squeeze a thought out of it.

Donnelly looked up from his paperwork. "Uh-huh?"

Cruz spoke cautiously, deliberately.

"On this Soto murder, the body on Twenty-first."

"Yes?"

"What we have is a suspect who probably killed the Soto girl," he said, "who is probably on the run from us, is probably a very disturbed human being and is probably very heavily armed."

The last two words made Donnelly's eyebrows go up.

"How heavily armed?"

Cruz took out the two ammunition boxes he'd found in the closet. Donnelly examined them and then whistled appreciatively.

"Jeez! Who is this soldier?"

"His name is Eric Hernandez, Hispanic, twenty-three years old, and he lives on Alabama. He's been in the country about two months." Cruz took out the photograph and showed it to him.

Donnelly got up from behind his desk and Cruz followed him out of that office, through the squad room, past the weapons room where the shotguns were stored, into the communications room, past the red-haired patrolwoman who sat at a desk full of telephones, until he sat down before a computer screen.

He typed "Eric Hernandez, male, Hispanic, dob 1964" and the address and punched the button, sending it searching the memory. The machine took a few seconds, then made an off-tone "beep" and the screen said, "No record."

"He hasn't had time to make a name for himself," Cruz said. He looked at a page in his notebook. "How about Julio Saenz, S-a-e-n-z, male Hispanic, Twenty-ninth Street address. He was supposedly mixed up with the girl and for some reason the family didn't mention him."

Cruz noted that Donnelly typed with all ten fingers. He could only use two. Words started to race across the screen and the Mule's arrest record poured out.

According to that record, Julio Saenz, born 1958, had been arrested four times in his life, all in the state of California. The first two arrests were both about ten years ago when he was a minor, one for disturbing the peace and another for car theft, joy riding. The usual kids' stuff. He had gotten off. Then seven years later, Saenz had been charged with carrying a concealed weapon and receiving stolen property and again had gotten a suspended sentence. Eighteen months later he had been charged with leaving the scene of an accident and had again gotten off. Apart from those arrests, he had two outstanding speeding citations, one from seven months ago issued down in Bakersfield and another two months old from near Big Sur.

"This guy's in a big hurry all the time," Donnelly said.

"That's because he's smuggling illegals up from the border," Cruz said. "At least that's what I'm told by Hernandez's sister. The faster you get back and forth, the more you make. He brought the girl, Gloria Soto, up here six months ago and was sleeping with her ever since, allegedly."

"Nice benefits in that job," Donnelly said.

"I have an explanation for the thumbs being tied too," Cruz said. "Death squads."

Donnelly's thick brows knitted.

"Salvadoran death squads," Cruz said. "The hoods you read

about in the paper who go around killing people down there. That's their signature: the thumbs and letters like this."

He took the note and the nine-millimeter slug, gave them to Donnelly and explained how he had gotten them from Elvira Hernandez. He gave Donnelly time to read it.

"Except Miss Hernandez wrote it herself," Cruz said.

"Ya think so?"

"I know so," Cruz said. "Her brother used to go out with this Soto girl before this Saenz character. He was crazy about her, and when he got here, he found out it was all over."

"So he kills her," Donnelly said, "and now he's walking around in the city with an M-16."

"Probably," Cruz said, "even though the dead girl's uncle left out a few things and she has a cousin who's a gun freak. It's still probably this Hernandez kid."

"I can't tell my guys probably," Donnelly said. "Somebody taps this guy on the shoulder and maybe he opens up with an M-16. I gotta tell 'em he's dangerous."

"That's why I'm telling you," Cruz said. "I have another name to check. Miranda. Dennis. Twenty-fourth Street."

Donnelly typed it in. "Who is this guy?"

"I'm told he's a friend of Hernandez and that down there he was a guerrilla leader."

"That sounds nice."

The machine beeped and the screen said, "No record."

Donnelly handed the photo of Eric Hernandez to the red-haired woman and asked her to photocopy two dozen copies. Calls crackled over the radio monitor. Through a narrow, horizontal window, Cruz looked into the small holding cells. A couple of drunks were in there, both chatting away, not to each other, but to the walls. Cruz followed Donnelly out of the communications room back into the squad room to the water cooler, the murderers tracking him wherever he went.

"You have any idea where he is?" Donnelly asked.

"A name or two, nothing much."

"If he's still in the city, he could be anywhere," Donnelly said. "We have illegals coming out of the woodwork around here. You know that. I got cases where they dig a hole in the backyard, camouflage it so you can't see it and they hide there if there's any kind of trouble. They tell me they do that all the time down in their country to hide from the soldiers. Some of these people think we're gonna shoot them or something if we find them. And the thing is we're not even looking for them. If we had to bust illegals, that's all we'd have time to do. And now we got this guy making believe he's a god-damned jungle fighter."

"How about trouble between the political groups here? Anything new like that?"

"We've got the demonstrations, the marches, like always," Donnelly said. "Both sides have their people and they make lots of noise."

Donnelly looked Cruz in the eyes.

"Your lady is out there sometimes," he said.

"Uh-huh," Cruz said, looking away. "What else do you have?"

"Sometimes we get phone calls. Some guy tells you the other side is threatening them and has guns hidden some-place. That they're planning something. But we never find anything. Maybe they have them. The two sides have their rough guys, we know that, but nobody's been hurt bad and nobody's dead. Not so far." He knocked on wood.

The policewoman brought back the photo and Donnelly told her to call in the squad cars so they could pick up a copy.

Another cop, named Martinez, came into the communications room. "What happened with that woman on Army Street?" Donnelly asked him. He turned to Cruz. "Another Central American woman who went nuts on us."

"She was an older woman," Martinez said. "We found her

on the roof of the apartment building screaming in Spanish. She was pulling her hair out, handfuls of it, for Christ sake. She said God appeared to her and told her she was going to die. Everything was going to catch fire and then God would come and take her away." Martinez shook his head and rolled his eyes. "I guess she expected Christ to come and pluck her off that rooftop in a helicopter. Her family couldn't explain it. They said all of a sudden she just flipped out."

Donnelly shook his head. "Must be the moon," he said.

"There ain't no moon," Martinez said.

"Yeah," Donnelly said.

Cruz said goodnight and started to leave, but Donnelly caught him at the door.

"Listen," he said. "I wanted to say I was sorry to hear about you and Alice."

Cruz bobbed, looked away and looked back again.

"It's not that big a deal," he said. "She was just a tourist in my life. You know what I mean? She was on vacation, that's all."

Donnelly grimaced.

"What's that supposed to mean?"

"Like a Mexican vacation," Cruz said with false humor. "You know. It's cheap, it's nearby, it's spicy and hot, and when it's over you just come back over the border to your own people."

Donnelly didn't smile.

"I don't think she's like that," he said.

Cruz bobbed, looked down, smiled.

Donnelly said to him, "Anyway, you were taking your own tours, David. You were screwing around on her."

Cruz shrugged, the smile gone.

"I think she mixed me up with some other Mexican," he said, serious now. "She had a lot of complaints. I wasn't what she wanted."

"You're too hard, David. You want to see bad everywhere you look. You think somebody's always trying to job you. You think everything works like it does on the street—if you're not getting the upper hand, then you're getting screwed with. But it don't work that way with a woman like that, David. She cared about you, she wasn't trying to job you."

Cruz ran his hand impatiently through his thick hair.

"What are you, her lawyer?"

"I told you I saw her on the street. She looked like she hadn't slept in a month. She talked to me."

Cruz bobbed.

"She talked to me, too," he said. "But it's over. It didn't work. She lives in her head, in her paintings, in her political movements. All these fantasies. And I live on the street. You want to do her a favor? Tell her to grow up. Tell her to start living in real life."

Donnelly was shaking his head.

"Real life isn't as bad as you see it, David."

Cruz stopped bobbing and stared at Donnelly.

"Tell that to the ones with the bullet holes in them, Phil."

Then he said good-bye and ducked out of the squad room and into the night.

It was in that squad room, before he made Homicide, that he had first met her, when he was taking evidence about a break-in at a gallery. Some of her "visions" had been stolen. She was high-strung, very white, with silver-blue eyes. She'd tried to describe the abstract paintings by the emotions they evoked and he'd written it all down. She'd looked into his black eyes and thanked him for his consideration.

She'd told him, "With those eyes, you should have been a painter. Another Diego Rivera." Within two days they were in bed, inside a month she had moved into his Bartlett Street flat and the place smelled of paint.

It was a long shot, which he had always known would fade in the stretch, but for a while it beat the odds.

She took him to the museums; he took her to hear salsa and perfected her footwork. On the dance floor, they were dynamite.

They spent a lot of time in bed. She talked of her life, a series of art schools, men and political causes. She asked him about his past lovers, but he would never tell her. They were like missing persons who had disappeared without a trace. Instead he told her of his cases, the victims and the killers. She worried about the danger. She looked at him with eyes that were full of love. And he began to get a premonition of what would happen. It had happened before.

Sometimes they fought. She called him cynical, morose, negative. He called her a space cadet artist, with her head in the clouds.

Then they went back to bed and made up. They always made up in bed. It was their antidote, their drug.

They lasted a long time. Then one day she told him she loved him. Cruz said nothing and she looked at him as if he had defrauded her. She didn't say it, but it was there in her wet blue eyes. He had known it was coming. From then on, he spent longer hours working, steeping himself in murder. When he came home she turned her eyes full of love on him and it seemed to him like the glint of a knife. He could feel her trying to cut a piece out of him, a piece for her to have. She told him more and more that she loved him and he ducked away. Cruz knew how to avoid a knife. She pleaded with him. She said he was killing their love; in his house, he was the murderer.

Then he began to plot his escape. He would tell her he was working at night. He would escape her eyes, her words, stalking the streets, looking down the dark alleyways, sitting in the dingy bars with the drunk and dying, listening to the sirens, sometimes meeting the gaze of a woman and going with her into the night.

At first when he dragged up at dawn, she screamed and came at him with her fists. That was all right. Fists he knew about. But later she just looked at him with those eyes that went right through his skin.

"You're afraid of me because I love you," she told him. "If you let me love you, then you have to change the way you see everything, that dark, hopeless way you see things. You have to be a real human being." Cruz could only shake his head and tell her it was over. He had to live in real life. She said that was only his alibi.

On the walls of the apartment where her paintings had hung, there were now blank white spaces, clearly outlined by time. He knew her artsy painter friends would interpret those spaces. They would call them clever minimalist commentaries on the emptiness of his personal life.

Fuck them.

CHAPTER 5

The building on Twenty-fourth Street was a quiet three-story gray stucco structure dating from the twenties or thirties with a narrow entrance leading off the street. It was so quiet that Cruz, who had patrolled this street for eight years, could not remember having been there before. Out in front, small brown boys spun tops in a puddle of streetlight on the sidewalk. Across the street, older boys hung around a car, sneaking clandestine sips from beer cans and bobbing to the brassy, thumping music that emanated from the car radio. They must have been very bored, because they watched Cruz carefully as he walked down the street, looking for the house number, and studied him even more closely as he entered the narrow foyer of the building.

He found the name Miranda on the button for apartment 2-B and pushed it. Then he turned to look at the street again and found all the boys watching him. He smiled politely; they didn't.

Next to the button was a speaker, but no one asked him who he was. The door was buzzed open and he went in. In the lobby sat a desk where a security guard might sit, but it was empty. He took the staircase to the second floor and found the door to 2-B standing open. He was looking down a car-

peted hallway and from somewhere in the apartment he heard
a baby screaming at the top of its lungs.

Cruz knocked on the door and heard an older man's voice
call from the back of the apartment. "*Pasen.* Come een."

Cruz walked down the hallway into the living room. The
baby, a girl, not much more than a year old, with dark ringlets
and minuscule pearls in her ears, was standing in a playpen.
At first she was gripping the edge, mouth open and screaming
like a banshee. But the moment Cruz stepped into the room,
the mouth swung shut like a trap door, the noise stopped and
she stood staring at him in amazement.

The apartment around her was crowded with old stuffed
furniture, the cloth faded and the wood scarred. There were
several plaster figurines about and, again, supermarket art on
the walls. Against another wall was a large console television
and on the screen a soccer game was in progress, a commen-
tator trying to keep up with the action in a torrent of Spanish.
Above the television were gold-framed family photographs
that caught Cruz's attention. He crossed the room to look at
them.

One of the photographs was a portrait of the wide-eyed
little girl who was in the room with him and who was watching
him even now. And next to her was a picture of a wedding
party, the two central figures being a tall, very white-skinned
blond woman and a short, very dark-skinned bearded young
Latino man with a fixed gaze. The third photo showed a group
of young men dressed in fatigues, carrying automatic rifles,
standing in a wooded setting. In the middle of the line stood
Eric Hernandez, his face partially covered in a beard, but the
serious eyes unmistakable. The fourth and last photograph
was an old sepia print of several men dressed in cowboy hats,
bandoliers crossing their chests and holding old Remington
or Winchester rifles. The photo reminded Cruz of others he
had seen of the Mexican Revolution, of soldiers belonging to
Zapata or Pancho Villa.

Cruz was still looking at it when a small old man with white hair came hurrying into the room holding a baby bottle.

He glanced at Cruz, called "Hello, hello," and went right to the playpen, where he laid the child down and inserted the bottle in her mouth. Then he smiled at Cruz.

"Dennis and Elaine, they are not here now," he said. "They had to go to see a friend of theirs."

He was a funny little man with a chipmunk face, a turned-up nose and periwinkle eyes. He came up only to Cruz's shoulder and spoke with a heavy accent.

"They probably went to see Eric Hernandez," Cruz said.

The little man's face grew suspicious.

"Do you know Eric?"

Cruz shook his head.

"Not very well," he said. "I only met him recently."

The little man was suddenly enthusiastic.

"At one of the meetings," he said, wagging a finger at Cruz. "Dennis told me there was someone who maybe might come and make a contribution."

Cruz nodded cautiously.

"That's right."

The old man brightened up then.

"Don't worry, Dennis, he come back soon," he said. "I heard them talking. They had to go see Eric. Some kind of problem."

"Did they say where they were going? I'm looking for Eric too, but he's not at home."

"*No dijeron*. They didn't mention, but they will be back soon," he said. "You can wait for them."

Cruz said he would and he looked again at the photographs. The little man pointed at the wedding photo.

"That is Dennis and Elaine when they were married," he said. Then he pointed at the sepia print of the old soldiers, to a figure in the middle of the line.

"That is me," he said. "Fifty years ago when I could still

walk the mountains and shoot a rifle. I didn't hit anybody, but I think the noise used to scare the government soldiers on the other side. I always shake too much to hit the army." He held his hand up as if he were gripping a rifle and made it shake with nervousness.

The little man laughed a dry, chipmunk laugh. Cruz looked carefully at the pug-nosed figure, who was a half head shorter than the other desperadoes in the photo. It was him all right, which meant he was at least seventy-five years old.

"So you were a bandido."

"Not a bandido, no." He shook his finger in the air. "That's what the government tried to tell everyone. We were truly the first revolutionaries in our country. We were the enemies of the rich and the friends of the poor," he said proudly.

He pointed at the other figures in the photograph. "Those were my *compañeros*. They were all better fighters than me. My friends were very brave soldiers. In the end, they all died," he said without sadness. "They are our heroes and martyrs now. Really, our revolution, it lasted only a few days. But the army took its revenge and their killing went on for months. Thousands and thousands of people were massacred by the army, mostly Indians. Even people who did nothing, who had no guns, no nothing, the soldiers chopped them down. Those of us who were left, we had to get out of our country. That was 1932."

"But the war is still going on down there," Cruz said.

"It started again," he said. "That's because in our country, for the poor people nothing changed. Hunger and disease, they went through the mountains cutting people down. The rich, they got fat in their castles. One generation it passed away and then the young ones like my grandson Dennis and his friends, they saw we were right back then. They pick up the rifles again and go into the mountains."

You could see the pride in the little man's face. He was the

original rebel who saw his rowdy genes at work in his grandson
and loved the idea. Cruz looked again at the photos. He had
been a rebel too, but what they called a rebel without a cause.
He had often tried to imagine his life if his family had stayed
in Latin America. He always pictured himself in the Spanish
Colonial houses or surrounded by the jungles of the tourist
brochures, but he never really knew who he would have been,
what he would have thought and felt and done. He thought
about it now, looking into the eyes of Eric Hernandez and
Dennis Miranda. Theirs wasn't the Latin America of the brochures.

"How long was Dennis in the mountains?" he asked.

"Very little," the old man said. "His specialty is working
in the cities. Urban guerrilla warfare," he said carefully, trying
to suppress his accent. "That's what they call it now. The
underground, that is where Dennis was a master. He was
very sneaky." The old man chuckled with delight. "Before
the army found out about him, Dennis led more raids in the
capital than anyone. He stole weapons right from under the
pillows of the army guards. He robbed the banks. He walked
out of the warehouses with medicines for the fighters in the
mountains. It was Dennis who organized the system of clandestine cells in the cities, recruited the whole underground.
He was like *un hombre invisible.*"

"An invisible man," Cruz said.

"That is it. He walked through the army defenses and they
didn't see him." He smiled and shook his head. "If we had
been smart like Dennis, we would have won forty years ago."

"Is that right?" Cruz asked.

"Of course," said the old man enthusiastically. "The money
you give us goes for a very good system, a system that has
worked in other countries. Everyone is working at his own
job and people in one cell don't know the people in the other
cell. One cell finds money, one procures equipment, another

makes false documents, or recruits new members, or paints the walls with sayings, and another makes armed attacks on the army. No one knows who else is involved. It could be that a friend of yours belongs to a different cell and you don't know. That way if one person or cell is betrayed, the damage stops there. Everyone else disappears, they turn into smoke and drift away with the wind."

"And Dennis was the chief of the underground."

He nodded proudly.

"That's right. Dennis, he was the one person who know the whole operation and everyone in it. He know where the cell members live, where the safe houses are."

"They used safe houses?"

"Of course. If someone from the mountains had to come to the city, Dennis's people had a place for him or if someone was found out and the police were after him, they could hide him." The little man tapped his skull. "Dennis carried the information all around up here. He never wrote anything down that someone could find. He was the master of the underground and still the system works."

"You must be very proud," Cruz said.

The old man nodded solemnly.

"It's just too bad the army find out about him. But it was by accident, by luck only," he said pugnaciously. "They captured that other boy and they tortured him very bad. Their torturers get lessons from the devil. Finally, he told them where one safe house was and by bad luck Dennis was there when the army comes. We are lucky that he escapes alive. Thank God. The wound in the leg it leaves him no good for the mountains anymore and now they know him and he can't operate in the cities. That's why I told him to come here. Here he can use his brains to do the solidarity and organizing work, help raise the money for the fight down there. He is also studying here and applying for permanent status. Now that he is married to Elaine and the baby is here, it is better that he stay."

"And Eric?" Cruz asked.

"Eric we have known since he was a boy. He is a born guerrilla fighter. He is not clever like Dennis, but he is very brave, very noble. He was wounded even much worse than Dennis, but he still talks of going back."

Cruz nodded and proceeded cautiously.

"Yes, he seems like a person who has suffered very much," he said. "He seems disturbed, a little crazy."

The old man shrugged it off.

"That is only because of the troubles he is having with this girl."

"Gloria?"

Again the old man's face screwed up in suspicion.

"You know Gloria?"

"Yes, I met Gloria first," Cruz said. "Over on Shotwell Street. That's how I heard about Eric and Dennis and the meetings."

The old man nodded. "They were both here last night, Eric and Gloria," he said.

Cruz suppressed surprise.

"Together?"

"No, first Gloria came and then Eric."

"What time was that? I was looking for them last night."

"Gloria, she came around eight o'clock, I think. Eric he came later, maybe nine."

"Gloria just came to visit?"

He shrugged. "Who knows? Gloria, you know, she is not well. The death of her father, the other killings. She's full of devils these days."

"How do you mean, full of devils?"

"Sick," the man said tapping his skull, "she's loco. You don't know what she'll say or do ever."

"How long did she stay last night? I couldn't find her any-where."

"Maybe half an hour," the old man said. "She talked to Dennis and Elaine. I was watching the television."

"Do you know where she went after she left here?"

He shook his head. "I don't have any idea."

"How about Eric? When did he leave?"

"Eric comes right after Gloria left. He only stayed a few minutes and then he goes too. I don't know where."

"Maybe they met up some place together."

"Maybe," said the old man with a shrug. "Dennis will be back soon and maybe he can tell you."

On the television the crowd roared and the little man was distracted. The baby was working on the bottle, keeping a close eye on Cruz. If the old man wasn't suspicious anymore, she was.

Cruz looked at the photo of Eric Hernandez, in his cam-ouflage fatigues with his automatic rifle. In the eyes there was the same look as in the other photo, the seriousness, the willingness to die for the cause. But maybe he had decided to take the girl with him.

"Someone told me the problems with Gloria have made Eric act crazy. And he's walking around with a gun and threat-ening her."

The old man got a pained expression on his face.

"I know they have some troubles," he said, "but Eric still loves Gloria. That's what he told me. I don't think he would hurt her. That's a match made by God."

"Or the devil," Cruz said.

He shrugged. "Could be."

"And the gun? I was told he had an M-16 here."

The old man was wary now. He squinted at Cruz and turned back to the television.

"I don't know if he does," he said, "but a guerrilla should

always have a gun to protect himself. Even here, there are enemies. Sometimes they call in the middle of the night to threaten us. You always have to be ready."

"I'm sure Dennis is ready," Cruz said. "He has his gun."

The old man started to speak, but then there was someone talking right behind Cruz's back. "Hello," a voice said.

Cruz swiveled quickly. Standing in the room no more than three feet behind him was the short bearded man who appeared in the wedding photograph. In entering he hadn't made a sound. He addressed his grandfather.

"Hello, Papa," he said calmly. He had a polite smile on his lips, but his eyes were looking Cruz up and down icily.

The old man smiled. "I was just telling your friend here about the days when I used to pick up the rifle and scare myself more than I scared the army."

The bearded man smiled but kept his cool eyes on Cruz. "And who is this amigo, Papa?"

The old man started to answer and then realized that he didn't know Cruz's name. He looked confused. "He told me he was a friend of yours."

Cruz put up his shield and introduced himself.

"Your grandfather has just been telling me about the old guerrillas and a little about the new guerrillas, including yourself," he said.

Dennis Miranda nodded, not a trace of annoyance or any other emotion on his face. At that moment, the tall blond woman in the photograph with him stepped through the doorway and into the apartment.

"This is my wife, Elaine," Dennis Miranda said. He told his wife that Cruz was a member of the Homicide squad. She wasn't as cool as her husband. Cruz saw the wariness in her eyes right away. She crossed the apartment and picked up the child.

"Is there something we can do to help you?" Miranda asked.

"You can tell me where to find Eric Hernandez."

"I'd like to help you, but we don't know where Eric is," Miranda said.

"Your grandfather told me differently. He said you and your wife were out seeing him right now."

Miranda smiled. "My grandfather was mistaken," he said calmly. "He is an old man and sometimes he hears things wrong. He makes mistakes. My wife and I were out taking a ride in Golden Gate Park."

The old man's face was full of consternation. "I thought he was our friend, Dennis. I didn't know."

"That's all right, Papa."

"But he said—"

"It's all *right*, Papa."

"I'm looking for Eric Hernandez," Cruz said. "I have some questions for him about the murder of Gloria Soto."

The old man's mouth fell open, but Miranda showed no surprise.

"Gloria is dead, Papa," he said. "She was murdered last night. On the way back from the park we stopped at Eric's sister's house. She told us."

The old man's mouth flapped. "But how?"

"We aren't sure," Miranda said.

"When was the last time you saw Eric Hernandez?" Cruz asked him.

"He was here last night," Miranda said. "He comes here all the time. We have been friends since we were children."

"Are you a good enough friend to try to hide him?"

A smile passed behind the other man's eyes. "That would depend on why he was hiding and who he was hiding from," Miranda said.

"How about if he's hiding from the police because he killed Gloria Soto?" Cruz said.

"Then it wouldn't be Eric," Miranda said. "Eric wouldn't do something like that."

Miranda crossed in front of Cruz to the window overlooking Twenty-fourth Street, walking with a pronounced limp. He raised a hand and waved to the boys hanging out there, one of whom waved back.

"Those boys friends of yours?" Cruz asked.

Miranda shrugged. "They are young fellows who keep an eye on the block. We had troubles with a break-in here not long ago. When I pulled up just now they told me a stranger had come in and they were concerned. You never know who might try to visit you these days."

He left the window and sat at the Formica dinette table. He shook a cigarette out of a pack, proffered the pack to Cruz, who shook it off. Miranda lit one for himself, exhaling languorously. Cruz knew he was dealing with someone who had been around. Already Miranda had dealt with Cruz's unexpected presence, lied to him about where he had been and informed the old man about the girl being dead, all without a twitch. Yes, he was very cool.

Cruz sat down across from him.

"Are you afraid someone might come after you?" he asked. "Is that why you keep the boys out there?"

"I wouldn't say I was afraid," Miranda said, "just careful."

"Death squads?" asked Cruz.

Miranda shrugged.

"It doesn't matter what they call themselves," he said, "but they are people who don't care for us."

Cruz's black eyes grew both skeptical and amused, as if Miranda were a low-key but clever salesman trying to peddle him a bill of goods.

"Eric Hernandez's sister tells me he's on the run because someone threatened his life," Cruz said. "What do you think of that?"

"Yes, I know they have threatened him, just as they have threatened me. They call here at all times of the day and night. They say they will shoot me dead."

Cruz raised his eyebrows in mock concern.

"But if these threats are true, why haven't you gone underground just like your friend Eric? Aren't you afraid they'll kill you too?"

Miranda puffed at his cigarette and shrugged. "Eric has just gotten here. He is still more nervous than I am about these people."

Cruz nodded. The woman and old man looked on as if the two men were about to arm wrestle or play a life or death game of blackjack.

Cruz drummed his fingers on the table.

"You certainly are a very cool customer, Mr. Miranda," Cruz said. "Your grandfather told me of some of your adventures down in your country working in the underground and all. Being in charge of the cells and the safe houses, it sounded very exciting."

Miranda glanced at the old man, not annoyed but amused.

"My grandfather tells a lot of stories," Miranda said. "He gets his own adventures that he lived years ago mixed with other people's lives. I wouldn't believe very much of what he says."

"He told me you were the leader of the underground forces in your country," Cruz said, "that you were very smart and fearless. Other people tell me you might still be involved in those activities. Like gunrunning, for example."

"Then they are very badly informed," the bearded man said. "Everyone knows for the past several years the guerrilla forces in our country have captured all the weapons they need from the army. There's no need to smuggle arms, unless, of course, you are smuggling them to the army."

Miranda smiled and flicked his ash.

"The other thing your grandfather told me was that Gloria Soto was here last night," Cruz said.

The faintest shadow of concern passed behind Miranda's cool gaze.

"That's right," he said, "she was here about eight o'clock."

"Why did she come here?"

"She wanted to talk to my wife and myself," Miranda said. "She has adopted us, as you say, as her big brother and sister here. She tells us her problems."

"What problems did she have last night?"

The answer came from behind Cruz, from Elaine Miranda, who was holding her child.

"She told us she was afraid someone was going to hurt her. This creep she's been going out with."

Cruz turned to her. The child was sucking on the bottle, still watching him carefully.

"Julio Saenz?"

"That's right. He's a creep who smuggles refugees up from the border. We told her she shouldn't hang around with a bum like that and I think she was going to break it off with him, but he wouldn't let her and she was afraid. That's who you should be looking for, not Eric. Eric wouldn't harm a hair on Gloria's head."

"You have to understand," Dennis Miranda said calmly, "that Gloria was constantly afraid something was going to happen to her. When she first came up here from our country, she was hearing voices, seeing people, reliving killings she had seen. It made her very afraid."

"The killing of her father?"

"Yes, the death of her father, but also the killing of the Hernandez family, Eric's people."

Cruz pulled a face.

"She actually saw them killed?"

"She saw that massacre with her own eyes," Miranda said. "It happened near her house. We think that was what drove her loco, that and her father's death."

Cruz scowled as if he'd taken a jab in the face. He was trying to picture it.

"Elvira Hernandez didn't tell me about that."

Elaine Miranda said, "If it was your family that had been gunned down, maybe you wouldn't want to talk about it. Maybe you wouldn't want to have to remember the details."

"Maybe," Cruz said. "And then Gloria became afraid someone would kill her too."

"She started telling us about a week ago that she was afraid something was going to happen to her," Miranda said. "We knew Eric wouldn't hurt her, so we figured it was Saenz she was afraid of. We told her to stop seeing him, but we didn't really think he would do anything to her. We just tried to calm her down."

"Why would he want to kill her? Because he was in the smuggling business and she knew about it?"

"No, it was more than that. She said she knew something she wasn't supposed to know. It wasn't just that Saenz was a mule. Everyone knew that. It had to be something more."

Cruz's tone grew cynical.

"She didn't say what it was she knew, not even to you, her adopted big brother and sister?"

"I didn't insist on knowing," Miranda said. "As I said, I thought it was all in her imagination." He smoked. "Of course, now we know her fears were real."

"So you're telling me it was this Saenz character who killed her, the mule?"

"Almost certainly."

"Almost," Cruz said, looking into the other man's eyes.

From his days on the street Cruz knew that the secret to being a good liar was building a whole story, a complete world in your head of which the lie was only a small part. Then you could say it without too much pressure, without the shaky eye. Miranda, Cruz could tell, was a man with a world in his head.

Cruz looked from one to the other. "It's funny, you just coming now from seeing Elvira Hernandez. It's interesting because this is the same story she was trying to tell me."

"It's the truth," Elaine Miranda insisted.

Cruz looked at Miranda, who remained unruffled.

"Did Gloria say where she was going after she left here?" Cruz asked.

"No. I thought she was going home," Miranda said.

"She didn't go home," Cruz said. "How about Eric Hernandez, what did he have to say? I understand he came just after Gloria left, stayed a few minutes and went out."

"He didn't say he was going to kill Gloria, if that's what you want to know."

"Did he see her going out? Did he ask you where she was going?"

"I don't think he saw her and he didn't ask me anything. He stayed a few minutes and I told him what Gloria had said. I said I didn't believe it, but it made him worried and he left right away."

"So maybe he went looking for her."

"Maybe." Elaine Miranda spoke again. "That would be like Eric to want to protect Gloria. That's what he was like. He didn't want to kill her."

"And even though your grandfather told me you were out seeing Eric, you still insist you don't know where he is?"

"I told you, Inspector, my grandfather is an old man, he sometimes gets confused."

Cruz drummed his fingers on the table.

"Elvira Hernandez just finished telling me what a loyal friend you have always been to Eric." Amusement flitted across Miranda's gaze. "And your grandfather has told me about how good you were at hiding people who were on the run. How you set up those houses—what were they called?"

"Safe houses."

"That's right. They were to hide guerrillas from the mountains hiding out in the city."

"Yes, that is so, Inspector. There were always people who would help us. Ordinary people who lived in the most ordinary houses. Nobody ever suspected them and it was almost impossible for the army to find those houses. They used to waste a lot of time looking," he shrugged. "But, of course, that was back in our country. Here those kinds of houses don't exist."

Cruz smiled. "I'm sure they don't."

Miranda became serious. "You could save yourself a lot of time and a lot of mistakes just looking for the people who really killed Gloria Soto," he said.

"Because you have Eric Hernandez hidden away so well in your underground that I won't find him."

Miranda was expressionless. "I don't know what you're talking about. What I'm trying to tell you is Eric didn't kill Gloria. Eric was a guerrilla fighter. He killed in combat. He doesn't go around shooting women who can't defend themselves."

Here was another one with "illusions" about his fellow man. Even with the killing he'd seen. But it was different in a war. He didn't have to look at the ones killed over a swallow of cheap wine at the bottom of a bottle, over a parking space or a few lousy dollars. If Cruz had Miranda's kind of illusions, he would never have found even one murderer.

"When he was here last night, was he carrying a weapon?"

"No, he wasn't."

"You're sure?"

Miranda nodded smugly. "I have a very good eye for that sort of detail, Inspector. He wasn't armed."

"And you, do you have a gun?"

"Not me," Miranda said. "I'm a student and on the side I'm a waiter at a restaurant. Why would I need a gun?"

"What restaurant is that?"

"The Quetzal. We serve both Salvadoran and Guatemalan food," he said. "You should come in some time."

"Maybe I will," Cruz said.

He got up, crossed the room and stopped at the head of the hallway.

"Harboring a suspect in a homicide is a serious matter. It's a felony. And for someone who is applying for permanent status in the United States and has a wife and a small baby it wouldn't be a good idea to get into that kind of trouble."

Elaine Miranda couldn't hide the concern in her eyes, although Miranda himself betrayed no emotion. Cruz smiled.

"Nothing shakes you, does it, Mr. Miranda?"

"I've done nothing wrong," he said. "And I've been threatened before, Inspector, all my life, in fact."

"You think you're protecting Eric Hernandez, but you may be putting him in more danger," Cruz said. "This isn't your old country, Mr. Miranda. Here when somebody goes underground, it means they're getting buried."

Miranda smiled, but the woman, the old man and the child all followed Cruz with enormous eyes as he walked out.

Cruz went out into the street and saw that the boys were still there, hands gripping beer cans, eyes on him as he hurried down the street. He glanced back up to Miranda's house as he climbed into his car and saw the bearded man standing there watching him. He glanced at his watch, drummed his fingers on the steering wheel for several moments, his lips pressed in thought. Then he cranked it up, figuring he'd get something to eat and then head for Stacy Stoner's house.

CHAPTER 6

Saturday night had arrived, but the cool breezes off the ocean hadn't come with it. Mission Street was neon and slow traffic, the electric buses knocking white sparks off the overhead wires and a heat as thick and still as the night itself.

Cruz stopped at a Chinese restaurant near Army Street, a place he had known since his days on the beat. The decor was nonexistent, the food was good, their service for cops extra fast and the beer always frosty. He ordered a cold Tsingtao, egg rolls and a plate of moo goo gai pan. He drained the Tsingtao quickly and they brought him another cold one. The egg rolls were crispy on the outside and hot inside and the moo goo vegetables were fresh and cooked just enough. He drained the beer, they gave him a check for half the menu price, he left a big tip and a half hour after he'd walked in, he was headed for Stacy Stoner's place.

Stacy Stoner was a fixture in the Mission District, a psychiatric social worker who had worked in the barrio ever since Cruz had been on the beat. She spent her whole life doing missionary work on the dark side of human nature; her clients were the desperate, the violent, the would-be suicides, the drug dependent, the psychotic. Cruz had once crouched next to her for five tense hours in a dark tenement apartment as she soothingly talked to an unemployed Mexican man who held a pistol against the skull of his terrified ten-year-old son. Finally, as if the hours of words had slowly filled the pistol and made it too heavy to hold, he let it drop and fell into her arms. With the sobbing man wrapped in her embrace, Stacy had turned to Cruz with a shrug: "Well, all's not lost, at least I have a date for tonight."

Stacy was the calm at the eye of people's individual storms and had saved a lot of them from worse troubles. Of course, sometimes the storms dragged them away and they ended up badly, like Gloria Soto.

Soft lights shone behind the lace curtains of the two-story white house on Nineteenth Street. Just a block and a half away lived Cruz's wife. She had moved there after the separation, and as he walked up to the porch, he caught himself wondering what she was doing that night.

When he rang the bell, one of the curtains moved, and then Stacy opened the door.

"Hello, David," she said. "I've been expecting one of you guys."

The other thing that set Stacy Stoner apart, besides her dedication to borderline people, was the way she looked. In her stocking feet she was six foot one, and her long natural blond hair fell way down her back. She joked that she was so big and different-looking that her patients were afraid not to get well. Her face was too long and thin to be beautiful, but her eyes were too blue and intelligent not to attract attention. Right now they were a bit bloodshot and he smelled a whiff of alcohol on her breath.

"Her uncle called me a while ago," she said. She led Cruz down a hallway and left him in a small study. On the desk sat an ice bucket, a half-empty glass and a bottle of Scotch with a large dent in it. Also on the desk was a manila folder with a sticker on it that said "Gloria Soto." He picked it up and beneath it found another folder, this one labeled "Eric Hernandez." He flipped it open and found a note on top of the file, dated August 15, the day before, the day of Gloria Soto's death. It started, "Eric called at 10:00 P.M. . . ." He heard footsteps and put the folders down.

"I tell my patients not to drink when something is bothering them and now look at me," Stacy said. She was carrying another glass for Cruz. She didn't seem drunk, just sad, worn out.

"You had Eric Hernandez as a patient also," Cruz said. "I didn't know that."

Stacy glanced at the files and back at him with mock severity. "You've been spying," he said. She took the files and stuck them into a drawer of a filing cabinet. "Yes, I treated both at the same time, ever since Eric arrived here two months ago," she said, pouring Cruz a drink. "It was a horror movie, a double feature, let me tell you. Do you know Eric?"

"No, but I'd like to," Cruz said. "I'd like to talk to him about all this."

Stacy peered over her glass at Cruz, her eyes suddenly full of suspicion.

"You're not thinking Eric killed Gloria, are you?"

There was an edge on her words that made Cruz proceed carefully.

"You don't think so?"

"No, I don't," she said flatly. She drained what was left in her glass and then put it on the desk before Cruz like a contestant in a drinking contest. "If you think he killed her, you're way off track."

Cruz sipped his drink and said nothing. He had seen Stacy Stoner like this before: the Mama Bear standing up for her clients, protecting her young. Her blue eyes were cool and wary. When she was like that, you didn't want to tangle with her.

Cruz changed tactics.

"I'm not accusing, I'm just asking," he said, crossing a leg. "I've heard different opinions about this Eric Hernandez. I've heard different versions about what happened down in their country and up here after he showed up."

"You've heard the version from her uncle, is what you mean?" Stacy asked, sticking out her chin. "Her uncle is no pillar of truth, let me tell you."

"I wouldn't doubt it," Cruz said. "He looked crooked."

"It makes sense he would blame Eric," she said. "He's accused Eric of everything else that's happened to his family. Why not accuse him of Gloria's death?"

Stacy took ice from a bucket, poured Scotch over it and, slouching in her chair, sipped it. She sank into her own thoughts. She had black circles under her eyes and her hand shook. Cruz could see she was taking this one hard.

"The first thing is what happened down in El Salvador," she said, stirring the Scotch with a finger. "What happened is both these kids went through hell, David. Absolute hell. These aren't kids with adolescent hassles. Both of them had the earth open up under their feet and they fell right into hell. They were both badly burned, especially Gloria."

"The killings of her brother and father," Cruz said.

"Her brother died a few years ago and I never got it straight who killed him," said Stacy. "I know it wasn't Eric. Gloria told me so herself. She said she was with Eric when her brother died. But I do know what happened six months ago. Eric's parents and his two young brothers were massacred."

"By death squads," Cruz said. "That's what I'm told."

"That's right." Stacy sipped her Scotch. "I know something else. Gloria's father was the one who sent the killers to their house and Gloria was a witness to the massacre. And there's a connection between that and her death."

"Yes, and the connection is Eric," Cruz said. "That's what Victor Soto says."

"No, it isn't," Stacy said flatly. "That's what Soto wants you to believe, but it isn't true. The connection is the killers."

It was Cruz's turn to sip his Scotch. "Did Gloria think that?"

Stacy grimaced. "I'm not sure Gloria 'thought' anything. She was too scared out of her head. Her only emotion was fear. Fear of her memories and fear that it would happen to her as well. Working with her was like walking through a jungle. You never knew what was going to come out at you. She screamed and she bit and she scratched."

Cruz nodded. He had dealt with the relatives of the dead and witnesses to violent death. It was one thing if you were a cop, you knew violence would come your way. It was like the wind, sooner or later you knew it would blow. But people who weren't expecting it, and even some who were, it could blow them away.

"But leave it to Stacy, Queen of the Jungle. I dragged the story out of her bit by bit. Then I understood why she was terrified. And now I think I know why she was killed. What she saw that day Eric's family was killed is what matters."

"So what did she see?" Cruz asked. "Who did she see? What does it have to do with anything or anybody up here?"

"She saw Eric's family—his parents and his brothers—put up against a wall and shot in cold blood and left for the vultures to eat. That's it in a nutshell."

"By this death squad."

"That's what they call them," Stacy said and she knocked back some Scotch.

"And you think they're here now?"

"One of them, or more, or friends of theirs," Stacy said. "Yes, I do."

"I see," Cruz said. He ran a hand over his face as if he were trying to wipe off the skepticism. Stacy wasn't a bleeding heart. But sometimes she tried to muscle you so you'd go easy on her people.

"But if she was standing watching all of this, why didn't they kill her too?" Cruz asked.

"They didn't see her. She was watching from the woods and they didn't know it."

"How did that happen? She just happened to walk by?"

Stacy shook her head.

"Eric was with the guerrillas for four years," she said. "Every once in a while he would send word to his parents and he would meet them at a shack they had in the hills near the plantation. Just to show them he was still alive. Gloria would sneak away and see him there for a few minutes or an hour. Sometimes her father found out, but it was always too late. Eric had already gone back up into the mountains. Sneaky as a fox.

"This time, a Sunday it was, Eric's parents and brothers all left the plantation, which is what they usually did on Sunday. But Gloria's father somehow got a notion something was up. He was sneaky himself. He went to the village to tell the retired colonel there who was head of the local vigilantes, the local death squad. A pillar of local society."

"And he took Gloria along for the show," Cruz said. "That doesn't sound right."

Stacy shook him off.

"No. Gloria heard her father talking to one of the farmhands and took off on foot for the shack to warn Eric before the squads got there."

Cruz gazed into the past as if he could see Gloria running.

"And she didn't get there in time," he said.

"She got there at exactly the wrong time. She had a bad sense of timing, that girl," Stacy said. "Eric wasn't even there yet, but that didn't matter much. She was just coming out of the trees when the trucks pulled up. They dragged the old man and his wife and the two sons out of the shack, lined them up against the wall. They tied their thumbs behind their backs. The colonel questioned them a bit. He asked them where Eric was, but of course, they said they didn't know. Then he walked away and the others just mowed them down."

Cruz was frowning now.

"And Gloria was watching it."

"That's right. With the shooting, she started to scream. Her father had come along with the killers. He discovered her there. He told his friends, the death squad people, he would keep her quiet, and he dragged her back home. Some way to spend Sunday afternoon, isn't it?"

"Yes. Very pleasant," Cruz said, but his face was twisted now with doubt. He drank some of his Scotch. "And Eric?"

Stacy shook her head sadly. "Eric didn't get there until dusk," Stacy said. "He told me from a distance he could see the vultures circling in the air and he got very scared. He approached carefully and from the woods he saw the bodies still lying where they had fallen. The colonel had left them there as a warning to other peasants: This is what happens to you if you collaborate with the guerrillas, even if it's just to visit with your own flesh and blood."

"So he went to kill her father?"

"No, he didn't," Stacy said. "Eric didn't know it was Gloria's father who had sent the killers. He waited until dark, to make sure the soldiers weren't waiting in ambush. Then he buried his dead and headed back to join his unit. It was another group of guerrillas who found out about it and showed up late the next night at the plantation to take revenge."

"And Gloria was there to see that one also."

"I told you this is the horror show of horror shows," Stacy said. Her words were starting to blur at the edges. "A double feature. Gloria was still hysterical because of what she had seen at the shack. She was in bed and her mother and father were taking care of her, trying to soothe her. Even though it was her father who had caused the killing to happen in the first place. All of a sudden some men in camouflage kicked in the door of the house and dragged her father out by the hair."

"Guerrillas."

"That's right. According to Gloria's mother, Gloria went running out of the house after them, just in time to hear the rebels sentence her father on the spot and see one of them put a gun to his head and blow him away. Bam!"

Cruz winced as if he'd been hit with a solid right. Stacy shook her head.

"I told you she had one sense of timing. This girl's life was like other people's nightmares, David. And her nightmares came true in real life. After a while, she couldn't tell one from another. She lived in terror."

Cruz nodded and sipped his Scotch. He thought about people you sometimes saw wandering the streets of the city, especially the refugees, who looked as if they were walking through mine fields. You were careful with these people because it seemed at any moment they might go off. They had brought a fear with them that always sat in their eyes and became part of everything they saw around them. It didn't matter that they were in San Francisco, to them it was still the jungle. And all you could do was wonder what had happened inside them to make them so scared.

"And then she came here," Cruz said.

"That's right. The land of opportunity. After her father died, her uncle, Victor Soto, brought her and her mother here. He smuggled them across the border and into California by coyote."

"That's where Julio Saenz picked her up."

Stacy frowned. "You know him?"

"No, I haven't had the pleasure yet."

Stacy closed her eyes and shivered all over. "You're gonna love it. He's a real piece of work."

"That's what I hear."

"It's the story of beauty and the beast. Gloria was beautiful and she took up with this three-hundred-pound animal who looks like something out of Aztec mythology. No offense intended."

"Why?"

"God knows," she said. "The whole relationship was sick. I know on the way up here from LA he had her ride in the front seat of the van with him while he kept the other people locked up in the back. Along the way they stopped off at a motel and had sex. I don't know how she did it, unless he forced her. Sex between those two people seems biologically impossible."

"You think he forced her?"

"I asked her over and over, but never got a straight story. Either she was afraid to begin with and just let him do it, or he raped her and then threatened her so she wouldn't tell. She would never talk about him."

"And she kept seeing him even after she got up here."

"That's right. Even after I told her she shouldn't and after I told her uncle too. Lots they listened to me. There was something going on there, some reason I never got out of her. But I know she was scared of him."

She took another nip of Scotch and then the telephone on the desk rang. She picked it up, said hello, and listened, her eyes focusing on something far away.

"No, don't come," she said. "I have someone here right now. I'll call you back." She listened again. "You call me back, then, make sure."

She hung up. "Where were we?"

"Nothing urgent?"

"In this business, it's always urgent," she said blithely.

"We were talking about Julio Saenz," Cruz said.

"How could I forget?"

"You said she was scared of him."

"Gloria was scared period. But lately even more. Something happened in the past week to put a real scare into her. Over the past few months she had made some progress. Her hallucinations were abating. I had her calmed down some. I thought I did. Then a week ago she started losing it again. She started having flashbacks, seeing the massacre. Or I thought they were flashbacks. All she would say was, 'I saw something I shouldn't have seen and the colonel will be angry with me.' She said that over and over. She was much more afraid for herself. She told me she was afraid she would die."

"But she had always said that."

"Yes, that's what I said to myself," she said. "Leave it to Stacy, the ace psychologist. I thought it was just a momentary relapse."

"And now you don't think so."

"Momentary relapses of that kind don't result in bullets to the brain," she said. "The girl's dead, David."

"And you're blaming yourself," Cruz said. "That's why you're hogging all the Scotch." She poured Cruz more, freshened her own, sipped at it and frowned into the past.

"She told me someone would kill her and I didn't believe it," she said.

"The girl saw ghosts everywhere she went and you're supposed to take her seriously?" asked Cruz.

Stacy stared at him emptily.

"And you think Saenz had something to do with it," Cruz said, "or maybe someone who wanted to shut her up about the killing of Eric's family."

"One of the rat's nest," she said. "That's what Eric calls some of his countrymen here, *un nido de ratas.*"

Cruz gazed down into his Scotch as if it were a golden crystal ball.

"But you don't think it was Eric himself," he said, "even though he was the one who was jilted, even though he's the one who was walking around with a gun, threatening Gloria, and even though he's the one on the run."

"Eric never threatened Gloria," Stacy said pugnaciously. "If he followed her, it was to protect her. He was afraid for her."

Cruz passed a hand over his face, trying to wipe the fatigue from it. If he looked anything like Stacy, he was very tired and sad, indeed. All the cleverness, the sarcasm had drained from her and they were back where they had started.

"Gloria's uncle said when she left the house last night she was heading here," Cruz told her.

Stacy shook her head. "She didn't make it," she said, "but around two o'clock in the morning she called here."

Cruz's head came up.

"So she was still alive at two o'clock. What did she say?"

Stacy shook her head.

"I don't know because I wasn't here," she said. "I was out at a party and didn't get back until three. My mother answered the phone and recognized Gloria's voice. When she said I wasn't here, Gloria hung up."

"Nothing else? She didn't say anything? Did she sound scared?"

"She didn't say anything," Stacy said, "and Gloria always sounded scared. It wasn't the first time she'd called late at night, so my mother didn't make much out of it. Neither did I, until I heard she was dead."

Cruz watched Stacy warily as if she herself was the terrible series of events she had related and he had to worry what might happen in her next.

"How about Eric, have you heard from him in the past two days?" Cruz asked.

Stacy looked him straight in the eyes, but said nothing.

"This is someone we want to talk to about a murder, Stacy. It's serious business."

She squinted and took a while to answer. "I'm worried about what's going on inside him, David. You have to understand.

Gloria was his whole life. His plans, his dreams were tied up in her. More than anything he wanted her to get well so that after the war was over in their country, they could make their life together. Now that she's dead, I don't know how he'll react. I don't know what he'll do."

"You mean suicide?"

Her eyebrows went up in surprise. "Not that. He could be dangerous to the people who killed her, David. It could get very nasty around here. He could go after them and then he could get himself hurt. I lost one of them. I don't want to lose the other."

"I understand," Cruz said. He glanced at the file cabinet. "How 'bout if you let me take a look at his file? It might help me put things together."

She shook her head. "No, I can't do that, David. Eric is my patient. My relation with him, including everything in that file, is confidential. So is Gloria's file, at least for now."

"We're dealing with homicide here, Stacy. Other people could get hurt."

She looked very tired, very sad. "If I thought it was Eric, it would be different. But it isn't him."

"You're the one who said all his dreams were tied up in Gloria," Cruz said. "She told him to take a walk. How do you know that didn't make him crack? How do you know that everything that has happened to him didn't finally drive him over the edge? He's a human being, Stacy, maybe he just couldn't take any more."

"Go to my supervisors," she said. "Maybe they'll agree with you."

She drained the last half finger of Scotch and placed the empty glass before him. Cruz sat in front of her, bobbing tiredly. Then he got up, took out a business card and laid it on the desk.

"Don't do anything foolish, Stacy," he said. "Like you said, you don't know what's inside him." She nodded at him but said nothing.

Cruz left her sitting there looking bad and let himself out. He started the car, turned at the corner and found himself on the street where his wife lived. He went a block farther than was necessary and passed the yellow clapboard house with the peacock painted on the side. He looked and noticed there were lights on. If she saw him, what would she think? She wouldn't believe he was staking out a house waiting for a suspect. She would think he wanted her back, that he couldn't stay away, that he was lonely for her.

He sped up like someone escaping the scene of a crime, went all the way around the block and parked where he could again see the Stoner house. He sat listening to the last of the Giants game. An occasional siren sounded and died in the night. He sat there forty minutes and then decided to give it up.

He had started to pull away when he saw the figure come around the corner beyond the house. Cruz hit his brakes and stopped in the middle of the street to get a good look at him, or as good as he could get maybe 150 feet away. The T-shirt looked black and the pants might be camouflage.

The individual had stopped as well, dead in his tracks on the sidewalk. Then he started to back away in the direction he had come. Cruz jammed it into reverse and turned the wheel. He saw Eric Hernandez pivot and sprint around the corner into darkness, and he put the gas pedal to the floor and turned the same corner, searching the street and seeing nobody. He braked and jumped out, then listened. He heard nobody running. He heard nothing. He got in and drove quickly around the block, then started knocking on doors, checking backyards, waking up people. When he got to his wife's house, he hesitated. She would think he was making it up, he thought again.

Then he climbed the stairs and pushed the bell. He heard it ring inside, but there was no other sound. He looked through the window into the living room: no one there. It was Saturday—she was probably out with her artsy friends, talking post-modernism and sampling wines. It was too bad; she had missed a chance to meet one of her guerrilla heroes. He rang the bell one more time, just to make sure, then left.

Cruz continued to comb the rest of the block but found nothing. It was like the man said, Eric Hernandez had gone up in smoke.

He drove around another half hour. He passed Elvira Hernandez's house, but there were no lights. Then he went back to Stacy Stoner's place to give her a hard time, but the car was gone from the driveway and the house was dark. He didn't drive by the yellow clapboard house again.

He started home, but his house was empty too and the Scotch Stacy had pumped into him had given him a start, that and the story she had told. He stopped at the bar on Valencia and ordered a double.

CHAPTER 7

A sharp sound penetrated his paper-thin sleep and even before he had opened his eyes, he was grasping for the M-16. He jumped up like a shot, the rifle turreting to all sides. He had committed a cardinal sin, he had fallen asleep on watch and let them close in on him. Son of a whore! He felt exposed, trapped in the bright moonlight that made him a sitting duck. With the intake of breath, he expected the shots to come.

But all that came was silence, except for the pounding of his own heart. Not even the sound of the wind in the trees or the pulsing of the cicadas, because there were no trees, no cicadas. He looked around the yard wide-eyed, like a maniac, as if the bush about him had suddenly disappeared, and he had been transported in his sleep to this strange place where he would die. What the fuck was happening? The light came not from the moon that softly flooded the mountains, but from a harsh streetlight beyond the fence, being battered by moths. There were no outlines of trees against the sky, only the spindly arms of a television antenna growing from the dark gable of a house. The sound, he knew now, hadn't been a twig snapping as someone approached or a faraway shot, but a window being closed or a car door slamming. And the shots didn't come, just the sound of his own heart.

He lowered the automatic rifle, and the pounding began

to slow. He sat back down, laid the rifle across his lap and rubbed his eyes. Somewhere nearby, a car roared to a start. The sound might have been the hungry growl of the jaguar. Given a choice, he told himself, he would prefer the jaguar. He would prefer the cold mountaintop, the tarantulas, the coral snakes, the fleas, the torrential rain. He would prefer it all to the city, or as his sister had called it, somebody else's jungle.

He looked blearily around the yard, at the tall wooden fence surrounding it and the three small tents pitched in a row. The tents would be good to have in the mountains. They were a waste here in the city. In the mountains, he had only used hammocks, which left you vulnerable. Even with mosquito netting over the hammocks and a canvas cover, the insects and rain still got to you. Sleeping was something you learned to do wet and with a buzz in your ear. Like planes coming to suck your blood. In a tent you wouldn't hear them and they couldn't get you. He would like to take these tents to his *compañeros*. What he didn't like at all was that right now the people in them, sleeping all around him, were strangers, possible betrayers. In the mountains, he slept surrounded by men he had fought next to, brothers for whom he would die. These people in the tents now, illegals like him, seemed like good, simple poor people, but he didn't know them and he couldn't trust them. They scared him, just as the whole city scared him.

He lit a cigarette, cupping the match carefully out of habit, not wanting the flame or the live ash to be seen. He had been in the city two months already and still he acted like a skittish animal. He was like a deer turned loose in the middle of this place with its buildings and lights and cars and buses. He had once heard of a deer running wild in a city. It had seen its own reflection in a window and jumped right through it. It thought it was seeing another deer. You need brothers, he thought. Everybody does.

A light went on in a window of an adjoining house and he

glanced up. In the mountains he used to look up for shooting stars or the first rays of moonlight touching the ridges. Here even the fucking sky seemed different. The stars weren't as bright and seemed much farther away. The whole sky was blurry, not the sharp pinpricks of cold light he saw above him there. Everything was different in the city, the sky, the earth, the air, the human beings.

"Just stay put," Dennis Miranda had told him. "You don't know this place. You don't know how to move here. You don't know how to survive on these streets."

He was right, too. Here, he was like a calf at the mercy of wolves. Not like back home, where he had learned to survive with nothing more than his will to live and his wits. There he had learned how to see at night, like a cat; how to find clean drinking water in the middle of nowhere; how to dig below wet soil to find dry earth to sleep on; how to make canopies out of banana leaves and slant them right so that the rain ran off and kept you dry, even in bad storms. The first time, he hadn't slanted it and the weight of the cold water had brought it crashing down on him in the middle of the night. But he had learned to survive.

There was a lot he knew. How to start fires in the rain. How to hide your fire so that army planes wouldn't see it. How to skin and cook an animal and salt it so you could carry it. When your bullets got wet, how to put them in the sun so that the powder would dry.

In the city, that was all useless, *he* was useless, a scared animal. With all its attractions and comforts, it was no place for a man like him.

When he had first come, he had thought differently. In his first days in San Francisco, the city had seduced him like a woman who made you feel warm and comfortable. For years he had been sleeping in the mud, eating beans and tortillas cold, dressing himself in clothes always wet with dew and rain. In the first days, the city had stripped him of his wet clothes, bathed him in hot water, put him to bed on a soft mattress, fed him warm food, meat even, and had told him, "Don't be afraid, sleep tight. No one here is trying to kill you. You are safe."

But, of course, it wasn't true. The fucking city was full of enemies. And the city itself was an enemy. It tried to lull you to sleep and when you needed it, it gave you nothing to survive. There wasn't even a bird to shoot, except for a dirty pigeon. You couldn't start a fire of any kind. You were surrounded by stores full of food and couldn't go into them. You could smell the food cooking around you, but couldn't make a deal to buy a plate of it, the way you could with the *campesinos*. You didn't know them, they didn't know you. You were like a man from another planet.

He smoked and looked at himself, at the camouflage that covered his legs. In the mountains these clothes helped you blend right into the bush. There were times he had sat just yards off a trail and made fools of the soldiers, watching them go by; they hadn't even gotten a whiff of him. Here these clothes made you stick out, like a moving pile of brush. In the city, to blend in, you had to wear the colors of concrete, steel and glass.

"And the people here are different," Dennis Miranda had said. "You won't know who is who. You don't know what the *guardia* look like and how they work."

That was true too. On the sidewalks and the streets, you couldn't read boot tracks, you couldn't decipher bent brush and the ashes left behind. The police wore uniforms, but there were some who didn't, like that one tonight outside Miss Stoner's house where he had almost fallen into the trap. He wore regular clothes and might have been anyone, that damned *policía*. He might have been one of the rat's nest. How was one to know? Either way, he would carry a gun. He could shoot you down.

Even Dennis seemed scared. Not just careful, but afraid.

"Don't call here," Dennis had said, "and don't call home. You don't know who may be listening."

If there was a master urban guerrilla, a magician in the city, it was Dennis. He knew how to hide, how to escape, how to live in their midst. You did what he said.

But how to put up with the loneliness? How to put up with being cut off from your people and not knowing what was happening? Dennis hadn't told him that. For that reason, he had called Miss Stoner. To try to know what was happening, to talk to someone who could tell him who was hunting him and how. And not to be penned up like a snake in a hole.

Once on the street, he had moved as the city people moved, minding his own business, looking at nobody, sticking to the shadows, the way in the mountains you stayed in the bush. And still it had scared him very much. All those windows, all those faces, the headlights that turned corners and scoured you like searchlights. Dozens of people staring out at you from the brightly lighted buses. The sparks jumping off the electric bus lines, making you flinch. No matter what route you took, there was no way to avoid the people and possible betrayal.

You had to be even more careful, more scared here. He had decided not to call Miss Stoner back because that seemed dangerous. She didn't know "who might be listening." She didn't know about these kinds of dangers. Instead he had waited a while and then tried to get close to the house, just like back home, approaching the houses of collaborators, making sure no strangers were visiting, and that the soldiers had not uncovered them and were not lying in wait to kill him. So he had waited down the block and across the street and when he thought it was safe he had approached carefully.

But the *policía* had been waiting. Son of a whore! Not in a police car with lights on top, but just as Dennis had warned him. Out of uniform in a car like any car. Then all he could do was run and that had scared him worst of all, because he didn't know how to run in the fucking city. In the mountains you ran up the slope so you could get the drop on those who wanted to kill you, or you ran them through a narrow pass and ambushed them there, or you just ran faster than they and put distance between you and their guns. But this one had a car and you couldn't outrun him. You had to hide.

So he had taken the first corner and started looking for alleyways, pools of shadows to dive into and disappear. Behind him he had heard the squeal of the tires, like a screech of pain, and the roar of the car engine. It was like having a big cat after you and no way to protect yourself from its teeth.

And then he had seen the house and recognized it—bright yellow with the peacock painted on the side—like a gift from God. He had been in that house one night when Dennis had talked to a group of gringos: artists, he said. "They know almost nothing," Dennis said, "but they are willing to help." He himself had sat in the back, understanding little, saying nothing, dark-skinned in that sea of white, like the displaced animal he knew himself to be.

But now he ran for it with the tires squealing, the jaguar's hunting call at his heels. Fifty paces up the street, he turned off the sidewalk, out of the streetlight, cut up the driveway, and then suddenly found himself up against a tall fence. In that moment he thought he had finally found the fence that bordered his death.

In the street he heard the screech again, the headlights came scanning around the corner and a spotlight appeared, its beam prying into the yards, coming toward him. In the mountains they fired flares into the air that lighted the hills like day and pinned you to the ground. Here they would pin him to the fence.

And then he saw it, the hatch door that led down into a cellar. He tried the door, it opened, he climbed down several stairs and let the door down softly, closing the night and the jaguar out behind him.

The strong odor of paint filled his nostrils. A light was on and he saw the room was disordered, full of rags and boxes, and in the middle, a painter's easel and a painting. It was the head of a man, a Latin with deep black eyes that looked straight at him and startled him. But it was only a painting. The person who had painted it had not done a good job on the nose, it was crooked.

He stood, his back against the wall, slowly gaining his breath, then came the sound of a door opening above, someone climbing downstairs toward him, and his fear became real. Son of the great whore! He went to his knees, like a fox scrambling to get beneath chicken wire, and crawled behind the boxes and other paintings stacked there.

He saw the shoes first, not a man's, but a woman's. Then next to the easel the face came into view, light-skinned, blond, *gringa*, good-looking like an actress in an American movie. He slipped his hand into his pocket and felt the cold steel of the pistol. He could not let her scream.

But she didn't see him; not at first. For minutes she just stood in front of the easel and stared at the canvas, as if the painted face was talking to her and she was listening. She nodded, she squinted, she moved her head one way, then another. She looked a little crazy, this *gringa*, and that worried him. Crazy people, you didn't know what they would do at any moment. Like Gloria. You never knew.

And then suddenly she was looking right at him. She frowned, but said nothing, only stared at him suspiciously. It was as if she were looking at another canvas and didn't remember painting it. Then she was looking at the pants, the camouflage.

He held a finger to his lips and his eyes implored her. The other hand stayed on the pistol in his pocket, just in case. There was something strange about the woman. She didn't scream or even back away. She just looked at him, curious and wary.

When she spoke, it was bad Spanish with a heavy accent, but good enough so he could understand.

"I know who you are," she said. "You were here one night and I just heard about you on the radio."

He shook his head.

"I didn't do it," he whispered to her. "I didn't kill her."

She stared at him and he knew she was deciding.

"I didn't," he said. "I loved her."

She watched him carefully, her eyes full of doubt.

Then suddenly the sound of shoes thudded on the wooden porch above and the bell sounded, like a shot going off just above them and echoing through the house. Without wanting to, he flinched. He looked at her and knew she could see his fear, smell it on him.

There was no other sound at first, only that of his heart trying to explode from his chest. She turned and walked to the basement window, showing him her back as if he didn't have a gun, and she had nothing to fear. Then the bell rang once more, the footsteps sounded again on the porch and descended the stairs. She stood to the side of the window and suddenly he saw her eyes get very big and her mouth open. In that moment, he thought she would call to the *policía*, that she would scream. He was sure he would have to kill her. His arm came up and his finger closed on the trigger. But she didn't make a sound. Just as quickly, her mouth closed and eyes narrowed. She stepped back from the window, as if she also didn't want to be found.

They both listened as the footsteps disappeared down the walk. Then she turned to him and watched him with that same look, as if he were a painting she didn't understand.

From one of the tents, a snore erupted, like the growl of a small, sharp-toothed animal. He smoked and held the rifle across his legs, remembering, then reached into the flapped pocket of the camouflage pants and took out the pistol as well. Here they used pistols. He was used to the rifle, but Dennis said it was too big, too visible.

"Don't take that thing," Dennis had told him. "Don't be crazy." But without it, he felt unprotected. You knew they were hunting you, so how could you not have your gun?

"A guerrilla is never without his rifle." That was what he had told Gloria and it was true.

In the distance, across the hills and valleys of the city, there was a howling. A city howling. A police siren chasing someone else. Some other poor son of a whore.

Then he thought of Gloria. Her eyes, terribly scared. He closed his own eyes, rubbed them. There were no tears left in them.

The flap of a tent opened and a woman came out. She was still half asleep and didn't notice him. She went to a hole in the corner of the yard and crouched. He heard the passing urine. She got up and walked back to her tent without a word.

Yes, definitely, the worst thing was the loneliness. All these people all around you and no one to talk to about Gloria, about his pain.

After a while, the blond woman in the peacock house had told him he could stay, that she would help him hide, and he had thought that if he did, he would tell her about Gloria, about everything. But he hadn't known her and he hadn't trusted that wildness in her eyes. He'd smelled danger.

"If you want to help me, hide me in your car and get me away from here," he had told her. "That's all."

Six streets away, near the grocery, he had told her to stop.

"*Gracias,*" was all he said to her, even though her blue eyes invited him to say more. He had waited until she had turned the corner before making for this goddamn hiding place, the tents and all the strangers.

CHAPTER 8

It was 9:15 A.M. Sunday, and Cruz sat slouched in an easy chair, his temples caught in a vise formed by his thumb on one side and his fingers on the other, his shaky left hand bringing a drink, made mostly of tomato juice, to his trembling lips. The window was wide open and the fan was working hard to cool the place off, tousling his hair with its breeze. He swallowed a mouthful of the drink and then sat still waiting for results. His eyes were frozen in discomfort, aimed at the silent television screen, which showed scenes of fighting in Beirut.

Through the open window came the sounds of the street: kids making noise just to make noise, it seemed to Cruz. In the background, he heard fuzzy, ghetto-blaster salsa.

For Cruz, Sunday morning in the easy chair, the sound off and trying to keep the tomato juice from spilling had become ritual. The only vestment he wore was a ratty red towel and the ceremony went on until Cruz could once again feel his body and blood in reasonably working order. The telephone on the side table rang, making Cruz squint with discomfort. He knew that was part of the ritual as well. He picked it up quickly before it could ring a second time.

"Hello, Mama."

"David?"

"Yes, Mama. It's me."

"¿*Como estas*? What are you doing?" His mother's voice was husky and heavily accented.

"I'm fine, Mama." He sipped his drink. "Right now I'm cleaning the apartment." On television, men with hand-kerchiefs pulled up over their faces were seen running through bombed-out streets holding rifles. Many of the buildings had walls blown out, holes in them, like gaping mouths. There were so many that way it seemed like a new style of archi-tecture.

"I don't believe you, David. You're not cleaning nothing."

Cruz squinted. "Why would I lie to you, Mama?"

"Because I know you, that's why. You don't clean nothing," his mother said. "You're sitting watching television, maybe already you start to drink. I know you."

"You've got my number, Mama," Cruz said. "That's almost right." He sipped his drink.

"At my age, I got all the numbers, David. You don't fool me," his mother said. "Are you listen?"

"Yes, Mama."

"That's why people come to me," she said. "Strangers I never meet before, they ask me to help them with their prob-lems. They say, 'Doña Concha, she knows everything.' You, my own son, all you do is lie to me and fool around."

For decades, Cruz's mother had run a shop in the Mission in which she sold both herbs and religious supplies. One side of the store was lined with large wicker baskets containing herbs, natural medicines, pungent spices, powdered animal bones and other remedies. She sold concoctions that made you smart, helped you to see, to hear, to make love. The other side of the store was dedicated to spiritual articles: books, images and amulets, dream code books that helped people pick winners at the race track, Christs who when tilted at the right angle would blink their sad eyes at you.

Now in her seventies, widowed and retired, she offered "private spiritual consultations" in her home. Using a candle and incense, she provided advice on a range of problems and it was even said by some that she could make contact with the dead. As for Cruz, he went to her house only to eat. In his job, he already had enough contact with the dead.

"Be careful with those consultations, Mama," he told her now. "The bunko squad is going to be on your case."

"Boonko, nothing. You be quiet." Cruz winced and moved the phone farther away from his ear.

"You're practicing law, medicine and God knows what else without a license, Mama. You hear me?"

His mother hissed at him. "You keep quiet. These are matters of the heart, of the spirit, nothing they have to do with your police. I don't charge these people money, they bring me a gift; a fish, some candy. So you keep quiet," she said.

Cruz smiled and sipped his drink. Arguments over his mother's consultations were as much a part of the ritual as the tomato juice. Ever since Cruz's father had died fifteen years before, she had dressed exclusively in black, further adding to the respect in which she was held by the women of her neighborhood. What they didn't know was that she had a taste for cheroots, but it was one she satisfied only in the privacy of her kitchen, never in public.

"It's not my consultations I called you to talk about," she said. "Are you coming to eat today? It's a feast day, the Virgin."

"I'll do my best, Mama."

"You're not coming," his mother said ominously. "I can hear it already."

Cruz gripped his temples again. "I didn't say that, Mama. I'm on a case. A girl was found murdered yesterday."

"I know," his mother said.

"How do you know?"

"I just know." Cruz's mother never read newspapers or

listened to any radio or television news. Instead, she belonged
to a network of rumor-mongering old Latin women that kept
her in close touch with the events of the barrio.

"Did she suffer barbarities?" she asked. "I was told she
suffered barbarities."

"No, Mama, no barbarities. We don't think so. Somebody
just shot her."

"Thank God for that," she said. Cruz could picture his
mother blessing herself. For his mother, rape was a much
worse fate than death. "With some of the creatures walking
around here, it's a miracle."

"Well, I still have a creature running around I have to worry
about. He killed her," Cruz said.

"Today is Sunday, David. People in this country, they don't
work on Sunday, and it's a feast day."

"I know, Mama. I'm going to church." Cruz sipped his
Bloody Mary.

His mother hissed.

"Don't play with me, David," she said. "You don't go to
any church."

"I have to go talk to Father Clarke," Cruz said. "The girl
who was killed was from Central America. Maybe he knew
her. Maybe he knew the guy who killed her too."

"So you're working. You're not going to church. Don't lie
to me. It's Sunday."

"People don't kill each other nine to five, Monday through
Friday, Mama. We've been through this."

"You and your killers." His mother made a sound of disgust
deep in her chest. "You work all the days and the middle of
the night. That's why the wife you had left you. That's why
they all left you."

Cruz pressed his temples and drained his drink. Of course,
that wasn't why his wife had left him.

"Don't be mean, Mama."

"You're never going to have a family like this, David. I warn you."

Cruz sat, eyes closed, in silence.

"David, your sisters are coming with their husbands and the children. The children, they ask for you."

"I'll do my best to get there, Mama."

His mother accused him with her silence. "God bless you, David," she said. "And you be careful, the city is full of crazy."

"I will and I'll try to get there."

His mother only grunted and then hung up.

It was near eleven when Cruz drove down Mission Street. The strip was almost empty, except for the harsh sunlight that exploded off his windshield. Despite the early hour, the street already pulsed with heat. Cruz, his suit jacket folded across the seat, tie loosened, rocked to a number by Willie Colon, trumpets blaring and congas rolling. Willie was cooking and so was the day.

The blocks around the church were a meter maid's paradise; cars parked in the median, up on sidewalks, beside hydrants. Cruz parked several blocks away and walked along the procession route, which had been decorated for the occasion. The lightpoles were garlanded with brightly colored crepe paper and imitation flower bouquets. The smiling face of the pope, printed on a poster, watched from shop and apartment windows along the route.

Cruz was still three blocks away when he began to hear the singing of the faithful. He turned a corner and found the street outside the church packed with worshipers who had overflowed from inside. The street was Latinos, wall to wall.

Many of the women had their heads draped in black mantillas, and the men wore dress shirts buttoned to the neck. Everywhere there were children in bright Sunday clothes, but imitating the somberness of their parents. The hymn they were singing was sad and somber and their bodies rocked to that rhythm like the slow sway of the sea. Their voices throbbed with grief.

"*Señor, ten piedad de nosotros.*" "God, have mercy on us." Many of the people sang with their arms lifted toward heaven, their eyes full of fervor. In some hands there were bouquets of flowers and in others, rosaries, with the crucified Christ hanging from the fingers.

As a boy, Cruz had attended these processions with his mother and sisters. It wasn't true, as his wife said, that he had never believed in anything. In those days he had believed in a God who knew every evil that was committed, especially Cruz's. In time, perhaps, he had come to believe only in the evil itself. But without a doubt he still believed in that. Now he pressed himself against a wall and watched the other believers. Visible in the crowd were men who sang more fervently and swayed more recklessly than the others. Their faces were like the faces of the saints in religious paintings and on holy cards, full of rapture, as if they were actually seeing God or the Virgin in the sky. These men had an edge on the others; they were full of religious spirit but they were also already drunk. Later in the day, they would be joined by lots of others. After all, a feast day wasn't a funeral, it was a celebration. This meant patrol would be busy; rapture often got out of hand in the inner city.

When the sad hymn ended, there was a moment's pause, the organist inside the church struck several high notes and the people swung into a livelier song in praise of the Mother of God. The crowd changed moods, as if a cloud blocking the sun had moved away. Near the doors of the church there was a commotion, then cheers broke out and flowers were being thrown in the air. Cruz caught sight of the Virgin, a small blue-and-white statue, not more than a foot high, covered by a dome of glass. She was being carried on a litter, balanced on men's shoulders, and came bobbing out of the church door and into the multitude. Just behind her another figure came dancing into the sunlight; the crucified Christ, pale, bare-chested, the crown of thorns dripping bright red with painted bloodstains.

The singing grew louder as the two figures came down the stairs, flowers raining down on them as they started down the street. People poured out of the church making the crowd in the street bigger, louder, more rambunctious. Cruz remembered marching with his mother and sisters as a boy, his fear of being trampled and the frightening knowledge that people weren't as they usually were, but had been taken over by something they called a spirit.

Cruz pressed himself against the wall, which vibrated with the force of the voices. Near the end of the march came a woman, dressed in black, crawling along the sidewalk on her bare knees. In her face could be seen the pain of the burning concrete, but also the rapture. It still touched something deep inside Cruz when he saw it: both excitement and fear.

As she and other stragglers moved by him, Cruz spotted Father Bill Clarke standing on the church stairs in his white vestments. Clarke, who was about forty with a gut under his robes, stood stroking his goatee, watching the last marchers as if he suspected some kids would make a break for it.

As Cruz climbed the stairs toward him, the priest frowned. "My Lord, the prodigal returns," he said.

They shook hands, Clarke squeezing so that it hurt Cruz's bones. The priest had grown up in the Mission and he liked to play the role of the tough guy taken to the cloth. The way Cruz remembered it, Clarke had never been as tough as he made out. Smart but no punch.

"The teachings say never to despair, but I'd given up hope," Clarke said, straight-faced.

"I stopped coming because I couldn't understand your Spanish," Cruz said.

Clarke glanced after the slowly moving marchers. "That's

the beauty of faith. You come even if you don't understand the *gringo* priest. How have you been?"

"I'm working on a case," Cruz said.

"I should have known it was that," the priest said.

"A girl from Central America shot to death two nights ago."

Clarke nodded. "Soto. Gloria Soto."

"You know her?"

"Not that I know, but the family called and I'm saying the funeral mass Tuesday morning."

They strolled into church and down the center aisle. The church dated from the last century and the nave was of beautifully carved stone, as ornate and finely worked as ivory fans sold in Chinatown. The only worshipers still in the pews were the very old, who wouldn't brave the midday sun. They sat, working the rosary beads, waiting for the procession to return.

Cruz brought out the photograph of Gloria Soto and showed it to the priest. Rivulets of sweat ran down Clarke's overheated face and disappeared into the vestments. After a good look, he shook his head.

"No, I don't know her. What did she do to get herself killed, or did she do anything?"

"It looks like she got mixed up with the wrong guy," Cruz said. "She was in love with him down in El Salvador, but she wasn't in love with him when he came looking for her here."

He handed the priest a copy of the photo of Eric Hernandez. They passed through the altar rail gate and climbed steps to the spare marble altar. It was buried in flowers and their smell was overpowering.

"Are you sure this fellow did it?"

"Pretty sure. He ran away the same day. We found ammunition boxes in his house and he had a motive."

They were behind the altar, facing the congregation now. The priest put the photograph down and began to tidy the altar.

"So what do you want with me?"

"You know a lot of these Central American people," Cruz said. "I thought maybe you had heard where to find this kid. I know he's still in the neighborhood because I saw him last night."

"Why didn't you talk to him then?"

"He wasn't in a talking mood," Cruz said. "He was in a running mood."

The priest nodded in commiseration. To the side of the altar, a young Latino man was wielding a broom, sweeping up fallen flowers and other debris. The priest called to him in heavily accented Spanish and told him to go clean up in the rectory and leave the church for later. The kid stopped sweeping and glanced at Cruz, then nodded to the priest and went.

Bill Clarke drank the wine left in the chalice and patted his lips with an altar cloth.

"Now, my friend, let's get down to business," he said. "The church we stand in is a sanctuary church. That means the members of this congregation have voted to give sanctuary, protection, to a number of illegal Central American immigrants, Salvadorans, and Guatemalans. These are people we believe would be in danger of their lives if they were forced to go back to their countries. Do you understand that?"

"Yes, I've heard that," Cruz said.

Clarke looked at Cruz, his eyes sly and amused. "Is that why you're poking around here? Because you think we have this kid hidden in the catacombs downstairs?"

Now Cruz looked amused. "Do you?"

The priest laughed. "No, we don't," he said. "We give sanctuary to innocent people, not to murderers." He wiped at the inside of the chalice with the altar cloth. "That is, if this boy you're looking for is a murderer," he said pointedly.

"You don't think he is?" Cruz asked.

Clarke shrugged. "I don't know the kid and it really doesn't matter what I think. What's important is what other people are thinking and saying."

"And what are they saying?"

The priest pulled a handkerchief out of the full sleeve of his vestments and patted his forehead.

"They're saying that this girl Gloria Soto was found killed in a very particular way," he said. "A bullet in the back of the head and the thumbs tied behind her back."

"Death-squad style," Cruz said.

"That's what they say."

Cruz pulled a face. "Don't tell me they have you spooked, too. Those things happened down in their country, Bill."

"That doesn't mean it can't happen here," the priest said. "There have been rumors running for some time, scary rumors. Then certain people received threats in the middle of the night. Now this girl shows up dead, the thumbs tied. For these people, it's like prodding a wound that hasn't healed. It brings back pain and fear."

"Anybody can tie up thumbs, Bill. Especially if they want to screw with the police, throw them off the trail."

"Yes, that's possible. Although in this particular case it seems like a very malicious twist. I understand this boy Eric Hernandez had most of his family wiped out in a death-squad killing in El Salvador. Thumbs tied and all."

"You don't know this kid, but you seem to know a lot about him, Bill," Cruz said.

The priest shrugged. "That's why you came to me. Because I know things."

"Did you know that this kid told Gloria Soto he had a gun; that I found ammunition boxes in his house; that he's on the run?" Cruz said. "Maybe having his family killed gave him that malicious twist."

"And maybe not," the priest said calmly. "Given what he has been through, you want to be extra sure you're fair with him."

Cruz ran his hand through his thick hair, impatiently.

"Listen, Bill—"

"No, you listen," the priest said sharply. "I don't think you realize the situation. As I said, this church is a sanctuary. The boy who was here a moment ago is one who has asked us for refuge and there are more in the rectory. Now a cop comes walking in here looking for some illegal and that is sure to cause fear in them and discomfort in the rest of the congregation."

"I'm not here to bother those people," Cruz said, "and I'm not here to arrest just any illegal."

"So you say." The priest's eyes were full of suspicion. "You have to realize, kiddo, we've been threatened by the immigration police. They tell us we sanctuary people are public enemy number one these days. They tell us we have prison terms hanging over our heads for the transport and harboring of illegal aliens from El Salvador and Guatemala. Now you come walking in here asking me to help you find an illegal. I haven't seen you in a couple of years. How do I know what you're up to? How do I know who you are collaborating with? How do I know what kind of orders you've gotten from up top?"

Cruz bobbed and anger flashed in his eyes. "So after all these years, I'm a worm who screws over a friend, lies right to his face."

"Go ahead and get mad. I don't give a damn," the priest said. "The issue here is too important. It involves too many lives for me to worry about hurting your feelings. That's the second thing I'm going to tell you, that the killing of this girl has many people in this community terrified. Absolutely terrified. And you better start dealing with that fear, David, or you could have big, big trouble on your hands in this neighborhood."

Cruz glared and said nothing.

Clarke poked him in the chest, egging him on.

"You haven't changed since your days on the street, David. You're a tough guy. I tell you people are worried and you just

shrug it off. That's because you haven't lived what these people have lived. Some of these people have seen and lived and
suffered things you can't imagine."

He pointed to the street. "Why are they out there marching
in the heat, do you suppose? Why are they out there singing
up at an empty sky? Listen and maybe you'll understand
something. These people believe in the whole ball of wax,
David: angels, saints, miracles, fiery chariots, paradise, the
resurrection of the dead. Why is it they believe, do you think?
It's because they've seen first-hand how cruel life can get,
how savage, how really scary it can be. These people don't
believe because the nuns told them they should, David.
They know God and paradiso must exist because they've already been through hell and they know the devil face to
face. And if hell and the devil exist, then why not God and
paradise?"

"So who's arguing with God and paradise?" Cruz asked.

"Now this girl shows up right at your feet with a bullet in
the back of the head and you brush it off," the priest said.
"You say they have no reason to be afraid or terrified. The
truth is these people have two reasons to be worried about
you: You're a cop who might bust them for being illegal and
you're a cop who doesn't know his turf anymore, doesn't care
about the people in his own neighborhood."

"Is that so?" Cruz bobbed with anger, but the priest got
right up in Cruz's face.

"Yes, that's so." Cruz glared at him, as if they were back
on a street corner twenty years before. It was just like Clarke,
with the robes and all, getting tough and knowing Cruz couldn't
lay a hand on him.

Cruz shook his finger at him. "Listen, Bill—"

In what had been a silent church, someone hissed. Cruz
turned and saw an old woman sitting in the first pew, scowling
at him. The rest of the old people in the church were looking
his way, frowning. One white-haired man rapped on the edge

of the next pew with a bamboo cane. Cruz dropped his hand and his voice.

"You're playing politics with me, Bill."

"Politics is exactly what I'm not playing," Clarke said flatly. He pointed out at the pews and the watchful, scowling old faces. "In this congregation I have many people who come from down there. Some of them back the government and some of them want the guerrillas to win. They all have relatives down there and it's a gut issue with them. Fears and emotions run very high, David.

"I once got up in the pulpit here and tried to address the issue of the war down there. I must have said something I shouldn't have, because part of the congregation got up and walked out on me. Just like that. They thought I was taking sides against them. Now I walk the tightrope between the two sides. So don't accuse me of playing politics. What I'm trying to do is make you realize how real and how contagious this kind of fear can be. When there's evil in the air, these people see the devil. That's how strong their faith is. Yesterday I had a woman in the confessional who asked me if it is true there are death squads operating here. Rumors that such killings might start to happen have been running through this community for a while. There have supposedly been fewer of these killings down in their country the last couple of years, and maybe the death squad people have come here to get their kicks. I'm trying to get you to investigate this murder in a way that will end those rumors, calm those fears and head off a possible showdown in this community."

"If I catch Eric Hernandez and he did it, that will calm them," Cruz said.

"And if you crucify him for it and people aren't convinced he did it, that will only make those fears grow. People will begin to think that here it is like in their own country: that some killers are immune to prosecution, that the plague has caught up with them. That the war has spread to here."

"I'm not crucifying anyone," Cruz said.

"When you have so much faith in your own notions, your own narrow experience, you can end up crucifying someone just out of ignorance." He lifted the chalice as if in a mass. "It has happened before. You don't know where these people are coming from; what has happened between them in the past in their country that has made them turn on one another. How can you be sure who is the victim and who is the guilty one? Who has interests to protect that make them willing to kill?"

From outside the church and down the block, the singing could be heard again, a tide of voices coming back.

"Maybe this kid Hernandez did do it," the priest said, "but take my advice and handle this thing the right way. Look into some of these other characters around here. When people say there are killers here, I know it's true."

"Like who?"

"I don't know their names."

Cruz threw his hands in the air and, again, there were hisses in the church. "Everybody knows there are killers, but nobody has names," Cruz said. "They tell me there are vultures and rats and ghosts. What are you going to tell me?"

"That they're human beings. I know because I get them in the confessional," the priest said. "You haven't been in years, but we still don't ask names in the confessional. Every once in a while I get one that comes to talk about his past sins. They were in the army or the National Guard or maybe death squads and they were involved in very bad business down there. I don't know if they want God to forgive them, or if they even believe in God. I think they just want to talk about these things to take the pressure off their souls.

"I hear some incredible and terrible things and I hear them in great detail, David. The way they forced people's mouths open and held cigarette lighters to their teeth until they cracked, making prisoners swallow fishhooks and yanking them back up, holding people under water, systematic cutting and dismemberment, castration, gang-raping girls twelve and thirteen years old and lots of killing, David.

"I've had a couple come in with stories like that from down there," the priest said. "I don't know what they're up to here. But when you have men carrying around those kinds of sins, I know they are disturbed, David. It makes me wonder and it makes me worry."

The Virgin climbed the stairs now and the faithful, singing at the top of their lungs, began to flow back into the church.

"Okay, let's say I look around for those guys," Cruz said.

"That's all I'm asking," the priest said.

Cruz tapped the photo of Eric Hernandez lying on the altar. "How about my friend here? What happens if you hear about him or if he shows up at your door looking for sanctuary?"

"Like I said, we don't give sanctuary to criminals, especially murderers," the priest said, "but we would have to know he was guilty."

Cruz squared his shoulders again. "What does that mean? We're looking to question him. How am I going to know if he did it if I can't question him?"

"Take it easy, David." The Virgin was halfway down the aisle, and the men who were carrying her were looking at Cruz as if he had come to rob the poor box. "God have mercy," they sang.

"You go ask about those other fellows and I'll find out what I can about this body of yours. If I can."

They stared each other down as the Virgin approached the altar rail.

"God bless you, David," the priest said, and he turned toward the congregation.

Cruz swore under his breath then hurried out a side door, like an evil spirit routed by the faithful.

CHAPTER 9

It was just after noon when Cruz rode the elevator to the seventh floor of the Hall of Justice and let himself into the Homicide office. It was Sunday, the office was empty like all the other businesses downtown. At a glance it might have been any other business—insurance, stocks, marketing—with its scarred desks stacked with folders, old filing cabinets and a bulletin board full of notices and for-sale advisories. It was only when you looked closely that the nature of the business became clear. The bulletin board notice was from the chief and had to do with extradition proceedings, and a for-sale notice was for a bullet-proof vest. The folders were full of macabre photographs and the chalk outlines of bodies. The cabinets held the records of past "clients," all murderers. The business was homicide.

Closed since Friday, the place was like a steambath. Cruz pushed open a window, turned on a stand-up fan and threw his suit jacket over a chair. He opened a folder waiting on his blotter and found the coroner's report on Gloria Soto. The report confirmed several of the medical examiner's observations made on the scene: According to tissue deterioration and the stomach contents, the girl had died late Friday or in the earliest hours Saturday; she had certainly died of a single bullet to the brain; she had not engaged in sexual intercourse, forced or otherwise, in the hours preceding her death. The report also said there were several small contusions on the body but those had been caused after the girl was dead, probably in the process of disposing of the body. In addition, a close examination of the girl's thumbs and the cuts left by the waxed string indicated the thumbs had been tied once Gloria Soto was already dead. It was just as Cruz had told Bill Clarke, somebody had probably tied the thumbs to throw the police off. The last item indicated that Gloria Soto's blood, at the time of her death, contained a considerable amount of alcohol, enough to mean she had been intoxicated. This thread of information made Cruz frown.

In a separate small envelope on the desk Cruz found the ballistics report and the bullet in question. He shook it out into his palm. The tip of the slug had been blunted, possibly from hitting the skull. The ballistics reports identified it as .38 caliber, the same kind of slug that would have come in one of the boxes he had found in the Hernandez house.

Cruz took out blank, official-sized paper, opened his notebook and began to type his report, covering the lot where the body had been found and his interviews with Victor Soto, Elvira Hernandez, Dennis and Elaine Miranda, Stacy Stoner, and Bill Clarke.

Lieutenant Weintraub, chief of Homicide, was a stickler for written reports. He wanted one at least every other day on cases under investigation. He wanted names, places, days, times and bloody details. But Weintraub was an amateur sociologist and he also expected what he called the inside story: He wanted evaluations of the people involved, where they came from, how much money they had, how they lived. He wanted to see reasons beneath the surface. Cruz listed the times and places of his interviews and the basic information gathered on each one. Then he looked out the window for a while before continuing.

"El Salvador is in a war and these two families, the Sotos

and the Hernandezes, got caught in the middle of it. One of them is rich and the other one is poor. There was bad blood already between them because of that, and when the war started up again in the seventies, they ended up on different sides. People in that country started killing each other and it spread to their families too.

"Eric Hernandez fell in love with the Soto girl, but from the beginning it wasn't going to work. I don't know if he killed the girl's father and brother, the way Victor Soto says. Soto is slippery and his son is worse. Given the bad blood between the families, they would accuse Hernandez of anything. It also seems like Gloria Soto was mixed up with some other bad eggs, like this Julio Saenz, the smuggler of illegals whom I have to see.

"Still, it looks like Eric Hernandez killed the girl. The ammo boxes, the ballistics test, the fact he's nowhere to be found. He had been through a lot, like Stacy Stoner said when she was trying to convince me it wasn't him. All his dreams were wrapped up in Gloria Soto. When she kissed him off, he snapped."

He sat for several more moments staring out the window at the San Francisco skyline. Then he closed the file, gathered his coat and headed for Julio Saenz's house.

The Saenz place on Twenty-ninth Street was a small green pastel house in a row of small pastel-colored houses a couple of blocks off Mission. The old woman who answered the door wore a cross around her neck and also a small idol that looked Mexican, as if she were covering all her bases, both Christian and pagan. She wore wire-rimmed glasses and told Cruz that Saenz was not at home.

"Maybe he's at Joe Ortiz's place," she said with a heavy accent.

"Where's that, ma'am?"

"The Cantina Bar on Twenty-eighth Street. Maybe he's there. His girlfriend she was killed and he doesn't feel good."

"Gloria Soto."

The woman nodded her head, yes, and said, "I don't know her. Julio he didn't bring his girlfriends to the house." This aspect of Saenz's deportment didn't sit well with the lady. You were supposed to bring *novias* home for inspection by the family.

"Did Julio see the girl Friday?" Cruz asked.

The woman shook her head. "Julio was out of town." To Cruz, it didn't appear the woman was lying.

"When did he get back?"

"He come back last night. Then they tell him. It was terrible." The woman shook her head, her face full of misery.

"Yes, it was," Cruz said. "Do you know where Julio was?"

"Julio was down in Los Angeles on business, he had something to pick up," she said. She tapped the Mexican Indian idol hanging around her neck, a cheap, poorly carved piece of onyx that went for pennies down in Mexico.

"Julio is in this business of the *artesanías,* the handicrafts. Clothes, blankets, jewelry. He brings them up here from down south." She got a canny, mischievous look on her face and rubbed her thumb and forefinger together suggestively. "He makes a lot of money, Julio."

"That's good for Julio," Cruz said. "I'm glad to hear he is doing well. I know he works hard and is always going down south."

"Two times a week, sometimes more," she said. "He works hard, Julio. He's a good boy."

"Yes, he's a very good boy," Cruz said.

He thanked her, climbed into his car and headed for the Cantina. During Cruz's days on the beat the building had housed a war veterans' hall. Now there were neon beer signs shining in the windows, salsa music sounding from inside and a couple of fetching brown-skinned women, dressed to the teeth, tottering on spike heels, making for the door. Among the parked cars was a red Firebird. Elvira Hernandez had said Saenz owned one, bought with "vulture money."

Cruz walked into the Cantina, just as a salsa group, all dressed in cranberry shirts with puffed sleeves, swung into a tune by Sonora Matancera.

The place was designed to look like a typical cantina from south of the border. It was brightly colored and rustic with bullfight posters on the walls and those square aluminum tables Mexican beer companies pass around to advertise their products. In the middle of the one large room was a good-sized dance floor strewn with sawdust—it reminded Cruz of a cock ring—and overhead were strung Japanese lanterns. The place was packed and the music was loud.

Cruz found a spot at the bar and watched the crowd on the dance floor. It was like watching a complicated piece of machinery, with all parts synchronized to the pulsing rhythm. Arms pumped, heads rocked, shoulders shimmied, hips writhed and swiveled. Cruz watched the faces; some danced happily, some seriously, others wore faces that reminded you of sex.

One red-haired woman, in a low-cut flowered dress, tight across the hips, came dancing out of the crowd toward the bar, one hand on her stomach, her hips swiveling, her eyes shining. She danced right up to Cruz, until she was inches from him, smiling into his eyes. Then she reached past him, picked up a drink on the bar, drank from it, winked at him invitingly and then turned and danced back into the crowd, her hips swaying rhythmically. Down the bar, several men burst out in wolf calls and raucous laughter.

The bartender was a lean, fastidious-looking older Hispanic with a few strings of white hair on his chin that made him look like an old wise Chinese. Cruz ordered a beer and then yelled into his ear, asking for Julio Saenz. The old guy worked the tap, giving Cruz the once-over with a cool, practiced eye.

"Julio had a friend who died and he doesn't want to be disturbed," he said, serving up the beer. He wiped the counter, waited for payment and studiously avoided looking at Cruz.

Cruz took two dollars out of his billfold and then let it flap open to his shield. The old guy glanced at it without emotion.

"Is he here?" Cruz yelled.

The old Hispanic Confucius thought it over a minute as he polished a glass and then flicked his eyes toward the back of the room.

"Last table," he said.

"Thank you," Cruz yelled. "Keep the change."

He grabbed his beer and threaded his way back through the aluminum tables. At most of the tables there were several people sitting around enjoying themselves with a quart of whiskey or rum, a bucket of ice, limes and mixers. Seated at the very last table next to a door that said "Office—Privado" was a man as big as a Sumo wrestler, sitting behind a quart of whiskey all by himself, and not enjoying himself. At first glance, he looked like some kind of Indian idol, big, ugly and lifeless. He was dark, with wiry hair that stood straight up from his shallow brow. His face was flat like the faces of gods carved into enormous boulders. His eyes were small, narrow and blank. He wore a brightly patterned Indian blouse as big as a tent, and around his bull neck hung a thick gold chain, carved jade, onyx and other charms, like offerings left there by worshipers who were afraid he might destroy the world. He stared blankly at his subjects now as if the music and the dancing were in his honor.

Cruz flashed his shield at the man and offered him a business card.

"I'm investigating the death of Gloria Soto," he said.

Only the idol's eyes moved at first, glancing at the badge as if it were another shiny offering. Then he took the card and stared at it for a while before putting it on the table, where it began to soak up spilled liquor.

"What is there to investigate?" he said sullenly. "Go find the Indian she used to go with, the guerrilla. That's who killed her." He talked like a recording at reduced speed, slow and wobbly.

Cruz sat down across the table from him. It was like sitting across from a jukebox.

"We're looking for Eric Hernandez, Mr. Saenz, but I'm also trying to establish Miss Soto's movements that night. I'm checking with other people who might have seen her before she was killed."

Saenz poured part of his drink down his throat. "I wasn't here. I was in LA."

"That's what they tell me."

"If I was here, she wouldn't be dead," he said. "I would have killed that guy." Saenz's expression turned fierce, as if he were imagining Eric Hernandez and what he might have done to him.

"I'm sure you would have," Cruz said, looking at the man's shoulders, which were like rolling hills. "I'm told you cared for her very much."

Saenz nodded, his big boulder of a head tottering on his shoulders.

"I heard you cared for her so much that you were the one who brought her up here from Los Angeles," Cruz said.

Saenz nodded again, but wariness had crept into his gaze.

"You cared for her so much, in fact," Cruz said, "that you only charged her a few hundred dollars and along the way you stopped and molested her."

Saenz turned and looked at Cruz for the first time now, as if Cruz were a species of animal that had never spoken before.

"I didn't molest nobody," he said finally.

"Uh-huh."

"If we did anything, it's because she wanted."

"Yes, I'm sure she did," Cruz said. "A handsome guy like you. She couldn't remember how to tie her shoes when she came up here, she was so screwed up, but she certainly knew a movie star when she saw one."

Saenz crunched ice between his teeth.

"I stopped at a motel to take a shower and she wanted one too," he said. He shrugged his mountainous shoulders as if to say, the rest is history.

"I guess she needed a shower pretty bad by that time, didn't she," Cruz said. "She's just come all the way from her country and crossed over from Mexico on foot. That's a few hours' walk. Then she was in the trunk of a car for a while and then in your truck. So you did her a favor and offered her a shower, didn't you, Mr. Mule?"

Saenz glared at him. "I don't know what you're talking about." He tilted the glass and crunched ice between his teeth as if it was Cruz's bones he was munching.

"You don't know what a mule is?" Cruz asked. "A mule goes hee-haw like an animal and charges scared people big money to bring them to the big city. Except that sometimes he takes the money and he leaves them in the middle of nowhere, sometimes in the desert to die."

"I never done nothing like that," Saenz said. "I'm an American citizen and a legitimate businessman. I bring merchandise, crafts, to sell here. That's how I make my living."

"You bring merchandise all right, merchandise like Gloria Soto. People desperate to escape the war down there. And you squeeze them for every penny. You get rich off the war, off other people's suffering."

"I got nothing to do with the war down there," Saenz said. "It's this Hernandez and his friends, the ones involved in that war. I don't get mixed up with politics. Some people been telling you lies."

"Who would do something like that?" Cruz reached over to the jewelry hanging around Saenz's neck and fingered the shark's tooth. "This piece of merchandise is exactly right for you. Did you give one as a present to your friend Victor Soto? I saw him with one."

Saenz was sneering at Cruz.

"Victor Soto is a respected person, a legitimate businessman like me."

"What makes you and Soto such good friends?" Cruz asked. "Was he selling you his niece, or what? I can't see her doing it on her own."

The idol's eyes smoldered. For a moment, Cruz thought Saenz was going to eliminate him. Maybe make the earth open under Cruz and swallow him with one fiery gulp. Instead, the eyes glazed over again.

Stacy Stoner had been right: Julio Saenz was not only ugly, he was an evil spirit. That petite, beautiful Gloria Soto had gotten together with this god of ugliness meant there was something strange going on, something very wrong in the universe.

As if he could read Cruz's thoughts, Saenz said: "Gloria and I liked each other." He crunched ice between his teeth.

"Yeah, that's why she was walking around scared out of her mind, because she was in love with you," Cruz said. "She was thrilled by your every touch."

"It's Hernandez she was scared of. He's the one who's crazy." He poured himself more whiskey, not bothering to invite Cruz.

The band swung into a *cumbia* and the energy in the place was jacked up another notch. In the midst of it, Saenz sat glum and grim-faced. The god of bad business. Even the women who passed to and from the nearby ladies' room didn't attract his attention, as fetching as they were.

"Maybe they'll sacrifice one of these girls to you," Cruz said, "maybe that would make you feel better."

Saenz glowered. "Whatchu talkin' about? I don't sacrifice nobody."

"Gloria was sacrificed," Cruz said.

Saenz guzzled his whiskey. "I don't know anything about it."

"Where were you Friday night and early Saturday?" Cruz asked.

"I told you I was in LA."

"Where in LA? Who did you see? I want to know every address you stopped at and every person you talked to."

"I was picking up merchandise. Jewelry and stuff. I can give you the names of the suppliers. I picked up Friday and came back Saturday."

Cruz picked the shark's tooth off Saenz's chest and let it fall again. "You're gonna tell me that you make a living selling this kind of garbage? You want me to believe that watch and your fancy car come from selling this junk?"

"It's a good business," Saenz said.

"Where did you stay Friday night?"

Saenz's hooded eyes feigned thought. "I don't remember the name of the place."

"That's too bad."

"But I have a receipt," Saenz said. He picked up the front of his Indian blouse and revealed a money belt strapped around the folds of his gut. He took out a piece of paper, unfolded it and handed it to Cruz. It said "Traveler's Hideaway, Rte. 101, Santa Barbara"; it was dated Friday, made out to Julio Saenz and signed by the clerk, who had even taken the trouble to print his name clearly beneath his scrawl. His name was Joseph Allen.

"The clerk will remember me," Saenz said. "I gave him a little statue of the rain god."

"I'm sure he could never forget you," Cruz said. He frowned at the receipt. "This is very convenient, isn't it? Receipt and all."

"I get them for tax purposes. Business expenses."

"Do you have a receipt for the people you brought back too? Ten refugees: three thousand dollars."

His brow furrowed again, like a growl.

"I don't know what you're talking about."

"Did you stop to molest one of them the way you did Gloria Soto?"

Saenz crunched ice. "I need that paper for my taxes," he said.

Cruz wrote down the name of the motel and the clerk and laid it on the table where it soaked up some water.

"When was the last time you saw Gloria Soto?" he asked.

"Thursday night. We came here and had a couple of drinks," Saenz said sullenly. "The bartender can tell you that."

"Did she tell you she was scared of you?"

"She wasn't scared of me. She was scared of Hernandez, he was the one following her around. I wanted to punch him out, but Gloria's mother didn't want it. She didn't want trouble because maybe they would deport her and Gloria."

"Did Gloria say what she was going to do last night by herself?"

"She said she was going to stay home."

"She didn't," Cruz said. "She came in here and did some drinking, didn't she?"

"That's what they tell me. I wasn't here and they can tell you that."

"I'm sure they can. You were in LA being a legitimate businessman, weren't you?"

"That's right."

"That's right, you associate only with legitimate businessmen and upright citizens." Cruz drained his beer and got up. "Too bad Gloria Soto didn't associate with legitimate people instead of an animal like you," Cruz said.

Big guys always brought out the wiseass in Cruz. He saw

the muscles in Saenz's neck tense, and all over the other man's body the fat quivered with anger. Cruz thought steam would come from him, or fire out of his eyes. Then the glass, clutched in his enormous paw, shattered. Saenz looked at his hand dumbly. A trickle of blood escaped the meaty fist and dripped onto the table. Saenz looked back at Cruz, no pain on the face, no feeling, apart from menace.

"Please let us know if you plan to leave town again, I want to order some jewelry," Cruz said. "And make sure and take care of that motel receipt, since you went to so much trouble to get it in the first place. It could save your fat neck."

He gave Saenz a wink and a nod and walked away. At the bar he crooked a finger at the old Confucius and showed him a photo of Gloria Soto.

"This girl was in here Friday night," Cruz said.

The other man glanced at the photo, took a swipe at the bar with his bar rag and a shot a look toward the back of the bar, toward Saenz.

"No need to look anywhere, Confucius. What time was she here?"

He polished the bar a bit more. "Maybe ten, ten-thirty."

"Alone?"

He nodded. "The only person she ever come in with before was Julio and he wasn't here. He was out of town."

"I just heard all about it," Cruz said. "She ever come in alone before?"

Confucius shook his head no.

"Who did she come in looking for?"

"Nobody. She sat at the end of the bar and she drank sloe gin fizz."

"Did she talk to anybody?"

He shook his head. "A couple of guys tried to hustle her. She didn't even look at them. She just drinks her drinks. She's loyal to Julio."

"Yeah, Julio inspires devotion," Cruz said. "How many did she drink?"

"Three, maybe four. I didn't give her no more."

"Why not?"

"She shouldn't have no more."

"She looked drunk?"

Confucius shrugged his bony shoulders.

"Then what?"

"Then she left."

"By herself?"

"That's right. Just like she come in."

"What time was that?"

"About midnight."

"And she didn't come back?"

He shook his head.

"You know anybody might have reason to kill her?" Cruz asked. Confucius shook his head again. "I don't know things like that. I just work around here."

"Yeah, me too," Cruz said.

He left then, as the band swung into a merengue.

CHAPTER 10

Cruz sat hunched at his mother's kitchen table eating dinner. From the rest of the house came the sounds of kids screaming, music playing, people laughing, ice ringing in glasses. Cruz had arrived late, just as the dinner was ending, had paid his respects to the aunts, uncles, cousins, sisters, husbands, and boyfriends and then had ducked into the kitchen to kiss his mother and get himself some of her chicken mole.

He sat in his shirtsleeves, the pistol on his hip visible. His small nephews came in to stare at it a while, but his mother chased them out. The old woman stood at the stove watchdogging two big coffee pots and heating tortillas for Cruz's dinner. She was a full-breasted, broad-shouldered, bulky woman, but her neck was long and elegant and on it sat a finely sculptured, strong-featured face. She wore a black dress and a yellow corsage. In her hair was a large, very feminine Spanish comb, but she had a dishrag over her shoulder that made her look like a cut man in a fighter's corner. She might have had a cheroot in the corner of her mouth, but there was at least one new boyfriend in the house and she didn't want to give any bad impressions.

She took another hot tortilla off the stove and brought it to Cruz. Attached to the wall above the kitchen table was a red glass dish with a candle burning in it. A candle had burned there, day and night, ever since Cruz could remember, even before his father had died fifteen years before. Whenever anyone asked his mother about its significance or importance, she would bless herself in the most elaborate way and put a finger up to her lips. "These are matters about which people do not talk," she would say mysteriously.

She had met Cruz's lateness with a stern look, a shake of the head and a sigh, but had heaped a plate and poured a beer for him and was heating the tortillas.

Marta, Cruz's younger sister, walked into the kitchen, a drink in her hand. Where Cruz was bronze-colored, his sister was light-skinned. She wore her dark brown hair in a shag and was dressed in a suit. She worked for a personnel agency, and after thousands of hours interviewing she had developed a slick, offhand way of dealing with people.

"So what's up, David?" she said, sitting down and crossing her legs so you could see a lot of them.

Cruz swallowed and speared more chicken. "The crime rate."

"I didn't mean that. I mean you, dummy." Cruz chewed and shrugged.

"Things are all right."

"Are you seeing anyone?"

"Yeah," Cruz said. "I see lots of people every day."

She made a face at him. "I mean women. What happened to this woman you told me about? The ash blond with the Mercedes. She was a bank officer, right?"

"That's right."

Marta called to Cruz's mother. "Did you hear about this woman David's seeing, Mama? A bank officer."

Cruz's mother raised an eyebrow but didn't respond. Although she loved her daughter, she also thought Marta was foolish. This was the same Marta who only a month after Alice had left him had begun to ask Cruz about who he was dating. That was because she had not liked Alice. His sister, Cruz knew, judged people on how easy they would be to place in a job. Alice, an artist and too much of an individualist, was not placeable.

"The new one's not like the women you used to attach yourself to," she said. "Women you meet on murder investigations or in emergency wards."

"There are some very nice women in emergency rooms," Cruz said, taking a pull of beer. "And they're already lying down."

"You're sick," Marta said, and she giggled. "So what happened with this bank officer? You made it sound like it was getting serious."

Cruz shrugged, shoveled mole onto a piece of tortilla and put it in his mouth.

"What happened, David?"

"It's a delicate matter," Cruz said.

"What's delicate?"

Cruz shot a look at his mother, who had her back to them, and then back at Marta and shook his head. His sister leaned toward him with interest. She lifted her eyebrows mischievously. Cruz talked between bites of tortilla and mole.

"She was perfect," he said softly. "And she was crazy about me. She wanted to give me money and take care of me forever. Perfect."

"So?"

Cruz leaned forward, his face just over the plate, so his mother wouldn't hear. "So we go to bed the first time."

His sister leaned farther forward.

"And I get her clothes off and I look at her. I tell her 'You're the perfect woman.' That's what I said to her. And she was, too." Cruz shoveled more mole into his mouth. "You could have placed her anywhere."

His sister nodded. She understood the type. A picture placement.

"So? Don't tell me she was frigid."

"No," Cruz said. "Not frigid. I told you she was perfect."

He shot a glance at his mother and then leaned forward again.

"I get my clothes off, too, ya know?"

"Uh-huh."

"I kiss her. I touch her. And we're just about to . . . ya know."

"Yeah?"

Cruz's face suddenly filled with fear and awe. "And suddenly she floated right off the bed." He brought his hands up slowly, as if he were watching a body levitate. His eyes followed the body as it went up.

"Right up into the air. And she just kept going up in the air, naked, light all around her," Cruz said as if in ecstasy. "Right through the ceiling. *Up*, up, up. I lost track of her at about five thousand feet." Cruz stayed looking into space a moment, then he looked back at his plate and speared more chicken. "The perfect woman, ya understand, she went back up to the gods."

His sister was scowling at him. "You're sick, David."

"That's not true. I never laid a finger on her."

"You made it all up, going out with her, didn't you?"

"Yeah, the last time you started sticking your nose in."

"So you're back to chasing whores, I assume. Or you never stopped chasing whores even when you lived with Alice, that's what some people say."

Cruz's mother hissed at the language.

"Have you heard from Alice?" Marta asked.

"No, I haven't," Cruz said, not looking up from his plate.

"When was the last time you tried to talk to her? She did put up with you for years." There was meanness in her voice now.

"Why don't we just leave it there?" Cruz said.

"Well, if all you're going to do is chase whores."

Cruz let his fork drop on the plate. His mother hissed.

"You leave your brother alone. Let him eat," she said.

"You're always bothering him about it, Mama." His mother just stared at her.

Cruz picked up his fork again. "How about if I tell you about my new girlfriend," he said.

Marta stood up and lectured him. "You're in love with your work too much, David. You spend too much time with murderers. You don't know how to be a normal person anymore."

"What can I tell you. I like murderers," Cruz said, sipping his beer.

His sister turned on a heel and left.

His mother, muttering, brought him another tortilla.

"You come late, then you argue with your sister."

"I'm sorry, Mama."

"You're not sorry. I know you."

Cruz shoved in more rice with mole sauce and chased it with Dos Equis.

"I came late because of that case, the girl we found on Twenty-first Street."

His mother moved back to the stove.

"You found the animal who killed her?"

"No, not yet."

"He didn't commit barbarities to her, thank God." She blessed herself.

"Yeah," Cruz said.

"But she had trouble with some man," his mother said suggestively.

"Yeah. She had trouble with two men. An old one and a new one."

His mother made a sound in her nose that said, "No wonder."

"She was a very screwed-up girl," Cruz said.

"Those people down there, they are suffering," his mother

said. "They come up here, they still suffer. They are afraid."

"That's right," Cruz said. "This girl was very afraid."

"I see it in my consultations. It's what happens to the people when they live in a war," his mother said. "I was a baby when the revolution happened in Mexico, but my mama she told me about the *miedo,* the fear of the people. She told me about all the dead ones and how the other people they were alive, but they were so scared they were sick. Their eyes went crazy. I remember, years after the war ended you still saw these people, sometimes they shake like they are nervous and always you saw in the eyes the sickness. These people from down there, they have that war sickness."

"This girl who was killed, she had it, Mama."

"I told you."

"People tell me she had crazy eyes and that she saw things and heard things."

"That's the way it is." She took the towel off her shoulder and removed the coffee pots. "Demons get into those people," she said.

"But it wasn't any demon that killed her," Cruz said.

"No, but the demons chased her so that she died. They chased her right toward that animal who killed her."

"I know where the demons chased her part of the night, Mama, now I just have to find out where the animal caught up with her." He sipped his beer. "And I then have to figure out which animal it was. They tell me it's one guy, but I just met another one. A big animal. You can't tell the animals without a scorecard, Mama."

Cruz's mother had the coffee pots on a tray. "You'll find him," she said. "Now come spend some time with your family and don't argue with your sister."

Cruz followed her and spent the next hour listening to his relatives. The big problem of the day was the Chinese who were coming from Hong Kong before the Red Chinese took

over the island and how they were buying up all the real
estate in the Mission and driving out the Mexicans. Cruz also
listened to personal complaints.

His uncle, Sixto, was near eighty and in mid-August was
wearing a tie on which was pictured Rudolph the Red-Nosed
Reindeer. He was having trouble with noisy teenagers outside
his window and Cruz gave him the name of a sergeant to
whom he could complain.

His aunt Aurora was also elderly and wore her stockings
bunched up just above the knee. This was the same aunt who
swore the Virgin had once appeared to her in her kitchen.
She said she had had a dream that the world would be destroyed soon and also that she had been assured by a reliable
source in the neighborhood that all the police were on drugs.
Cruz told her he wasn't and she thanked God.

The younger relatives complained about "niggers" and no
parking.

Before the hour was out, Cruz was restless and starting to
rehearse his strategic retreat. Then the telephone rang and it
was for him; Donnelly at Mission Station.

"We've been looking for you. We know where your boy,
Hernandez, is hiding and we're getting ready to go in after
him."

The red-haired policewoman was behind the Dutch door
in the weapons room handing shotguns to four cops. Cruz
found Donnelly in his glass cubicle, in civilian clothes, but-
toning a plaid shirt over a bullet-proof vest.

"The call came in half an hour ago and they called me at
home," he said. "A woman telling us where to find him."

"Who was she?"

"She didn't say. All she said was Hernandez is hiding at a
building on Florida Street. There's a grocery on the first floor
and a house above. Used to be run by a Greek."

"I know the place," Cruz said. He was watching the uniformed men crack the breeches of their shotguns and slip in the shells. He didn't like what he saw.

"The place is called Tony's now; run by some Latin," Donnelly said. "It isn't doing good business, I guess that's why the Greek sold it in the first place. My men on the beat say Tony has been giving illegals a place to stay as a way of making some extra money. He puts them in tents in the backyard. Do their necessities in a hole. He was busted once for health violations a year ago."

Donnelly clipped his gun to his belt and let his shirt hang over his belt to cover it.

"Did the woman who called say he was armed?"

"She didn't mention," Donnelly said. "I figure we put a pair of guys behind the place, in case he tries to jump the fence, and another outside and that you and I either go in or call in."

"We have to figure if it's him that he's armed, so we better call in. Give him a chance to come out without any shooting."

Cruz found the telephone number of Tony's and jotted it down. He also checked the street directory to find the names of the grocery's closest neighbors and wrote down those names and addresses as well.

A few minutes later they turned onto Florida Street. Donnelly pulled over, walked back to the two patrol cars following them, talked there for several moments and then the cars pulled away to take up their posts.

Cruz and Donnelly, both in civilian clothes, walked down the street toward the store. Florida Street, at that level, was passing through bad times. On the southern corner stood a dark bar painted inside and outside in black, frequented by men and occasionally women who dressed in tight black leather fixed with studs and chains, drove gleaming black motorcycles and got their kicks, it was said, by beating each other black and blue. On occasion they put each other in the hospital.

At midblock directly across the street, one from the other, stood two storefront Evangelical temples whose faithful sang at the top of their lungs almost every night trying to drown out one another and the sound from down the block of roaring motorcycles and clinking chains. The members of the temples were convinced, like Cruz's aunt, that the world would soon end. In fact, to hear them, they couldn't wait for it to end.

On the far corner of the block was a long storefront with whitewashed windows, which was known to be a sweatshop where illegal Latin women working for about three dollars an hour sewed the latest fashions that sold for who knew how much. Catercorner from that operation was the burned-out husk of a warehouse whose owners had decided that arson was a better business than running the warehouse. Everyone in the Mission knew it had been arson, except the storefront preachers, who insisted it had been the work of God, showing his displeasure with the entire society.

In between these establishments there were houses, two-family walkups, most of which were going to seed, and planted right in the middle of the block was Tony's Family Grocery. Not a good location, to say the least, Cruz thought.

He and Donnelly walked down the opposite side of the street. Despite the heat, the street was empty; the gray light of television screens was visible through many of the house windows. Fluorescent lights were on inside the store and a man in a red shirt stood behind the counter. Otherwise the place was empty.

Cruz checked his list of names and addresses. Then he led Donnelly up the stairs of a well-maintained house just across the street from Tony's and rang the bell. The door was opened by a short, red-faced man with graying hair and an enormous gut that stretched his T-shirt so that it was skin-tight.

Cruz looked down at his list. "Mr. Manzelli?"

"That's right."

Cruz flashed his badge and introduced himself and Donnelly.

"We're investigating a complaint on your block and were wondering if we could use your telephone."

Manzelli nodded.

"Which one of the freaks is in trouble now?"

"Nobody's in trouble yet, but we're investigating someone who may be living across the street at Tony's Grocery."

"Uh-huh." He ushered them inside. "That guy, either he has a real big family or he's turning the place into a flophouse."

They were led into a living room and introduced to a woman in a pink bathrobe and matching curlers in her hair.

"Police," said Manzelli. "They need the phone. Something to do with the greaser across the street."

Cruz took the phone from a table in the hallway and made the cord stretch until he was standing at the front window, looking across the street to Tony's. Donnelly excused himself to the Manzellis and turned off the lights.

"What's this with the lights?" the woman asked.

Donnelly asked the couple to stand back in the hallway away from the window.

Cruz took out his notebook and dialed the number for Tony's Grocery and watched as the man in the red shirt picked up the wall phone behind the counter.

"Hello, Tony's." He talked with a thick accent that made it "Eh-toneese."

"Is that Tony?"

"Yes, it's me. Who's there?"

"This is Inspector Cruz of the San Francisco Police Department, Tony."

"Police?"

"That's right. How is everyone at your place this evening?"

"I'm all right. No problems here," Tony said. Even from across the street, Cruz could see the scowl on Tony's face. For a guy like Tony, things were never all right.

"That's good, Tony. Just checking."

Tony was nodding his head. "Just fine here. No problems."

"There's one thing, Tony."

"What?"

"We understand you have a house guest staying with you. His name is Eric Hernandez."

Cruz and Donnelly watched as Tony's head swiveled quickly and looked to the back of the store where there was a black door.

"Who?"

"His name is Eric Hernandez, Tony. A young fellow from Central America who dresses in army clothes. We're told he's staying with you and we would like to talk to him."

Tony was stock still, his eyes glued to the back door. "What's that you say?"

"We must have a bad connection, Tony," Cruz said. "I said we want to talk to Eric. Can you please put him on the telephone?"

Tony was shaking his head as if Cruz were right in front of him. "It must be some mistake. This is a grocery, not a hotel. I don't have no guest."

"We know it's a grocery, Tony. We also know that along with the Cheez Doodles you stock a few refugees there. We just want to talk to one of them."

Tony was shaking his head, rocking back and forth on his feet, as if the floor were a griddle.

"There must be a mistake," he said.

"Listen, Tony, don't hang up. If Eric is there, we want you to tell him that we're waiting to talk to him. We know his life may be in danger and we want to help him. Can you tell him that?"

The grocer had his face to the window now, searching the street.

"Yeah . . . no. I mean there is some mistake," he said. "I'm sorry."

Then he hung up.

Cruz and Donnelly watched from the dark bay window as Tony hurried around the counter and disappeared through the back door.

"He's in a hurry," Donnelly muttered.

A minute later, Tony came back through the door accompanied by another man, dressed in a black T-shirt and camouflage pants, carrying a black duffle bag.

"That's him," Cruz said.

Alongside Eric Hernandez, Tony was talking agitatedly, motioning with his hands. Cruz and Donnelly went out the door and down the stairs, just as Eric Hernandez hit the street and turned north, away from the backup patrol, and started to walk away quickly.

Cruz called his name and the man swiveled toward them.

"It's the police. We want to talk to you, Eric."

At first the kid froze, as if he didn't know where the voice was coming from, as if God had spoken to him out of the darkness. Then he rammed his hand into a pocket and pulled it out again in a way that sent Cruz and Donnelly diving behind a parked car. Three shots rang out and the windshield of the car exploded, showering the two cops with glittering diamonds of glass. Donnelly, stretched on his stomach right next to Cruz, reached for his pistol, took aim from behind a tire, and with the pistol very near Cruz's left ear, pulled off a shot. After that, Cruz heard nothing, only ringing.

He saw Donnelly jump up and run into the street. He saw him plant his feet and hold his pistol in both hands, leveled at Eric Hernandez, who was running north. Donnelly's mouth was moving, shouting. Cruz, ears ringing, reached out and pulled Donnelly's arm down. He shouted at the top of his lungs in Spanish for Hernandez to stop. His voice sounded as if he were underwater.

The kid didn't stop. Donnelly grabbed Cruz and yelled something at him angrily, but Cruz couldn't make it out. The unmarked car that had been stationed down the street came charging toward them. It slowed and Cruz and Donnelly jumped into the backseat.

Eric Hernandez, with almost a block's head start, disappeared around the corner of the blackened warehouse building. The cop at the wheel floored it all the way down the street, past the temple, where people were standing and looked to be singing, although Cruz couldn't hear them.

The cop at the wheel hit the brakes at the cross street and went around the corner on two wheels onto a long block of warehouses and darkness.

Then came the only sound that penetrated the ringing in Cruz's ears. It sounded like a string of firecrackers going off. About ten small pops, one on top of the other. In the darkness ahead, he saw the reflection of the firing, the mouth of Eric Hernandez's automatic rifle. Then the windshield of the car was disintegrating in front of his eyes and Cruz faintly heard someone scream.

The car went into a slide, the back end fishtailing out of control, jumping the curb, whiplashing a lightpole and slamming, tail-first, into the warehouse building.

The crash into the lightpole knocked down the power line and the lights went out all the way down the now pitch-dark street. Cruz heard screaming, but it sounded muffled, far away. For all he knew, it was himself. He pushed open a door and threw himself out onto the sidewalk. Hanging out the driver's door was the dark outline of a body. It was writhing. The mouth was open as if the man were screaming. Cruz pulled the body out of the car and onto the sidewalk. The uniformed man was clutching at his upper chest.

"He's hit," Cruz yelled, but still it sounded muffled, underwater, as if no one could ever hear him. But then he made out someone else screaming. He turned and saw Donnelly stretched on the sidewalk behind him, yelling into a pic microphone attached to his shirt.

"Code thirty-three, code thirty-three. Officer in trouble, all cars come at once."

Cruz crawled back to Donnelly, who screamed something at him.

Cruz caught only the last words, "assault rifle."

"Where is the son of a bitch?" Cruz yelled, but Donnelly was yelling into the pic again for help.

Cruz peeked over the back fender of the car now. The street was dark and the only sounds were the faraway howl of a siren, the moaning of the wounded man and Donnelly. Cruz could make out the corner of the warehouse building from where the shots had come.

Then at the far end of the block, a patrol car turned onto the street, its roof lights careening wildly off the sooty brick buildings, its headlights racing up the street. A rat scampered down a gutter, but there was no one else to be seen.

Donnelly was screaming, "Caution! Caution!" and the car stopped.

Cruz pulled his gun, pressed himself to the brick wall of the warehouse and advanced. Donnelly was yelling at him now, but he kept going.

At the corner of the building he found a bunch of ejected shell casings on the ground from some kind of automatic rifle. Cruz poked his head around the corner, pulled it back quickly and then peeked around it again. It was a loading dock, empty of trucks or anything else for that matter.

Donnelly was at his back now. With their guns drawn, they moved across the empty lot.

The metal bay door of the loading dock was warped from the fire, but not enough to allow a person to slip through and into the warehouse. There didn't appear to be any other way to enter the building. The chain-link fence at the back of the lot, however, was pulled away from the wall just enough to allow someone to slip through and to enter a very narrow alleyway that ran between the buildings. Donnelly sent a beam from his flashlight down the dark alley. It was empty, but it had to be the route Eric Hernandez had used to escape.

Donnelly was on the pic now, telling all cars to scour the area. He gave them a description of Hernandez and warned that he was carrying a black duffle bag in which an automatic rifle was hidden.

Cruz went back to the car. Ambulance attendants were already lifting the wounded cop into the back of an ambulance. His partner was next to him, covered in the other man's blood. The careening red rooflights of the police cruisers played over them, making them look even bloodier.

Donnelly came up to him now, ice in his eyes. When he spoke, Cruz heard him clearly, no ringing in the ears. Donnelly said to him: "Your ass is in trouble, friend, and you better hope he doesn't die." Then he turned away.

Cruz walked back down the block to Tony's Grocery. On the sidewalk, the congregations from the storefront temples were watching him as he walked up the middle of the street.

"Sorry, it's not the end of the world, folks," he said. He shouldn't have said it, but he did.

He entered Tony's. Inside the store, a uniformed cop stood guard over Tony, who was in a chair, handcuffs fixed behind him. He was jabbering at the cop about his innocence. Cruz walked right by them into the backyard, which was surrounded by a high wooden fence. In the yard were pitched three pup tents and, standing against the fence, guarded by a young Hispanic cop, were several people—three men, a woman, two small children—all looking very scared.

"These people act like we're gonna kill them or something,"

the young cop said to Cruz. "They say they been paying fifteen dollars per head per week to live in these tents and that doesn't include food, of course. They could buy food from the store, but at the regular prices in there."

Cruz greeted the people courteously. They told him that Eric Hernandez had arrived Friday afternoon, had left around nightfall and had not returned until after daylight Saturday. He had spent all day Saturday and most of Sunday in the yard and had not said one word to anyone. No, he hadn't received any visitors, but he had received a phone call, which had angered the grocer. After the phone call he had gone out for a while Sunday afternoon. That was all they knew. They hadn't known that he was carrying an assault rifle in the bag.

Cruz went back into the store. Tony stood up and started jabbering at him, but Cruz pushed him back into the chair.

He stood bobbing, like a fighter who had just floored his opponent.

"Who brought the Hernandez kid to you?"

"Nobody bring him," Tony said, scared now. "He comes by himself."

"Did anyone come to see him or call him while he was here?"

Tony shook his head. "I don't know anything about anybody else or this boy. I don't know what he's done."

Cruz squinted hard at Tony and Tony got worried.

"You better start remembering, Tony, if you don't want to be an accessory to murder."

Tony's eyes bulged and his head started moving nervously like a rooster's.

"Whaddyou mean murder? I'm nothing to do with keel anybody."

"Did he get a telephone call?"

"Yeah. He gots a telephone call."

"From who?"

"I don't know. How I supposed to know?"

"Man or a woman?"

"A womans. A young womans."

"Did she give her name?"

"No name. Nothing. Just she ask for him. That's all. She don't tell me he's a killer."

"When did he get the call, Tony?"

"Today in the afternoon and then he go out."

"Did you hear what he said?"

Tony looked offended. "I don't listen to other people when they talk."

"Yes, you wouldn't do that. You have people living like animals in the backyard, but you don't eavesdrop."

Cruz walked out and walked all the way back to Mission Station for his car. He drove to Emergency at San Francisco General and stayed there an hour until a doctor told him the cop, Joe Klein, had taken a single slug in the upper chest, but it had missed the heart and other vital organs and the odds were he would pull through.

Cruz then drove back to the warehouse and started patrolling the area. Like in the old days on patrol, Cruz fell into a rhythm of crossing and crisscrossing streets, his eye probing alleyways, entranceways, parked cars, looking for a hint of camouflage. It was the middle of the night before he got so tired he had to go home.

CHAPTER 11

He had the animal in his sights, tracking it as it crept unaware out of the pool of streetlight and across the grass. Suddenly, sensing danger, it stopped and turned its brilliant emerald cat's eyes right at the dark window, at him where he sat with the assault rifle. Behind the glass, he tightened his finger on the trigger. "Pow," he whispered. He would have hit it right on the white blaze that covered its heart. In the mountains, he would have had himself a rabbit or an armadillo, a warm supper. Instead, he watched the cat, its life spared, sprint away from him, into the shadows.

"That's my cat," she said. "Don't worry, he won't tell anyone you're here."

They sat in the living room with all the lights out as they had the past two hours; he on a low stool with his eyes just at the level of the sill of the bay window, with the rifle again across his lap, and she in a chair at the other side of the window, watching for anyone who approached from that other end of the block.

He looked at her now, still in the nightgown in which she had answered the door. A coffee cup was balanced on her lap, and she wore that same composed expression she had had the night before. There was no fear on her face. She had even made a joke about the cat, as if it were a time for fucking jokes.

The question remained. Would she tell? Would she call them down on him? At least one person had already betrayed him tonight. He wanted to know who it was. A fucking traitor! Now this woman insisted she wanted to help him, but why? In all his years in the mountains he had never had to trust his life to a collaborator like this one. The situation was a son of a bitch.

With the sharp clap of the M-16 still ringing in his ears, sweating and out of breath, sirens howling, he had pounded on her back door. A light had been switched on, she'd parted the curtain and, without a question, opened the door and given him a place to hide. He'd asked her to turn off the lights, and then gone to the window and taken up his lookout. Only then did she ask him what had happened. He looked at her suspiciously and told her it was always better for a collaborator to know as little as possible about a guerrilla. With the sirens howling on the streets all around them, she looked at him and said nothing in a way that made him nervous. So he told her the truth, that he had been betrayed, that someone had come after him, men in civilian dress, maybe his enemies, maybe the police. In order to escape, he had done what he had to do.

"Was anyone killed?" she asked.

"I don't think so," he told her, "but I can't be sure."

She took that in, made coffee for both of them, assumed her own lookout post in the chair a few feet away and sat quietly in thought in a way that made him even more uneasy. Any collaborator, even the best of them, could be uncovered, he knew. They could give in to the pressure and turn against you. This woman hadn't been cultivated slowly. She had agreed so readily, he had to be suspicious. And sometime, he knew, he would have to sleep.

Now she made her comment about the cat, a joke about betrayal.

"You don't joke about such things," he told her.

"You can stay here as long as you have to," she said. "They probably won't come here again looking for you."

"Oh, yes? Why is that?" he asked.

He thought he saw her smile in the dark.

"Because I'm just an artist with her head in the clouds," she said.

"They will look everywhere," he said. "In my country that is what they do. They go house to house and the artists' houses are some of the first places they might look."

"Here the police don't work that way," she said, looking out onto the quiet houses on the other side of the street. "Here they will put out an all-points bulletin, just in case you have left the city, and they will talk to the bus lines and the railroad. Hospitals and doctors will be notified, just in case you were hurt in the shooting. They will put your photograph on the television if they have one, and the police on the beat will show it to people on the street and have them look out for you. They'll also go to the houses of friends of yours and look for you there or put policemen to watch those houses and wait there to grab you. Most people being hunted for murder don't go very far, and most show up at some familiar place eventually. Homicide police have too many cases at one time to devote too much time to one of them. Most of the time it isn't that the police catch killers, but that the killer gets careless. You have to realize, most murderers aren't very smart or very organized. That's why they ended up killing somebody in the first place."

He was squinting at her suspiciously across the dark space that separated them.

"And how is it you know so much about how the police do things?" he asked.

He saw the white cup go to her lips as she sipped the coffee.

"I had a friend once who was a policeman," she said.

He stared at her hard as if her words were a pointed weapon she had flourished suddenly. In his own country, a collaborator could never have said that, a policeman as a friend. It would be impossible, like a lamb saying he had friends who were wolves. This was a different country, but still it made his stomach clench.

"Is he the one in the painting?" he asked. "The one downstairs?"

All he needed was for this policeman to show up at the door and spot him.

"Is that him?"

She was staring out the window into the darkness.

"Yes, that's the man," she said now, "but I don't see him anymore."

In her voice was a sadness, a pain because she was no longer with this policeman. It seemed an impossible thing to him.

"You were in love with this policeman," he said. "Maybe you still are. And if he shows up at the door here looking for me, then what?"

All the time you had to question collaborators to be sure they were telling you everything they knew. Often they were simple peasants who could be careless and naive. Other times they hid things from you because they knew they had made some slip and were afraid you would get angry. What they didn't tell you might cost you your life. Now this woman who consorted with the fucking police . . .

"He won't come here," she said.

"How do you know? He may decide tonight that he wants you. He may change his mind and tonight he wants to have you again in bed."

She was shaking her head.

"No, he won't come near here," she said. "He's a coward."

He nodded and his hands tightened on the rifle. But she looked at him and shook her head.

"No, it's not you he's afraid of, or that either," she said looking down at the rifle. "He's afraid of me."

He squinted at her. She sipped her coffee and stared out the dark window.

"The last time I talked to him, I called him a coward. I don't think he wants to hear that again. I told him I could no longer love someone who believed in nothing. Someone who was convinced that any man was capable of murder, that there will always be greed and violence because that is the nature of the beast, and that there's no sense dreaming of something different. I couldn't take that. That's why he said I was only an artist with my head in the clouds."

She lit a cigarette with a lighter, openly, without cupping it, and he frowned.

"Maybe that's why I'm helping you," she said. "You see the chance to make something different in your country. I've read some Marxism. I've studied the situation in Central America. I know about your movement. I don't know everything or how it will come out. But you believe in something and that, I guess, makes me believe you when you say you didn't kill that girl."

Things were becoming clearer now. Her willingness to help him, that strange look on her face the night before, became more understandable, but no less dangerous. It was a romantic fascination. She was the kind you were always warned about, because the person who became fascinated so easily with a guerrilla or the movement, and had no personal stake in the victory, could also become uninfatuated quickly, and treacherous. Maybe that was what had happened to the policeman: She had become treacherous.

"Or do you want to get revenge on this police friend?" he said.

She glanced at him defensively and he knew it was at least partly true. She looked away and drew at the cigarette.

"I told you I believe in your cause," she said. "And when you believe in something, you should do something besides go to meetings. You should take risks. You should live in real life. He used to say that to me, and about that, he was right."

On her face was seriousness and fear, like that on the faces of the youngest recruits, who made pledges to die fighting and were frightened by their own words. He cupped his hands, lit a cigarette and filled the space between them with smoke.

"I believe only in surviving," he said bluntly, as if he wanted to puncture her dream with the words.

Back home it was not the sort of thing he would have said to a collaborator. You didn't want to question his enthusiasm, but to inspire him. There, during a night like this one, he would have used the time for political organization, for explaining to the peasant his place in the guerrilla network, his importance to the cause, the absolute need for secrecy. Along the way, he would recount the sins of the army, the sons of bitches. The peasants knew those crimes only too well already, but it was good to stoke that anger. You wanted to create more and more of it, until it became part of the air the people breathed, like the heat at night, building until it filled the air with electricity. Then suddenly it would explode and the night would seem like day.

But now he had to deal with this woman, who had read Marx. In his life, he had never read Marx. He knew *compañeros* who had read him and sometimes talked about how the country would be after the final victory. That was their dream. His was less complicated. He wanted to avenge his family and get back what had been taken from them. It wasn't a matter of books and theories, it was all about family and avenging your own blood. Maybe someday, he wouldn't get along with the brothers who had all those other dreams—but

there was no time to think about that now. It was like he had
told her, he thought about just one thing: how to survive.

"If your police boyfriend doesn't come here, who does?"
he asked her.

"Friends," she said, "just artist friends. And sometimes my
students come by. That's how I make a living, giving classes.
But they always call first and if I tell them I'm working they
don't come. And then there are the vacuum cleaner and en-
cyclopedia salesmen and Jehovah's Witnesses, but I don't open
for them. Sometimes I don't see anyone for days."

"Do you go out for anything? Does anyone expect you to
be somewhere tomorrow to work? Would somebody come
here looking for you?" he asked.

"I work here and there is enough food in the house to last
for more than a week. There's no need to go out."

"How about clothes for me?" he asked. "Did your police
boyfriend leave any clothes?"

"Downstairs there are some boxes," she said, "and you are
about the same size."

He got up and backed away from the window until he could
look down the hallway through the darkness to where there
were other rooms. The house was well-furnished, clean and
comfortable, not like the hovels he had hidden in back home.
Of course there you didn't have to worry about telephones
and people selling encyclopedias and women who knew more
than you did.

"You could sleep in the spare bedroom," she said. "We'll
keep the shades drawn and no one will see you."

His eyes narrowed and his mouth turned grim. Sleep was
something he wouldn't do. You didn't make it easy for them.
You didn't let them shoot you in your sleep.

You also didn't get separated from your *compañeros,* and
if you did, you tried to rejoin them again as soon as possible.
But what could he do? He could have her call Dennis or his
sister, but Dennis had said that maybe they were listening

and they would trap him. The other possibility would be to send her to see Dennis at the restaurant, let him know where he was hiding. For that he had to trust her. After years in the mountains, he knew trust was something that grew slowly, like a tree, or it broke as soon as you tried to go out on its limb. He looked at her from behind, as if looking for the betrayal that she held behind her back, like a sharp knife.

She got up, crossed the room to the television and switched it on. The room filled with its gray light.

"It's eleven o'clock and the news is on," she said. "Let's see if they mention it."

They did. It was the first matter they talked about, a man with a microphone standing in front of a hospital emergency room with ambulances and many policemen milling about. He couldn't understand everything the man said, but he knew one policeman was wounded and it was serious. They also showed the car that had chased him, its windows shattered, its side crushed, the red lights of the police cars covering the whole scene with blood. He heard his own name and Gloria's and the word murder. It ended and he told her to turn it off.

"It's a policeman who was hurt. That's not good." She spoke with the same assurance she'd had before when talking about the police. "For a few days, they will be looking for you and only you. When one of theirs is hurt they get nasty. You shouldn't move from this house, not even if you change those fatigues you're wearing. They'll probably still spot you and they'd just as soon shoot you as talk to you."

He sat back down on the stool and rested the rifle across his legs. She made it sound like an unusual circumstance, but to be shot on sight was the threat he had lived with the past three years.

She brought the pot and poured more coffee for both of them. Then she sat again, sipped from it and smoked, the ash glowing in the darkness.

"This girl who was killed, who was she?" she asked.

He didn't even look at her. She broke all the rules, this one. Collaborators weren't to ask personal questions, weren't to have any information that might compromise them or their contact person.

"I know you didn't kill her," she said. "I could tell the way you said it last night. You said you loved her."

Again he made his voice hard and final, the way you had to be sometimes with collaborators.

"She was a girl from our country," he said. "That is all you need to know."

"I was just wondering," she said. "I thought you might want to talk about it."

He felt the toughness, the hard shell of an armadillo forming over his heart.

"Everyone who has been killed in our country in this war was loved by somebody," he said. "Even the son-of-a-bitching soldiers, their mothers probably loved them."

He cupped the cigarette, the red light escaping through the fingers.

"When you heard a policeman had been hurt, were you afraid it was your boyfriend?" he asked, squinting at her. "You were. I can tell. See, everybody has somebody who cares about him."

He smoked and allowed himself to smile.

"This is one son of a bitch of a situation I have myself in. My collaborator is worried that her policeman will get hurt." He laughed out loud and then let out a string of curses.

"No one has to get hurt," she said. "You can stay here and he won't know."

Then a car turned onto the street, and when it was still six houses away he saw the rooflights and recognized it was a police car. He moved to the side of the window and put both hands on the assault rifle. The patrol car came down the street very slowly, its spotlight prying into every shadow. He could sense the eyes inside the car prying into every window. He pressed himself against the wall and watched it until the red taillights disappeared from sight.

"I told you, they won't look for you here," she said.

"Because you had a policeman as your lover," he said sarcastically.

"Yes," she said. "You're lucky."

CHAPTER 12

Cruz was in a foreign country, standing in a bamboo shack surrounded by jungle. Through the gaps in the walls came spears of smoky sunlight. With him in the shack were peasants—men, women and children—dressed in ragged white clothes, all of them standing around a pile of gunpowder so big it reached the peaked thatch roof of the hut. Then a man came through the only doorway and pointed at the gunpowder with a shiny, black, evil-looking pistol. He was dressed like a gangster in an old movie, all in black, except for a white Panama hat. He had a dark complexion, but Cruz could not see his face because he had the brim of the hat pulled down across his eyes. The situation went from bad to desperate. The man waved the gun at the pile of blue powder and told Cruz to light it. Although they did not make a sound, Cruz could sense the terrible fear in the peasants. The gangster again waved the pistol at Cruz and Cruz did what he was told. He struck a match, at arm's length he touched it to the powder and held his breath. It started to smoke. To Cruz's surprise, the powder turned out to be incense, and the hut was filled with a smell he recalled from the church the morning before.

At an order from the gangster, the peasants dutifully formed a line and began to leave the hut in a silent procession, as the people had done Sunday morning, and marched into the dark jungle. They did not offer any resistance. Cruz recognized the last person in line. It was Gloria Soto. Knowing she was dead, this scared him. The people were marching to their deaths. When the gangster waved the pistol at him and ordered him to follow the others, Cruz refused. The gunsel advanced on Cruz, wedging him into a corner of the hut, pointing the pistol right at his stomach. The thin lips under the hat brim twisted into an evil smile and then the finger slowly tightened on the trigger. There was a flash from the mouth of the gun and then a greater explosion, as the pile of blue powder, which turned out to be gunpowder after all, exploded. The explosion was so large, Cruz knew in that last split second of recognition, that it would take him, the gangster, the hut and possibly the entire jungle up with it.

Cruz's eyes snapped open. At first he thought his ears were ringing from the explosion, as they had the night before from the pistol. They weren't; it was the phone. He glanced at the clock, which said 7:32, looked at the phone warily and picked it up.

"Hello."

"Inspector Cruz?" Cruz grunted and the boyish, wide-awake voice on the other end said, "This is Officer Detlof at Mission Station, calling at the request of Captain Lara."

"Uh-huh."

"The captain says he'd like to see you first thing this morning."

"Okay," and Cruz began to hang up.

"Excuse me, sir."

"Yes."

"The captain said no later than 8:30 A.M. sharp, and earlier if you can get here. He told me to tell you that."

"You've told me," Cruz said and he hung up.

As Cruz walked into the lobby of Mission Station forty minutes later, an old Latina woman in a full-skirted flower-print dress was yelling in Spanish through the bullet-proof glass at the front desk officer. She held her hand over her head and brought it slowly down toward the floor, as if she were watching something fall from the sky. She threw her arms in the air and then made a loud noise like an explosion.

"*Bombas*," she told the officer. "*Bombas*." Cruz noticed the cop had dark bags under his eyes. He was staring at her as if he were shell-shocked.

He buzzed Cruz through into the squad room, which was milling with cops, the way it usually was during a shift change, but 8:30 wasn't the hour for a shift change. The Dutch door to the weapons room was open and cops were checking out shotguns. Their faces were hard-set, serious.

Young Officer Detlof, whose bright voice had woken Cruz, now asked him to wait and offered Cruz a chair outside the captain's office. Throughout the station came the sounds of phones ringing, the static of police radios and the shotguns being cracked. Above him, fluorescent lights hummed. Cruz wiped sweat off his brow and the base of his neck. His eyes were bloodshot and in his stomach his mother's chicken mole was still moiling.

When Detlof finally waved Cruz into the office, Captain Arthur Lara didn't bother to stand, or even to greet him. Instead, he glanced away from a sheaf of typed incident reports and, peering over his wire-rimmed glasses, shot a glance at Cruz which, if it hadn't been for the intolerable heat, would have frozen Cruz's blood on the spot. Then he glanced away again.

Cruz had a premonition of trouble that made his stomach clench and made him grimace in pain.

Arthur Lara was a slim, silver-haired man who had the ramrod bearing of a military officer. Five years before, the Mission District had been ridden with crime and racial tension that touched all the ethnic groups, and the neighborhood had been on the point of exploding. Many businesspeople were saying the police had lost control and some were leaving the barrio, fleeing to safer parts of town. Lara, a career cop with twenty-five years in patrol and a reputation for bravery and diplomacy, had been transferred to "recapture" the barrio. He had quickly put the street gangs on the run and driven them indoors, cut the crime rate, reassured the business community and improved the badly deteriorated relations between the police and the ethnic populations. Now when people talked of the next chief, he was prominently mentioned. He was smooth as silk and hard as nails.

"Sit down, please, Inspector," he said without looking at Cruz. He spoke without anger, without any emotion at all, which made it worse. From a folder on the desk he removed several typed pages, and for the next minute he studied them in silence while Cruz read the criminology diplomas that covered the walls and weathered the sloshing of acid against his stomach walls.

"I have here three documents, Inspector," he said finally. "The report of Sergeant Donnelly on the sighting and attempted capture last night of a suspect in a homicide; a shooting incident report, also by Sergeant Donnelly, on the use of a firearm by the suspect, his attempt to answer fire and your behavior at that juncture; and last, we have the latest hospital report on Officer Klein, who was wounded by this suspect, Hernandez."

"How is Klein this morning, sir?" Cruz asked.

Lara gave no impression he had heard the question.

"According to Sergeant Donnelly," he continued, "the suspect was seen leaving a grocery on Florida Street, was asked to stop and pulled a pistol . . ."

Cruz, lulled by the heat, picked out only words from there on out: "shots," "danger," "interfered," "wounded."

Cruz had won two commendations for bravery in shooting

incidents, but that had not impressed Alice. At the end she had told him what she thought of his medals. "You do things like that because you don't value your life," she had said. "Cheap thrills, because you can't find what to live for, what to believe in. Nothing worthwhile, at least."

Cruz knew what she considered worthwhile would be having a kid. She had hinted at it. But Cruz had said this world wasn't a place into which he wanted to bring a child. Too many bodies in empty lots, too many hushed confessions to priests about bloodletting. Too many people with screwed-up lives he would have to protect the kid from. Every stiff was once somebody's baby.

". . . And then there's the condition of Officer Klein," Lara said and Cruz snapped back. Lara was glaring at him. "You're very lucky he's going to live, Inspector, because if he hadn't . . ."

He left the rest unsaid, but it was enough so that Cruz saw visions of a patrol car again, dark nights with the radio squawking.

"Donnelly and I were both dressed in plain clothes and the car we used to go after him was unmarked," Cruz said. "I wasn't sure this Hernandez kid knew who we were and there's a chance some other people are out to kill him. This girl was mixed up with bad guys."

Cruz's voice tailed off in a lack of conviction. Did he really think that? It was a story Elvira Hernandez had told him, probably as phony as the note. Bill Clarke had tried to defend the kid too, but Clarke was a missionary, a defender of the refugee, just like Stacy. Was Cruz going soft too, with the heat, or what? The truth was he didn't know why he had done it.

"You weren't sure, but Donnelly was sure," Lara said. "He knew this Hernandez had probably killed one person already and now he was shooting at two police officers and shooting to kill. He also knew his department guidelines for use of firearms. He knew that as long as there is no danger to bystanders he could use his gun and should use it in order to insure that this man did not harm someone else, either policemen or civilians. And a minute later he almost killed Klein and everybody else in that car, including you.

"He's out there now somewhere with an M-16 and there's a chance he won't give us another clear shot at him," Lara said. "I have guys working extra shifts looking for him and guys from neighboring stations helping them. They don't like it when a policeman gets hurt. They get angry and some of them ask questions about how it happened that Klein, a white officer, got gunned down by a Latino suspect, when you, *Inspector* Cruz, could have stopped it or let Donnelly stop it."

Cruz frowned, but Lara just bore down on him with his slate-gray eyes.

"And that's not the worst of it. We have people in the district, particularly in the area of the shooting activity last night, who are now scared out of their minds. They started calling around midnight and the calls haven't stopped. A lot of them speak only Spanish. If you'd like, you can listen in and you'll hear what they think about last night's incident. We've had people tell us that bombs went off last night, that battles went on in the street with dozens of men on each side, that the war has spread from down in the jungles all the way up here."

Lara swiveled in his chair, so that he was looking out the window at the sun-blinded street.

"Do you know how a rumor spreads in an area like this, Inspector? It works like an illness, a plague; it spreads fast and it kills all the commonsense explanations and reasonableness it finds in its way. Many people around here will believe the craziest, bloodiest story they hear. They come from places where anything could happen and lots of bloody things have happened. It's safer to believe the worst."

He swiveled again toward Cruz, like an artillery gunner zeroing in on a target.

"I've spent four years here trying to bring some peace to this barrio, and in one night some people are saying they live in a war zone. I want the rumors stopped, Inspector. I want this suspect in custody as quickly as possible, and for your sake, you better hope it happens without further violence and without anyone getting killed."

Lara swiveled again, turning his guns toward the street. "That's all, Inspector."

Cruz left the office and headed right for the door, not wanting to talk to anybody, but Donnelly cut him off before he could escape.

He lifted his dark tangled eyebrows and glanced toward the captain's office.

"He's not too happy," he said.

"What makes you think that?" said Cruz.

Donnelly pulled Cruz away from the door.

"Before you leave, you should go back to the drunk tank," he said. "I have Joe the Actor back there and he keeps talking about the girl who was found dead. He says he saw her that night. He's pretty spooked."

Cruz frowned.

"He's a drunk and he's got an imagination," Donnelly said, "but you never know."

Cruz cut through Communications and went out to the holding cells. Joe the Actor was by himself in the drunk tank, holding on to the bars, combing his white beard with his fingers, mumbling to himself, just as he had been the day Gloria Soto was found dead. Cruz walked up and said hello and the other man looked at him, his deepset eyes filled with fear.

"I hear you know about this girl who died, Joe," Cruz said. Joe started shaking his head.

"I didn't know she was dead," he said. His voice was very low for a small man and for a drunk his diction was very precise. "I swear I didn't. I'm an actor, a professional, but in this instance you have to believe me."

"I believe you, Joe," Cruz said, filling his voice with sincerity. "Just tell me what you know about the killing."

The other man stared into nothing, as if he were seeing the girl's ghost.

"I saw her lying there and she had her eyes open," he said. "I thought she had swallowed something. Some sort of narcotic. Like Juliet, you know. To sleep perchance to dream. But not that she'd given up the ghost. Not death's cold kiss."

Cruz was squinting at him.

"When did you see her, Joe?"

"I saw her lying there," he said, "and then I started to go away. It was not my place to interfere. I didn't touch her. I swear that to you on my honor! And then I saw the other one come."

"Who's that?"

"A man," he said. "I was across the street and I watched him go near. He had a stick in his hand and I thought he was going to do her harm. I was prepared to go help, but he didn't hit her."

"He didn't?"

"No. He stood there a minute. I saw him talk to her and then he went away back into the night. At that point I went back to talk to her myself, to make sure she was all right, and I saw it in the dirt. The drawing, that is."

"The drawing of the animal?"

"That's right," Joe said. "It was a drawing of a sacred bull. He drew it there and then he left. It was some ritual. A religious matter. I was sure of it."

"You watched some guy draw that bull in the dirt after she was already dead?" Cruz asked. "And he didn't see you there?"

"No," Joe said. "I was under the cover of darkness. Then I tried to talk to her, but she wouldn't answer. I touched her and felt she was kind of cool. But I still didn't know she was dead. Really I didn't. I'm not capable of taking life. I'm an artist."

"What time was this, Joe?"

The drunk thought, then looked at Cruz bleakly and shook his head.

"What did the guy look like, Joe? Remember!"

Joe looked into his memory again, struggling to see something through the alcohol fog. He shook his head forlornly.

"It was dark," he said. He looked spooked again. "But it wasn't me who harmed that poor girl."

"Okay, Joe," Cruz said.

He left the drunk hanging on to the bars, muttering to himself. He went out the door of Mission Station to the sounds of phones ringing and shotguns being cracked.

In the eastern sky, the sun pulsed like a distant explosion. There were fewer people on the street than usual. Cops there were plenty of, angry-looking cops. He drove down Mission, passing two patrol cars in four blocks and then another parked outside a walkup transient hotel. Patrol was on the prowl and looking under rocks in the dingiest corners of the barrio. They rode around with their jaws set, their eyes hidden behind bad-looking shades. Right behind their heads, clipped to the wire mesh, rode the shotguns. On South Van Ness, outside a dingy bar, sat another patrol car and the patrol wagon, its back doors open and waiting for cargo. You didn't have to be Eric Hernandez, just anybody who had been up to no good and you were going to get leaned on. You were in trouble and you better watch out.

Cruz was in trouble too and he didn't like it.

He stopped at a pay phone and got the number of Pan American Import-Export from information. A woman with a Latin accent there told him Elvira Hernandez had been expected at work at 8:00 A.M. but had not shown up. No, she didn't know why. Cruz called the home number and listened to it ring, rocking back and forth on his bantamweight's feet, but no one answered.

A minute later he pulled up outside the ocher-colored house on Alabama. This time there were no kids outside playing war. No one at all was out on the street, as if on that block the air itself was dangerous. The same yellow Chevy was in the driveway. Cruz climbed the stairs. The house was dead quiet and behind the living-room window Elvira Hernandez's jungle lay still.

He rang the bell, waited seconds, pounded the door and rang again. If she was gone, if she had made a fool of him, he would track her, just like one of the beasts she liked to talk about. Cruz would turn predator.

He pounded again. Then in the window giving onto the porch someone moved a palm frond, and Elvira Hernandez was looking at him out of her jungle. She opened the door wrapped in a flowered housecoat, her black eyes searching his.

"You found my brother," she said.

Cruz went by her without a word, climbed the stairs to Eric Hernandez's stark room, checked the other upstairs rooms, came down the stairs, went through the steamy kitchen and inspected the overgrown backyard. When he went into the living room, she was slumped in a chair rubbing at her eyes.

"Why don't you guys give me a break?" she said. "I had cops here half the night."

"What cops?"

She shrugged. "Who knows? Guys in uniform. They were

beating at the door at two in the morning, four of them with shotguns in their hands and a warrant to search the house. It scared the hell out of me. I didn't sleep again until after dawn."

He stood over her, bobbing.

"Is that so?"

"Yes, that's so," she said, temper flaring. "In my country, people hear knocks on their door in the middle of the night, it makes their hair turn white. Their hearts stop. We have seen too many people disappear that way. You don't do something like that to one of us."

"That's too bad it scared you," Cruz said, "but you should have seen the guy your brother shot last night. He was really scared and he didn't sleep much either. He was busy fighting for his life. Of course, he was lucky. Your brother didn't have a chance to put the gun to his head, to kill him in cold blood the way he did Gloria Soto."

"My brother didn't kill Gloria," she said through clenched teeth.

"Right," Cruz said. "That's why when we asked him to stop last night he shot at us. He thought we wanted to give him a ticket for jaywalking."

"I told you he has people who want to kill him."

"That's right, again. Every cop in the city would like to kill him, and they're all out looking for him."

"I don't mean the police. I told you already."

"Yeah. The vultures and the coyotes and rats. Tell me that scary story again." He ran a hand impatiently through his thick hair. "I gave your brother a break last night. They wanted to shoot him down like a dog and I stopped them. Then he turns around and almost blows my head off and almost kills another cop. So now there ain't no more breaks. Your brother shot a policeman and that's all that matters. Everything else stops until he gets arrested—or he gets killed. You understand?"

She glared at him, trying to look as cool and tough as the last time they had talked, but now her bloodshot eyes couldn't hide the fear. When she lifted her hand to push back her hair, it trembled from fatigue and nerves.

"So you come to my house to scare me," she said. "Is that it? You barge in here. No warrant, no nothing, and you bully me. Because you figure I'm just a dumb Latin girl and you carry a gun and you can scare me easy."

Cruz turned away.

"Why don't you just shoot me?" she said to his back. "You're acting like the police in my country and that's what they would do. If one of them got hurt, they would take vengeance. They'd kill me and anybody else in the family. Of course, first they'd rape me. For good measure they would burn down the house."

"Where's your brother?" Cruz said, turning on her. "That's all I want from you."

She fixed on him now with a strange look, as if he were changing right in front of her from a person into some kind of animal.

"What do you mean that's all you want? You talk as if there is something else in the world that should matter to me more than my brother. I told you we're the only two left, so what else could matter? Without him, my daughter and I have nobody. I lose him, I might as well cut out half my heart."

She clutched at the cloth over her chest. Cruz could see down to her breasts, which were dark at the top, turning to milky brown.

"Is that what you'd do with your own family?" she said. "Turn them in to your buddies on the police force? Maybe that's the way some people are in this country. They don't have family in their veins. People like you are bloodless."

Cruz shoved his hands into his pockets and drifted across the room.

"Did you even talk to Julio Saenz?" she asked.

"Yes, I did. He was in Los Angeles Friday night," Cruz said. "He has an alibi. Everyone has one, except for your brother, but that's because they didn't kill Gloria Soto."

"Because they aren't running, like my brother? That's why you think that," she said. "Eric knows if there is trouble he will be blamed, so he runs. They kill Gloria and they don't move. They sit fat and comfortable because they know they will never be suspected. They grow fatter all the time because they eat up other human beings. They are cannibals. In my country, we recognize them."

"And I'll tell you what I recognize," Cruz said. "I recognize that you didn't tell me how your family was murdered." An animal caution took control of her again and her eyes grew wary.

"You didn't want me to know it was one of the Sotos who had caused their killings," Cruz said. "That it was Gloria's father who had fingered them. If I know that, then I know your brother's motive for murder."

"Not to kill Gloria," she said. "Maybe her father, because he told the death squad people. But not Gloria."

"I have an idea about that, too," Cruz said. He leaned against the vine-covered mantel. "Maybe Gloria's father found out by himself that Eric was coming out of the hills, and laid a trap for him. But maybe he didn't find out by himself. Gloria said it happened that way, but the one who knew for sure Eric was coming was Gloria herself. And she was at the scene too. She told Stacy Stoner all about it. Maybe she told her father Eric was coming. Or maybe she let it slip somehow. She was the one who caused the deaths in your family. And Eric knew it and killed her. That's what I think."

Elvira Hernandez was shaking her head, her black-rimmed eyes fixed on Cruz.

"He didn't think that and he didn't kill her," she said. "Why would Gloria do that? She loved Eric. And he loved her. She was sick and he was trying to help her."

"Maybe it was the fact that she felt responsible for all the deaths that drove her crazy. Maybe that's why she was seeing faces and hearing voices and having nightmares."

"But if Eric knew she was responsible, why didn't he kill her when he first came here?" she said. "Why did he wait? Why did he try and be good to her?"

Cruz shrugged. "Who knows? Maybe he only found out this week. Victor Soto said it was only in the past week or so that Eric had started to act strange, dress like a guerrilla."

"That's because they were threatening his life."

"Yes, that note that was typed right in this house."

"I mean the phone calls."

"I think it was your brother who was doing the threatening, Miss Hernandez," Cruz said. "I think he's still doing the threatening—scaring the hell out of everybody around here."

She shook her finger at him.

"That's because Soto, the worm, he told you that," she said. "And you believe him. He has you fooled. But Soto didn't have to be afraid of Eric, he had to be afraid of other people and that's why he wants protection from you. He told you he fears my brother, but it is really his own friends he's afraid of."

Cruz drifted about the room and the palm fronds nodded as he passed. There had been the question of Soto's phone call and the fact that he had lied to Cruz. The .38 caliber bullet dug out of Gloria Soto and the .38 on the hip of Robert Soto. Julio Saenz and his convenient receipt.

"Who would be after Soto and why?" he asked.

"Why! Because they are mixed up in no good together. Smuggling people or whatever."

"Who? the vultures, the coyotes, the cannibals?"

"Soto and Robert Soto, Saenz, maybe Colonel Ortiz and

others. I don't know them all, I don't associate with animals."

Cruz's eyes narrowed.

"Who's Colonel Ortiz?"

"Joe Ortiz. He runs the Cantina Bar on Twenty-ninth Street. In my country he was a colonel in the National Police. He was one of the leaders of that pack of wolves."

"Was he down there when your family was killed?"

She shook her head.

"I don't know. He has been here for years and he goes back and forth, but I'm sure he knows all the killers still working down there. His kind, they never forget the old friends they hunted with and killed with. Soto and Julio Saenz sit with him at the owner's table at the Cantina, like a nest of vultures."

Cruz frowned and drifted across the room. He could feel her eyes on him, like a creature watching him from a hiding place in the bush.

"You stopped them from killing Eric last night because something told you he didn't do it," she said. "Why can't you follow those instincts?"

She was looking into his eyes. Maybe it was just Cruz, but every time she talked about instincts her voice grew musky and he saw sex in her eyes.

Cruz jabbed at his chest.

"I helped him and now I'm up to my ass in trouble," he said. "Anyway, I don't have instincts, remember?"

"Even you sense enough to know that Soto and Saenz are bad news," she said. "Talk to them again, talk to Colonel Ortiz. If you're in trouble anyway, why not try to find out the truth? If you care about the truth."

Cruz looked at her and made a face. "Give me a break."

"Every other cop in San Francisco is trying to kill him now," she said, "but you could still help him. That's not too much to ask, just one of you on his side and everyone else out to kill him."

"Those are exactly the odds your brother has," Cruz said.

She shrugged and when she spoke, it was with a voice without emotion.

"He probably won't survive," she said. "But then he wasn't going to survive anyway. That was all decided a long time ago from the time we were both born. You're born poor in our country, you may survive, but there's a good chance you won't really be alive. The life you have won't be worth living. My brother knew that and he made his decision to try to change things. Most of our people, the ones born the way we were, they make that decision or they put themselves in God's hands early on and look forward to the next world, because this one will be sad and will probably end up very bad for us. The ones who come here, this is like a fantasy, but we never really get away from our country and the suffering there. For my brother, even though he is very good, noble, it looks like it will end up bad."

Then behind Cruz's back there came a sound, a creak of a stair. He turned quickly, swiveling on the ball of his foot and dropping to one knee, his hand groping for the gun in his belt. He looked up and found crouched on the staircase a little girl. She was dark and pretty, but looking down at him, her eyes were full of fear. She looked like her mother, but strangely, it seemed to Cruz she bore a greater resemblance to someone else: to Gloria Soto with her look of terror.

"See, even she is scared of you," her mother said, crossing to the girl and taking her in her arms. "You're so anxious to kill my brother, who knows what you people will do?"

Cruz got up and holstered his gun. Elvira Hernandez was looking at him warily, a lioness protecting her cub from a rabid animal that had wandered into their den.

Cruz wiped the sweat off his face. Then he patted the little girl on the head and left.

CHAPTER 13

Back at the same pay phone on Mission, Cruz rang the Cantina, but it was still early in the day and there was no answer. Under Ortiz, he found a dozen Josés. On the third try he found "the colonel's" house, but the woman who answered said he wasn't home and didn't know where Ortiz was. Cruz left his name and office number. Then he went looking for Victor Soto at the Central America Travelrama.

Business had been bad the last few years, according to Soto, and the place certainly looked it. The sign above the door pictured the Earth, but it was faded and the paint had chipped off in various places, as if certain regions of the planet had been obliterated. On the sidewalk right in front of the office stood a handwritten sandwich board advertising "One-Day Jackpot Tours to Casinos in Reno: Low Cost, Big Winnings." On weekend mornings, Cruz had seen small groups of people, mostly old and down at the heels, waiting there to take those tour buses to make their fortunes. They always looked ghostly and sad, like rags-to-riches dreams fading right in front of your eyes. They certainly hadn't gotten rich, and neither would Soto with that brand of clientele.

Through the window, Cruz saw Soto sitting alone at a desk at the rear of the long, narrow office. It looked musty and the walls were plastered with travel posters curling at the edges. The sign in the window said "Open," but when he tried the door he found it locked. He rapped impatiently on the glass with his car key and Soto's head snapped up nervously. He grimaced and then came to the door. He looked at Cruz suspiciously through the smudged glass.

"I need to talk to you, Mr. Soto," Cruz said. "I have some questions."

Soto frowned, but let Cruz in. He immediately locked the door behind him, as if someone else unwanted might grab the opportunity to barge in.

"Interesting way to do business," Cruz said. "You only sell trips by appointment?"

Soto showed his yellowed teeth.

"Eric Hernandez almost kills a policeman and you wonder why I am afraid," Soto said. "It was all over the radio. Instead of bothering me, you should be out there looking for him."

He hurried back to his desk, bent his bald, freckled head over some papers and puffed nervously at a soggy nonfilter cigarette. Cruz settled into one of the two empty customer chairs and looked at a poster of a Mexican tourist site on the wall over the desk: an old Mexican Indian temple on which was carved a long, curling stone snake, its mouth open, poised for a fatal bite.

"You want to go to Mexico?" Soto asked. "Very nice beaches, ancient ruins, colonial cities. The dollar is very strong there now and there is no war."

"Next time I go, I'll look you up," Cruz said. "Right now, we're going to talk more about Gloria."

"I told you everything I knew the other day. I don't know where Eric Hernandez is. That's what you need to know."

Cruz nodded impatiently. He leaned forward in the chair, hands on his knees, and fixed his eyes on Soto.

"I need to know a few other things," he said, "like why you

didn't tell me that Gloria had a new boyfriend. Julio Saenz."

There was a sharp edge in Cruz's voice. It made Soto's brow furrow, but he kept shuffling his papers.

"Julio was out of town when Gloria was killed. He was down in Los Angeles."

"So he tells me," Cruz said. "He even carries a motel receipt around to prove it. Very convenient, very thorough. Still, it's strange you didn't mention him, since he was the love of Gloria's life."

The other man was shaking his head in short, nervous twitches.

"I didn't want to cause him any trouble. He was already hurt enough by Gloria's death. I saw no need for him to be dragged into a police investigation if he had nothing to do with the killing."

Cruz nodded.

"I see. Just trying to save a friend some inconvenience."

"That's right," Soto said.

One thing was clear: Soto could never match Dennis Miranda as a liar. On his bald head there were already pinpricks of sweat that hadn't been there before.

"Yes, I guess poor Julio was already suffering enough," Cruz said. "From what I hear he was very in love with your niece. Maybe he would have married her. And a very lucky man you would have been to have such an excellent young fellow in the family. Handsome, charming, a pillar of the community."

Soto blew out of the corner of his mouth a cloud of smoke that rose like mist and fogged a poster next to the desk. It was a poster of Greece, some ruins.

"Julio is an honest businessman like me," Soto said.

"Yeah," Cruz said, "except his business is trading on people's misery. Is it true he got to know your niece by raping her on the way up from the border?"

Soto made a face.

"My niece wasn't raped by anyone," he said.

Cruz leaned forward, put an elbow on the desk, reached over and fingered the jade shark's tooth that hung around Soto's neck.

"There are a few things about all this I don't understand, Mr. Soto. Maybe you can explain them to me," Cruz said. "To begin, I wonder why an upstanding businessman like yourself, respected in the community, has anything to do with a creep like Saenz. I really do wonder about that, Mr. Soto. I understand if he brings Gloria up from down south for you, you pay him and he goes his way. That's the way it should be. But he did more than that with her, didn't he? And still you two seem to like each other." He let the tooth go, so that it fell back into Soto's damp chest hairs.

"What is it that makes you and Julio Saenz such good friends?" Cruz asked.

Soto puffed at the cigarette as if he were trying to put up a smokescreen.

"Those stories aren't true about him," Soto said. "Julio didn't do anything to my niece. He treated her like a gentleman."

"Uh-huh. Julio Saenz is honest, gentlemanly and as gentle as the wind," Cruz said. "You're quite a judge of character, Mr. Soto, I must say. Why don't we try someone else? Let's see how much you know about Colonel Joe Ortiz."

The documents were still moving in Soto's hands, but his eyes were blank, like those of a blind man making believe he could read.

"What can you tell me about Colonel Ortiz?" Cruz asked.

"He owns the Cantina Bar," Soto said. "Everyone knows that."

"What else can you tell me about him?"

"Nothing."

"That's funny. I understand he's a good friend of yours.

That you sit at the owner's table at the Cantina with him. What do you talk about at that table?"

"We don't talk about anything," Soto said.

"That sounds interesting. You just look at each other."

"I don't know anything about anybody," Soto said. He pulled open a drawer, but before he could put papers in it, Cruz saw stowed there a pistol, a .22 by the looks of it. Soto's eyes jittered, he shoved the papers in and slammed the drawer shut. He looked at Cruz, and Cruz smiled and raised his eyebrows.

"My, my, everybody is walking around with a gun these days."

"I told you from the beginning, Eric Hernandez will try and kill me. I warned you he was dangerous. I have to protect myself."

"I know what you told me, Mr. Soto. What interests me is what you didn't tell me," Cruz said. The bald man's eyes throbbed and Cruz nodded at him.

"Yes, you forgot a few things," Cruz said. "How about if I tell you a few things you left out last time. First of all, Julio Saenz is a mule, a smuggler of aliens. He brought your niece up here from the border for you and for that reason she knew he was in the smuggling business and maybe some other bad business that she found out about later. She was close to Eric Hernandez, and Dennis Miranda too, and maybe they were telling her to turn Saenz in. That gave him and his partners reason to kill her. Because he has to have partners, Mr. Soto. I don't think Julio Saenz is intelligent enough to shine his shoes, let alone run a big-money operation like this. Somebody else runs it."

Soto swiveled abruptly in the chair, got up, opened the drawer of a filing cabinet and made believe he was busy there. Cruz watched him like a hunter tracking a deer through a gunsight.

"Saturday afternoon, after you identified your niece's body, you went home and made a phone call," Cruz said. "Who did you call?"

"A member of the family," Soto said.

"Which member? What's his name and telephone number?"

"I called a cousin down in San Diego, but he wasn't home."

"You talked to someone in Spanish," Cruz said. "Who was it?"

"I . . . I don't know. Someone answered the telephone, but it was a wrong number."

"You're lying," Cruz said.

Soto sat down again and ran shaky hands over his sweating bald head.

"Why don't you leave me alone?" he said, his voice trembling. "Can't you see I have enough problems already? My niece is dead. My business is dying. My family is threatened. They . . ."

Whatever it was caught in his throat.

"They what?" Cruz asked. "Who are 'they'?"

Soto began to shuffle papers again, but Cruz put his hand over them. The bald man's fingers scrambled across the desk to the ashtray, grabbed the cigarette and sucked on it.

"I don't know anything and I don't know anybody," he said.

"You don't know anything, except that you're afraid someone will kill you. They're probably the same people who killed your niece, but for some reason you want to cover up for them."

"Hernandez is after me. He is the one you have to get."

"Maybe he is," Cruz said. "And maybe Hernandez killed your niece and maybe he didn't. There's someone else besides him that you're afraid of."

The other man was shaking his head nervously.

"You don't understand," he muttered.

"What did your niece know that she shouldn't know? What did she see? Was it the massacre of the Hernandez family or something here?"

Soto just shook his head as if he were trying to shake off a bad dream. Cruz was squinting at him.

"Who did Gloria go to see at the Cantina the other night? If it wasn't Saenz, who was it? The Colonel?"

"I don't know. I told you."

"You weren't there?"

"No, I wasn't," Soto said, meeting Cruz's eyes. "I was at a meeting of travel agents at the St. Francis Hotel, downtown. We were discussing the problem of terrorism and how it has affected our business." He jabbed his chest. "Me, I know more about that than anyone else. I told them so. They can tell you I was there."

"Was it the Colonel she was going to see then? She told people she was afraid of the Colonel. Why was that?"

"That's crazy."

"Is it? I understand Mr. Ortiz was in the National Police in your country. I understand the police there aren't always very courteous with people. Sometimes they tie people's thumbs and shoot them."

"The Colonel is a legitimate businessman," Soto said. "He has nothing to do with killing. And he didn't even know Gloria."

"Everyone you know is a legitimate businessman. It's a wonder anyone ever got killed," Cruz said. "What are you afraid of, Mr. Soto? Tell me. We'll protect you. Nobody will get to you."

Soto nodded sarcastically behind a veil of smoke.

"You will protect me. That's fine. And the others? What about the others?"

"Your son and your sister-in-law, we can protect them too, if you're afraid they will be hurt."

"And the others besides them? The ones still down in our country? How will you protect them? Will you send a police car from San Francisco to park outside their farmhouses? Is that how you plan to keep them alive?"

He laughed and a burst of smoke came from his mouth. Cruz was frowning at him.

"Who would hurt your family down there? Why would they hurt them?"

Soto looked back at his papers.

"Let Gloria rest in peace," he said. "That's all. She was a good girl. She's in heaven. She's better off. Just leave her alone and the rest of us too."

"It doesn't work that way, Mr. Soto."

Soto shook a yellowed finger at him.

"You're the one who doesn't know how it works."

"How does it work, then? What's going on here? What is it that's scaring you?"

"Everything scares me," Soto said.

"But some people scare you more than others."

"You scare me more than anybody else," Soto said. "Just leave us alone. You'll only bring more killing. Do you understand? You're the one I have to be afraid of."

"What's going on here?" Cruz insisted. "Is it money? Is it politics? What is it?"

"I don't know anything about politics," Soto said. "All I know is what many people in my country have learned. That when trouble like this begins, you keep your mouth shut or somebody will shut it for good. They will write you a one-way ticket, a super-saver, to the next world, Inspector. Do you understand that?"

Then, red-faced and issuing smoke like a steam engine, he went back to his papers.

Cruz wrinkled his nose and watched the man a full minute. Then he took out a business card, put it on the desk and told him to call him if he changed his mind. The other man followed him to the door and locked it behind him.

On the sidewalk, the heat hit him as if he had walked into

a wall. Directly across the street a car was parked and Cruz recognized the man in the dark glasses sitting in the driver's seat.

As Cruz crossed the street, Robert Soto got out of the car and saluted. He was in his uniform.

"Good morning, Inspector," he said. "I'm glad to see you safe. I was just hearing on the radio all about the shootout."

"Staking out the place?" Cruz asked.

"That's right," he said. "Making sure Eric Hernandez, or one of his friends, doesn't bag another member of my family. If he comes anywhere near this place, he's one dead guerrilla."

He hefted his gunbelt, adjusting the .38 on his hip.

"I'll bet he is," Cruz said.

"I see you guys are going all out, sweeping the neighborhood," the other man said. "That's exactly what you have to do when you are hunting one of these monkeys. You have to let everybody know you are out for his blood; to convince everyone that he's bad business, not to have anything to do with him, to turn him in the moment they see him or things will be rough for them. To trap one of these guys, you have to turn everyone against him. Even if you scare people a little."

Cruz nodded, watching his own reflection in the black shades. Robert Soto probably enjoyed scaring people more than a little.

"In my country, the army has a saying," he went on. "They say first you have to dry up the sea, then the fish will die on their own. They mean you make sure no one helps the guerrilla, that he has nothing to eat, no place to stay, no one to hide him, and he will walk into your sights." He tapped Cruz on the chest. "That's why you should arrest that sister of his. That's who will try and help him when you really start to squeeze him."

"Thanks for the advice," Cruz said.

"Think nothing of it," Robert Soto said. "I know this kind of people."

"I'd like you to do something else for me," Cruz said. "I'd like you to lend me that gun on your hip."

The fat over Robert Soto's sunglasses wrinkled.

"You need a pistol?"

"I need that one," Cruz said. "Just for a day or two."

Robert Soto nodded.

"Ballistics testing," he said. "You want to compare it with the bullet that killed Gloria."

"Just routine," Cruz said.

Soto's smile was more of a sneer.

"Of course, just routine," he said.

When his hand moved, it moved quickly, making Cruz flinch. The gun came out of the holster, twirled on Soto's finger and then he was offering it butt-first, still smiling.

Cruz took the gun. "I'll get it back to you," he said.

"Don't worry, I'll get another from the company," Robert Soto said, and the sun glistened on his black shades.

CHAPTER 14

Cruz rang his office and was told by Sally Sessions, the secretary, that Mr. José Ortiz had called and that he would meet Cruz at the Cantina Bar around noon. It was 11:45.

Then he called Immigration and Naturalization and left a message for Irv Hicks, an investigator. He asked for anything on Julio Saenz or anybody else who was using the Mission as a place to drop illegals.

Last of all he called Stacy Stoner's office to see if she had heard from Hernandez. The receptionist told him that Stacy hadn't come in to work, so he called her house. Stacy's mother told him Stacy had gone out late the night before, "an emergency of some kind," and not yet come back. It had happened before and the mother didn't sound concerned. No, Stacy hadn't told her anything else. Cruz thanked the woman and hung up. He could picture it: Eric Hernandez getting away from the cops, reaching a phone, having Stacy Stoner rescue him. They were now hours away somewhere and maybe still driving. Stacy! This time they'd nail her ass to the wall.

Cruz walked down Mission toward his car, but stopped when he saw the headline screaming from the *Examiner* machine. "Latin Guerrilla Ambushes Cops in Mission."

He pumped a quarter into the machine.

A man dressed in camouflage fatigues and wielding an M-16 assault rifle of a kind used by U.S. combat troops fired Sunday night on police who wanted to question him in connection with a Mission District homicide, police sources said. One patrolman was wounded and was listed in critical but stable condition Monday.

The suspect was identified as Eric Hernandez of Alabama Street. Hernandez was wanted for questioning in connection with the murder of Gloria Soto, twenty-one, of Shotwell Street, whose body was found Saturday afternoon in an empty lot in the Mission with a bullet wound in the head. Police said she had been shot once with a .38 caliber pistol. They also said the dead woman had been found with her thumbs tied behind her back, a procedure followed in political executions in some Central American countries, particularly El Salvador.

Miss Soto was a native of El Salvador. Hernandez, also from El Salvador, is known to have belonged to a guerrilla force in his country and to be a veteran of three years of combat.

Police said they received a tip that Hernandez was hiding out at a Florida Street address, and when they closed in on that building, Hernandez tried to escape by pulling a pistol and firing on the officers.

According to police, Hernandez ran, carrying a duffle bag. The officers gave chase, but were stopped a block later when Hernandez fired a burst of automatic weapons fire at them. One patrolman, Joseph Klein, twenty-nine, was hit in the chest and seriously wounded. He was at San Francisco General Hospital Monday.

Police said Hernandez made his escape through back alleyways as police proceeded cautiously, because the suspect was heavily armed. Mission District Captain Arthur Lara said it is believed Hernandez is still in the city and that Monday morning the hunt was continuing.

"He's armed and very dangerous," Lara said. "We have every available man looking for him. We'll get him."

The article went on and on an inside page included the photo of Eric Hernandez in camouflage holding an M-16.

A drop of sweat fell from Cruz's brow and spattered the photo. He threw the paper into the car and headed for the Cantina.

The sign said "Closed," but the door was ajar and he went in. He found Confucius alone in the place, behind the bar working over a block of ice with an ice pick. The ice pick and Confucius looked alike, equally skinny, equally dangerous. Cruz was told that the Colonel was expected any minute.

He ordered a Dos Equis, sat at a tin table right under a whirring ceiling fan, read the sports page and listened to Rubén Blades on the jukebox sing about a shark coming up on the shore.

> *Es el tiburon que nunca duerme*
> *Es el tiburon que va acechando*
> *Tiburon de mala suerte*

He finished the sports page, the local news and the foreign news, including an article on battles between guerrillas and the army in Central America in which a dozen soldiers had been killed. About 12:40, a man walked in and stood at the door. He was a young Latin, dark, short and stocky, with a pug nose and cheeks badly scarred by acne. His build and his face reminded Cruz of a fighting dog, a pit bull. Even though it was a hundred degrees out, he was wearing a bright yellow sport jacket and under the left arm there was a noticeable bulge. He gave Cruz the once-over, like he was measuring him for a box.

Only then did Joe Ortiz come in. The owner of La Cantina, the former police colonel, wasn't at all what Cruz had expected. He was a tall man, with a powerful upper body narrowing to a waist that was unnaturally slim for a man his age. He looked to be at least sixty, but his face was unlined and he might have been eighty or a hundred for all Cruz could tell. His body still looked limber and powerful. His skin was dark and was set off by silver-gray hair combed straight back from a narrow forehead. For someone who ran a beer joint, his clothes were also out of character. He wore an expensively tailored pearl-gray suit and matching tie, with a diamond stick-pin twinkling from his chest. The outfit made him look not like a whiskey peddler, but more like a banker or predatory corporate lawyer.

He homed in on Cruz, a hand held out like a fin cutting the water, wearing a large smile that seemed to have more teeth in it than human beings were supposed to have.

"Inspector Cruz, I'm Joe Ortiz," he said. Cruz stood up and shook hands. Ortiz must have just left an air-conditioned car, because his hand was very cold. Cruz also noticed that the man's eyes, like his hair, suit and tie, were gray. They were set very far apart, good for seeing who was coming at him from either side, and their gaze was as emotionless as a razor blade.

"I understand you have been looking for me," he said, holding on to Cruz's hand. His voice was a raspy whisper, like sandpaper.

"That's right," Cruz said. He was looking into the man's smile, trying to count his teeth. It seemed there were at least forty of them. "I need some information and I'm told you're the man who can help me."

Ortiz was nodding and searching Cruz's eyes, as if he were trying to read something written on the bottom of the ocean.

"Certainly, Inspector," he said. "Anything I can do to help the police."

He waved to Confucius, asked him to bring Cruz another Dos Equis and himself a daiquiri and invited Cruz to sit. He also motioned to the Pit Bull, who closed the door but stayed posted there to take a bite out of any unwanted visitors.

"We don't want anyone interrupting our business," Ortiz

said. "I know what you want to discuss with me is a very serious matter." Cruz said it was and moved his chair so that he was not giving his back to Confucius, the ice-pick artist.

"How do you like my Cantina, Inspector?" Ortiz asked. "Very authentic, no?"

Cruz said he supposed it was, although he had never had the pleasure of visiting Ortiz's country.

"My people, they come here and they tell me, 'Colonel, this is just like back home.' They like that. The decorations, the posters, the music. It makes them feel like they are back in their villages. All I do is open the doors and they fill the place like the tide coming in to the beach."

"I'm sure it's very authentic, Colonel," Cruz said, "but then again the whole Mission District is getting to be like one of their villages, isn't it? It's not everywhere that people are found dead with their thumbs tied behind their backs."

From the doorway, Cruz thought he heard the Pit Bull growl. The smile disappeared from Ortiz's face. In his raspy voice was sadness now.

"It's a terrible thing when such a young, beautiful girl is killed," he said. "There is war in my country, and when I was there I learned to live with death every day of the week. But when the victim belongs to a family you know, to Victor Soto, it pains you very much, Inspector."

On the jukebox, Rubén Blades was singing

> *Tiburon, que busques en la orilla?*
> *La tuyo es mar afuera.*

"I'm sure it must," Cruz commiserated. "That's one reason I wanted to consult with you on this case, Colonel, because you knew the dead girl. I'm also told you were one of the top men in the police in your country and that you're an expert on these kinds of killings, these executions."

The Pit Bull whined again. Behind the bar Confucius stopped

chopping ice and stood with the ice pick vaguely pointing toward Cruz. Ortiz had no reaction, in fact Cruz couldn't even detect his breathing.

"I'm hoping, with your experience, you can help me find Gloria Soto's killer," Cruz said finally.

Ortiz nodded, not taking his eyes off Cruz.

"I will do anything I can to help you," he said.

The drinks arrived then, and Ortiz raised his glass.

"It's a shame that the fish got away from the police last night," he said, "but I hope it is you, yourself, Inspector, who puts a bullet in the heart of that guerrilla killer."

He drank, his opaque gray eyes peering over the salty edge of his daiquiri glass. Cruz sipped his beer.

"So you would say for sure it was Eric Hernandez who killed her?" Cruz asked.

Ortiz licked the salt off his lips thoughtfully.

"Her uncle told me there was no question who killed the girl," he said. "This Hernandez wanted her and when she decided there were other fish in the sea, he killed her."

"He says that's how she died," Cruz said, "but there are people who say it might have been someone else who murdered her."

"Is that so?" Ortiz asked, although no interest flickered in his eyes. "Who do they suspect?"

"Some people say it might have been this new boyfriend of hers, Julio Saenz, who killed her."

The other man squinted.

"But, if I remember correctly, Inspector, Victor Soto told me Saenz was in Los Angeles when the girl was shot."

"He says he was," Cruz said, "but who knows? I don't believe it. We're checking out his whereabouts Friday night and early Saturday."

"I see," Ortiz said. "That changes things." He dabbed at his mouth with a napkin. On the ring finger of the right hand a large diamond twinkled.

"I'll tell you the truth, Inspector. When I first heard that poor girl was dead, I, too, suspected Saenz might be the killer. He was a rough character. A real barracuda. Victor should never have let his niece go around with such a person and I told him that. But, as a former police official, I still don't see what motive Saenz would have to kill the girl."

"The way I hear it, Saenz was in a certain illegal business," Cruz said. He watched Ortiz's eyes but there was not even a blink. "The girl knew and was threatening to tell the police. Maybe Eric Hernandez encouraged her to do it, to get rid of Saenz, or maybe it was just Gloria's idea because Saenz molested her when he brought her up here from the border."

"By 'illegal business,' you mean the smuggling of aliens," Ortiz said.

It was Cruz's turn to raise his eyebrows at Ortiz.

"Everyone knows that Julio Saenz has been bringing illegal aliens into the Mission the past two years," Ortiz said. "Besides, Inspector, I am a former policeman. I still know things that others don't."

Ortiz smiled in his fashion. With the set of teeth he had, nothing was more menacing than his smile.

Cruz lifted his glass to the Colonel and the two men drank. From the back room a waiter appeared and placed between them a plate filled with ceviche, raw fish salad.

"This is one of our specialties," Ortiz said. "The fish is very fresh and very tender. Just hours ago it was swimming in the sea."

Cruz passed, but watched as Ortiz jabbed a piece of the fish with a toothpick, popped it into his mouth and apparently swallowed it without chewing.

"You were talking about Julio Saenz and his criminal activities, Inspector."

"This smuggling racket is big business," Cruz said. "Saenz stood to lose a lot if he got busted. And his boss, or bosses, stood to lose even more if Gloria Soto decided to cause trouble. He had vital interests at stake, maybe enough to drive him to kill."

In his own voice, Cruz could hear shades of Bill Clarke. Ortiz considered the information carefully like a piece of bait bobbing on a hook before his eyes. He circled it once before answering.

"Then you don't think he was in the smuggling on his own?"

Cruz shook his head.

"Saenz is a mule in more ways than one. Behind him there's a mule driver. Someone smarter, someone with the whip."

Ortiz speared another chunk of fish, popped it and swallowed it.

"But if Saenz can prove he was in Los Angeles?"

"Then maybe the mule driver had someone else do it," Cruz said, "or maybe he even did it himself."

"I see," Ortiz said. Unlike Soto, the Colonel wasn't at all nervous. He didn't blink an eye or sweat a drop. The third degree, trying to make someone squirm, that was his element.

He put down his toothpick and dabbed with the napkin at his mouth.

"As a former policeman, I would have to say I still consider Hernandez to be guilty," he said. "He is on the run and that would make one think he really is the killer, especially when he starts taking shots at policemen."

"Possibly," Cruz said. "But it may also be true that Hernandez is running from someone else, not from the police. That someone threatened his life to make him run at the same time they were taking Gloria Soto and killing her."

Ortiz again flashed his killer smile.

"Your theory is very ingenious, Inspector," he said. "You certainly have the mind of a detective."

"And there's one thing in particular that makes me think it can't be Hernandez," Cruz said.

"And that is?"

"The thumbs," Cruz said. "We found her dumped in that

lot with her thumbs tied behind her back and one bullet in
her head. I understand in your country, that modus operandi
has a very specific association with certain killers, Colonel.
People tell me that it's not the guerrillas who use that signature, but assassins on the other side. The death squads."

The Pit Bull stirred again. Ortiz speared another piece of
fish and twirled the toothpick in his fingers.

"And you believe Gloria Soto was killed by one of these
squads of killers? You think that even up here that kind of
crime could occur?"

"I don't know," Cruz said. "That's why I wanted to talk to
you, Colonel. I figured you would know."

"I see," Ortiz said.

He took out a silver cigarette case and proffered it to Cruz,
who shook it off. He removed a cigarette, tapped it against
the dial of his silver Rolex watch, lit it and exhaled luxuriously.

Then he sat quietly several moments, his eyes on Cruz,
but showing no emotion, no sign of warm-blooded life. When
he did talk, his voice was cold, detached.

"In my country, there are always many stories, many rumors, about killing, Inspector. There are also many accusa-
tions made behind the backs of reputable people." In his voice
now was a hint of menace. "The common people, the simple
people, they scare themselves with these stories. Just like the
people of the old legends, my people create monsters who
supposedly prey on them. I believe it's the Indian blood. In
the sixteenth century, when the Spaniards came on horses,
the rumor spread that strange creatures with the top of a man
and the four-legged body of an animal had come to kill the
Indians. Such rumors still spread down there, or up here,
wherever my people are."

"Maybe it's because some people wake up dead with their
thumbs tied behind their backs," Cruz said, meeting Ortiz's
gaze. "It wasn't a myth that shot Gloria Soto."

"That's true, Inspector, but everyone knows these stories,

and anyone could tie the girl's thumbs behind her back. Especially if he wanted to take suspicion from himself and put it on someone else, some enemy."

"Who would he want to implicate, Colonel?" Cruz asked. "Who in this city right now has those death-squad connections? Who might have tied some thumbs in the past?"

Cruz could feel eyes on him, those of Confucius behind the bar, and leaning near the door, the Pit Bull with the bulge beneath his coat. They were like contestants at a lottery waiting for their names to be picked out of a hat.

"There have, of course, been some killings in my country of the kind you have described, Inspector," Ortiz said. "But the murderers have never been identified."

Cruz frowned.

"You were never able to apprehend the killers or those who paid them to kill, Colonel?" Cruz asked. "Not even one? That doesn't sound too efficient, especially when there have been thousands of people killed. In San Francisco, you would have lost your job."

Ortiz didn't bother to smile this time. His eyes narrowed and he spoke deliberately.

"They are very efficient killers, Inspector," he said. "Quick, neat, silent and very well-connected. Their victims include all kinds of people, even policemen. A victim never knows when they are about to get him and they leave no traces."

Cruz looked around at Confucius, the Pit Bull and back at Ortiz.

"They sound like very talented people," he said. "It's not everybody who can tie up women and old people and children, thousands of them over the years, shoot them and not get sick about it eventually."

Ortiz's eyes reflected no light.

"War does things to people, Inspector," he said in his gravelly voice. "It makes them capable of terrible actions."

"So I see by the looks of Gloria Soto," Cruz said. He sipped his beer. "Gloria was here Friday night just hours before her death."

"I know," Ortiz said. "I saw her sitting at the bar. I said hello to her. I told the bartender not to let her drink too much."

"Did she say anything to you that would make you think she was afraid of someone, afraid for her life?"

Ortiz shook his head.

"Nothing. She was always a nervous girl, but I don't believe she was expecting to die. I have known people who were, Inspector, and you can smell it on them."

"Is that right?"

"Yes, it is," Ortiz said. "But given some of the people Gloria Soto knew, it was only a matter of time."

"Which 'people'?" Cruz asked.

"Eric Hernandez, Dennis Miranda," Ortiz said. "Those people have always lived underground. They get nervous very easily. Gloria maybe knew some secrets she shouldn't have known and they were afraid she would tell the wrong people. I understand she was not discreet."

"What sort of secrets could she have known that cost her life?" Cruz asked.

"Maybe she knew how many people a certain faction had," Ortiz mused. "And how many of them were armed and what kinds of weapons they owned. At a certain moment, that information might be very valuable. By knowing it, the girl was in over her head. Maybe that caused her death."

He drained the last of his daiquiri as if he were drinking to her memory as she sank beneath the surface.

"When was the last time you saw Miss Soto?" Cruz asked.

"Sitting at the bar," Ortiz said. "I left early and she was still there. Very alive, very pretty."

"And very scared," Cruz said.

Despite the overhead fan, Cruz's face ran sweat and he

mopped it now. Ortiz, on the other hand, was dry as the desert. It was as if Ortiz had been doing the grilling and Cruz was the grilled fish.

He took out a card and laid it on the table.

"If you can help me in any other way, give me a call, Colonel," he said.

"Certainly, Inspector."

Cruz walked to the door, stopped there, reached into the yellow sport jacket of the Pit Bull and pulled out a .32-caliber pistol.

"Jesus, I hit the jackpot," he said. "Do you have a license for this, amigo, or any other ID?"

The man glared into Cruz's eyes, bared his teeth as if he would go for his neck and took out his wallet. A driver's license showed the same pitted, ugly face and said it belonged to Carlos Ramos of Twenty-second Street.

Cruz held the gun up.

"When you get a license, I'll give it back to you," he said, and tucked it in his pocket. "That is, if you didn't shoot somebody with it."

Ortiz was smiling at him, showing all his teeth. Cruz thanked him for the beers and then went out.

He walked down the street to his car, thinking of his back and how a bullet would feel there, but not giving anyone the pleasure of seeing him turn around. He got into the car and sat there in thought. Somewhere in that conversation he had heard something that didn't click. It was a piece of information the Colonel had left in his wake, which now floated out of reach. Cruz reached for it, but the wave of effort pushed it away. He stopped trying; maybe it would drift back to him in time. Meanwhile, he wanted to have another talk with the mule, the vulture, the barracuda—Julio Saenz.

CHAPTER 15

Cruz was putting on the somber black pin-striped suit he always wore to wakes. He was also sipping a rum and Coke. He always had a couple of drinks before he walked into a funeral home. Stiffs he could deal with; what made him uncomfortable was grief. He was working on his second drink, his own brand of embalming fluid, putting a knot in his dark funeral tie and looking around him at the blank spaces where her paintings had been. Then the phone rang.

"David." Her voice stopped him cold, as if she had called knowing he was thinking of her. She had caught him.

"Uh-huh."

"Are you all right? I read your name in the newspaper, about that patrolman who was shot."

"I'm fine," Cruz said. He sipped his drink.

"It sounded like a close call."

Cruz shrugged as if she could see him.

"Close enough. Like you always said, 'Cheap thrills.'"

She had stopped calling him two weeks before. Now he knew that seeing his name in the newspaper was just an excuse to talk to him again. He bobbed and sipped his drink. "So what's new?"

"I wanted to make sure you were all right," she said. "What are you doing?"

"I'm on my way to a wake."

There was silence on the other end and then she sounded very concerned.

"That patrolman didn't die, did he?"

"No. He'll live," Cruz said. He sipped and stared at the blank walls. "Did you read in the paper it was one of your guerrilla heroes who shot him?" he asked.

Again there was silence.

"Don't be unfair, David," she said finally. "The people I support aren't murderers."

"Okay, I won't be unfair," he said blandly. "You ever run across this guy in one of your meetings?"

"No, I've thought hard ever since I saw the paper, but the name rings no bell. No one I know would do something like this, David."

He sipped and bobbed. He knew she was right. All her revolutionaries were tame, domesticated, safe-for-Anglo-consumption. For her and her friends, a real guerrilla would be too scary. In the background, he heard Mercedes Sosa on the stereo playing the guitar and singing. She said when the singer stops singing, the rose dies because what good is the rose without the song.

"They say this guy also killed a woman," she said.

Cruz pursed his lips.

"That's what they say."

"I read in the paper he was in love with her," she said. "Her own family said that."

"Uh-huh." Cruz nodded into the phone.

"You said once people didn't kill for love."

Cruz nodded again. "Well, sometimes they do, ya know? Not often, but every once in a while."

"Do you think he killed that woman?"

"That's whose wake I'm going to," he said.

"But do you think he killed her?"

"Maybe," Cruz said. "I don't know. But that doesn't matter

anymore, now that he shot the cop. Every guy in uniform is looking for him. Every cop on the beat wants to make sergeant by bagging this guerrilla."

He reached for the bottle, poured another drink, topped it with Coke.

"Is it your case, David?"

"So far."

There was a brief silence.

"Don't take chances, David."

In her voice, he heard a pointed effort to let him know she cared. It was that tone of voice that had made him duck away from her. Jump away from the point of the knife. Day after day it had insisted: Let me worry about you, let me keep hold of you. But now it had been weeks since he had heard it and it no longer made him squirm or pull away. She had said to him that last night: "If the world is so vicious, you don't want to be in it alone." He waited for her to say that again, to say she still loved him. For the first time, he didn't know what he would say to her in return.

"My mother says hello," he told her. "She wants to see you."

I want to see you, he thought, but he didn't say it.

There was a long pause.

"Tell her I can't this week," she said finally. "I'm trying to finish a project."

"Okay," he said quickly.

"I'm locked up day and night," she said. "You know how I can be. I don't even answer the door. But tell her I'll call her when I'm finished."

"Uh-huh."

In the background Mercedes Sosa was singing about how if the singer stops singing, the song of life dies.

"Take care of yourself, David," she said.

"Yeah, you too."

They hung up. Cruz finished getting dressed, had another drink and headed for the wake, shutting the door on the blank walls.

The tall, broad-shouldered white man standing at the door of the funeral home wore a thick beard, longish hair and a black suit. Cruz didn't know his name, but he recognized him. The man had once worked as the bouncer in a honky-tonk on Valencia Street before he started working with the dear departed. The new job had at least one advantage, Cruz figured. The clientele would usually be quieter and better-behaved.

"*Baynos notches,*" he said to Cruz.

"*Baynos notches,*" Cruz repeated with the same tortured accent. "Can you tell me where I find the Soto family?"

"*La Senoreeta Soto aysta . . .*" said the doorman, reciting from a memorized statement. Then he stopped and frowned at Cruz, his smile turning upside down. "You speak English."

"*Si, señor,*" Cruz said. "Where do I find them?"

The big man looked at him sternly. Given the competition among funeral homes in the Mission for the expanding Central American market, doormen these days had to put up with the wiseasses. The man smiled falsely and resisted any instinct he had to kick Cruz out on his ass.

"The Red Chapel, all the way to the back," he said.

"*Gracias,*" Cruz said.

He walked in and passed under a large archway painted with angels who floated in the air and played long trumpets. Although the ownership was trying for the Latin market, the cherubs were still all white people. Cruz decided that on the way out, he'd mention it to Saint Peter at the door. Among the clientele mingling in the main hallway, however, there was greater racial balance; in fact there were blacks visiting a loved one in the Blue Chapel; a white family that looked

Irish in the White Chapel, naturally, and then the Sotos and their largely brown-skinned acquaintances at the rear. With the mixture of people coming and going in the hallway and the angels floating on the walls, the place looked like a kind of United Nations reception or union hall in the next world.

Cruz threaded his way through them. That was another thing Alice had told him, that he was too callous about death, too hardened. Cruz argued that he wasn't callous, but that if he had cried for every dead person he'd seen in the last fourteen years, they could have floated Noah and his Ark and all the dead Italians in New York harbor to boot.

Cruz knew what had made him that way was working as a cop. It was always having to intrude on people's grief, ask them questions about crummy things someone had done, when they were trying to think about God and eternity, the flight of the soul and lost loved ones. This time he had to butt in on the Soto family, to put the squeeze on Julio Saenz, ask him about smuggling, rape and murder, while everyone else was crying over the death of the youngest of the Soto children. That's why he had a couple before going to wakes and why he made half-ass jokes about death.

Cruz wasn't drunk, but he hadn't eaten all day and now the three drinks he'd knocked back had left him feeling a bit lightheaded. But as he approached the Red Chapel, the smell of hot food reached his nostrils and led him by the nose to a doorway across the hall. On the other side of the argument was this: If you had to have a wake, better do it the way the Latins did, giving the loved one a chance to fill his stomach and drink before he headed for the other side. In the room across the hall he found a table covered with tortillas and various meats, a large bowl of creamy refried beans, fried bananas, a tub of guacamole, *papusas* with unknown fillings and more Central American delicacies. On another table stood open bottles, and, sitting in folding chairs, people talked quietly and respectfully and knocked back rum. Cruz popped a banana chip into his mouth, poured himself a finger of rum, topped it with Coke and smiled at the other guests.

Standing by the food table, dipping a corn chip into the guacamole, he overheard an old Latin woman explaining to a little boy about paradise.

"In heaven everyone speaks the same language," Cruz heard her say. "It's a language that on earth sounds like nothing, a bunch of stupidities, but everyone in heaven understands it."

Cruz shoveled the guacamole into his mouth. He could remember going to the funeral of his grandmother when he was five years old and being told by his crazy aunt Aurora, the one who was visited by the Virgin, all about the other world. He learned that in paradise people didn't eat.

"They just eat air and their blood is clear like water. It isn't red and people never bleed. God is in charge and he doesn't allow pain either. No pain and no fear. The saints are there, and the Virgin, and they protect you from all those miseries. You work for the saints and they treat you well. They don't cheat you ever or steal from you. You don't even have to count your money because it is always right. It's also very hygienic and there is no sickness. Even having children in heaven is pain-free." Paradise was a fine place, his aunt had assured him, and people cried for the dead only because the living are very stupid.

Cruz finished his rum. Then he stepped across the hall, through the plush red curtains, and saw Gloria Soto lying in her coffin dressed like an angel. Cruz hadn't seen the girl since the day she had been found with her terrified eyes staring at the sky, searching for God. Now her hands were folded over her white lace angel's gown and her eyes were closed behind a white veil. She was the one missing from the paintings outside, the mahogany angel.

Behind the coffin stood a statue of the Virgin. All around

the body were wreaths and vases of flowers that gave off powerful perfumes. The mourners were mostly women, draped in black mantillas, beads swinging from their hands, who recited the sing-song cadences of the Spanish rosary:

> *Padre nuestro*
> *Que está en los cielos*
> *Sanctificado*
> *Sea su nombre*

Standing next to the coffin, still in uniform and wearing dark glasses, was Robert Soto. He was the honor guard, Cruz supposed. In a chair right next to the coffin, a middle-aged woman draped in a mantilla was weeping. Cruz hadn't seen her before, but it had to be Gloria Soto's mother, grieving for her angel. Right next to her sat the old man, Gloria's grandfather, wearing a dark suit, a white shirt buttoned to the throat, but no tie. His expression was the same it had been two days before, his mouth open in a roar of mindless rage in the face of death.

Victor Soto sat in the next chair, and whispering into his ear was Colonel Joe Ortiz. Right behind the Colonel stood the Pit Bull, his guardian angel. He still wore his bright-yellow blazer, but there was no bulge under the arm, which made Cruz wonder where he was hiding his gun. Around the room, Cruz recognized several other men he had seen at the Cantina. All of them were doing their best to look sad and devout.

Robert Soto swiveled on one heel and came toward him in parade march. He stopped and saluted.

"Good evening, Inspector. Thank you for coming."

Across the room, his father and the Colonel stopped talking, looked at Cruz warily and then went back into their huddle.

"Is Julio Saenz here?" Cruz asked.

"No, he isn't, Inspector," Robert Soto said.

"Do you know where he is?"

"Not exactly. That's something I should tell you," he said. He got a conspiratorial look on his face. "Julio is out looking for Hernandez. We think he went gunning for him."

Cruz made a face.

"What do you mean you 'think'? Is he carrying a gun?"

"He has a nine-millimeter Browning. He showed it to me last night and he said he wanted himself to kill the guerrilla. He said he couldn't stand to see Gloria's body without taking revenge. I told him not to take the law into his own hands, but he wouldn't listen to me. I'm afraid now that something will happen to him."

Cruz stared into Robert Soto's black glasses as if he were watching a film projected there. He saw Julio Saenz, big as a house, shooting down Eric Hernandez. He also saw a court giving Saenz a light sentence because he was avenging the death of his girlfriend. There was always a degree of sympathy for that brand of killer. Once Eric Hernandez was dead, it wouldn't matter whether he was guilty. No one would question that he had killed Gloria Soto. He would take the fall without a murmur. If Hernandez killed Saenz, they would have that one against him and tack on Gloria just for good measure. Saenz was stupid enough to lend himself to a game like that and it might just work, if he could find Hernandez.

"When did you see Saenz last?" he asked.

"Last night at the Cantina," he said. "I thought it was talk, but now he isn't here."

Then Robert Soto's head turned away toward the hallway and Cruz saw him frown. The person who was "here" was Elaine Miranda. She was standing in the doorway wearing a black dress, a long mantilla over her blond hair, and her green eyes were wary. She walked by Cruz with a furtive glance, went to Gloria Soto's mother, offered brief condolences, knelt before the coffin just enough time for a couple of fast Hail Mary's and then got up.

Cruz caught up to her in the hallway.

"Can we talk a second, Mrs. Miranda?"

Before she could answer one way or another, Cruz had taken her by the elbow and guided her into the room across the hall.

"Have some food," he said.

He popped a fried banana chip into his mouth and spread refried beans onto a corn tortilla and bit into it.

Elaine Miranda was watching him with her nervous green eyes.

"What do you want with me?" she asked.

Cruz chewed and swallowed.

"I want to know where Eric Hernandez is," he said.

"I don't know where he is," she said.

Cruz popped another chip.

"Since it was you who tipped off the police last night about him, I thought you might know where I can find him tonight to help save his life."

As soon as he shot the arrow, he knew it had hit home. Her mouth opened and she started to shake her head.

"Don't bother to deny it," Cruz said. "It wasn't his sister who called in and I doubt it was Stacy Stoner. So it had to be you. You have no reason to stick your neck out for Eric Hernandez. You hardly know him and he's already putting your husband's life here in jeopardy. The question is where he is now, because Julio Saenz is out gunning for him, not to mention every cop in town."

She was still shaking her head like a wind-up doll.

"Don't worry, I won't tell your husband," Cruz said. "Just tell me what you know and maybe we'll be able to save your family situation."

Already pale, she turned a bit whiter then. She watched him a good twenty seconds before speaking, as if she were hoping he would choke to death on a corn chip before she had to answer.

"I swear I don't know where he is," she said in a trembling whisper, "and neither does Dennis. The only reason we knew the first time was that Eric came to us and begged us to help him."

"When was that?"

"Saturday morning, just after dawn."

"And he told you he had killed Gloria Soto."

She was shaking her head again.

"No, he told us he knew she was dead, but it wasn't him who killed her. He said it was Saenz and some other guys who murdered her. He was crying his eyes out. It was terrible."

"How did he know that?"

"Because he had been following Gloria and she had gone with Saenz and the others to this house. He was outside and he heard a shot. A few minutes later they carried her out dead. He watched them."

"He was sure it was Saenz?"

"Yes."

"But Saenz was supposedly in Los Angeles."

"Eric saw him carrying the body and putting it in the trunk of the car," she said.

"Where was this house?"

She shook her head again.

"Eric wasn't sure. He doesn't know one street from another around here. But he said it was on a hill and not far from the Cantina. Maybe it was Bernal Heights. He didn't know."

"So the story you and your husband told me Saturday about Gloria being afraid Saenz would kill her, that was all made up to go along with what Eric told you?"

"No," she said. "It was true. She was afraid someone was going to do something to her and she wouldn't say who it was. Then when Eric told us what had happened we knew it was Saenz."

"And why didn't you tell me all this Saturday if you knew Eric was innocent, if you knew who had really killed Gloria?"

"Because Dennis didn't think you would believe it," she said. "If we told you we knew where Eric was, you would want to talk to him and then you would blame it on him because of the troubles he was having with Gloria. So Dennis decided to put you on to Saenz without telling you about Eric seeing the killing."

"Or maybe Dennis didn't tell me Eric's story because *he* didn't believe it," Cruz said. "He knew it wouldn't hold up. Or maybe you just made it up. So he stashed Eric at Tony's Grocery and tried to get his old friend out of a jam. But then you called the cops to turn Eric in, because you didn't believe one word of that story either. You thought he really had killed Gloria."

She was shaking her head and staring at his words as if she were looking into a mirror.

"Or maybe Dennis knew it wasn't true," Cruz said. "Maybe he wanted Gloria dead because she knew things she shouldn't know, and when Eric killed her it was just as well. Or maybe he got him to do it."

Her face crumbled.

"That's not true," she said. "Dennis didn't want Gloria dead. She was a friend." Her voice started to crack. "I don't know who killed Gloria. Maybe it was Eric, maybe it wasn't. All I know is Dennis is the kind who would risk himself for his friends. Maybe even risk his life. And then what happens with me and the baby . . ."

Cruz popped another banana chip.

"I understand," he said. "And you're sure you haven't heard from Eric since Sunday night?"

"Not a word. I swear," she said. "He's probably out there hiding in some sewer."

"And your husband, where is he?"

"He was at work, but he said he was coming here."

Cruz's eyebrows arched.

"No kidding," he said. "That should be interesting."

Elaine Miranda looked at him as if there were something wrong with him. Then she went back into the hallway, where she lit a cigarette and began to pace.

Cruz took the opportunity to make himself a taco, spreading refried beans on a tortilla, topping it with diced steak, some cheese, a dollop of guacamole and a dash of hot sauce.

Next to him the old woman was still talking to the young boy, just as Aunt Aurora had instructed Cruz in the mysteries of the other world.

"No, not everybody goes to paradise," she had told him. "Many go down to hell. There you always live in a nightmare. It is always dark and there is no one with you from your family. The food is all poisoned and makes you sick and the water is boiling and burns your mouth. The dogs are poisonous like snakes. Day and night, bombs are falling, you hear the sound of them coming and you never sleep." His aunt Aurora knew her heavens and her hells.

Cruz hadn't finished the taco when he saw Dennis Miranda walk into the funeral home. Cruz wiped his mouth and went into the hallway to see the reception they gave him.

Miranda greeted his wife and then stepped into the doorway of the chapel. The rosary stopped and a hiss escaped the people there as if someone had punctured the sanctity of the occasion. The Pit Bull stirred and Robert Soto showed his teeth. The Colonel and Victor Soto stared at him. The other watchdogs around the room forgot about being devout and went back to being thugs.

Miranda, on the other hand, did not alter his look of grief and solemnity. He walked right up to the casket, with his pronounced limp, knelt right under the nose of Robert Soto, blessed himself and proceeded to pray. He stayed there a full minute, offering his back to anyone who wanted to get a good look at it. He blessed himself again, got up and went to Gloria Soto's mother who, dazed with grief, accepted his condolences. Victor Soto showed his yellow teeth but didn't move. Miranda turned away from them and, as pious as any boy receiving his First Communion, walked back out of the chapel.

Cruz was waiting for him.

"Very cool," he said.

"She was ours, too," he said soberly, "and we wanted to be with her."

"Saenz has a gun and is out hunting for Eric," Cruz said to him. "You should know that, because he might be hunting for you, too,"

True to form, Miranda didn't show concern.

"Thanks for the information," he said calmly.

"It would be safer for Eric if you tell me where he is," Cruz said.

"I don't know where he is," Miranda said. "And I don't think Julio Saenz represents a threat to Eric. Saenz is no guerrilla. He's too fat."

Cruz saw the Colonel approaching then. If Miranda was characteristically cool, the Colonel seemed to have lost his. He was jabbing a finger at Miranda.

"This is the one you should have in jail," he told Cruz. "He is helping hide Hernandez and he is a killer himself. If you are looking for killers, this is the one you should arrest."

Miranda smiled coyly.

"That is a kind of compliment coming from Colonel Ortiz," he said. "Very few people know more about killing than a colonel from the National Police."

Ortiz, a head taller than Miranda, leaned over as if he would bite his head off, pinching Cruz between them.

"You are the one who has been spreading lies about me," he said. "You should be careful how you talk about a real man who has fought for his country. Not hiding behind trees and ambushing and running away like you, but like a man."

"Yes, you fought like a man, Colonel," Miranda said, "but you only shot women."

All the men had crowded out from the chapel and they were jostling now. Even some of the Irish and the blacks had joined the mob. There was trouble in paradise. For a moment Cruz thought Ortiz would go for Miranda, but Victor Soto grabbed him by the arm.

"Not here, Colonel. Please."

He glared at Miranda, who smiled.

"And then there is Victor Soto," Miranda said to Cruz. "He comes from a family that stole everything they own. They were land-robbers. Everyone in our part of the country knew the Sotos were a family of thieves. So he came here so he could make believe he was a respectable individual, just like the Colonel here."

In the crowd, the Pit Bull barked and the others were growling. Cruz felt surrounded. Above him the angels were looking down without a care.

The Colonel jabbed his finger again at Miranda.

"You and your friend Eric Hernandez killed Gloria Soto," he said. "We know you want to kill more of us and I'm warning you, if the police don't protect us, we will protect ourselves. You will come after us and we will be waiting for you."

He turned on his heel and stalked away, the others following in his wake. Miranda watched them, the wheels turning behind his eyes. Then he headed for the door.

Cruz waited at the door until Miranda and his wife climbed into their car and got away safely. He understood now why the funeral home had a bouncer at the door. He said goodnight to Saint Peter and then he went to try to find Julio Saenz.

CHAPTER 16

It was after midnight that it hit the fan.

Cruz, lying in bed, listened to the news about Police Officer Joseph Klein, who was still in critical condition, and how the cops were combing all of Northern California looking for Eric Hernandez. According to one report, he had been sighted near Sacramento, and local authorities there were searching the area, trying to pick up his trail. Cruz sipped his rum and thought of Stacy Stoner. He saw her behind the wheel of her car driving somewhere with a very disturbed Eric Hernandez. What would happen if they were stopped? Was he armed? Would he try to get away? What would happen to her? Stacy had finally gone too far. They would bust her this time.

Cruz sipped his rum and listened to the ball scores.

That's when it came. In the distance he heard a sputtering that might have been firecrackers. There was silence and another burst, and then the explosion that sounded like the night cracking open.

Cruz jumped out of bed as more sputtering sounded, which he knew now was weapons fire. In a minute he had dressed and was out the door. The explosion had come from the south, and six blocks away, right around the Cantina, black smoke hung in the air. There was more firing in the distance, but it seemed to come from all sides. Neighbors hung out of windows, their faces gripped in fear. The neighborhood around him was a place suddenly changed, suddenly wired and dangerous.

Cruz jumped into his car and pulled out. On the radio, Celia Cruz was telling her lover to kiss her very much. *"Besame mucho,"* she said.

About halfway down the block, another car pulled out behind him. It was a Cherokee square-back and it didn't have lights on. Cruz turned the corner on squealing tires and the van did the same. Cruz frowned into the rearview mirror. He floored it, heading south on Bartlett for the Cantina, but the Cherokee was more powerful and it loomed behind him and bumped him. Cruz's car swerved out of control, sideswiped a parked car with a shriek of metal and bounced off. He glared into the rearview mirror, but saw only the black-tinted windshield.

"What the hell are you doing?" he yelled.

From behind, the Cherokee came at him again. The bumper came up close to Cruz's trunk and smashed it. The car swerved and Cruz fought to straighten it out, like trying to control a scared horse.

He jammed on the brakes, jumped out the door and groped at his belt for his gun, but it wasn't there. The Cherokee was coming again. Cruz cursed at the black windshield and jumped back into the car just as he got rammed again. He stepped on the gas and turned hard onto Twenty-fifth.

At Mission he ran the light and barreled east away from the Cantina, but the Cherokee ran it also and was right on him. The streets were empty. All around he heard distant shooting. Sirens were sounding, but there was no cop in sight. There wasn't a person to be seen, as if something had happened to everyone.

At Harrison a car crossed the street, forcing him to slow,

and they caught him, coming up on the left, cutting him off and pinning his fender against parked cars. There was no one on the block. The window was tinted and he couldn't see in. Then it was rolled down, and a rifle came out the window and stared right through the windshield at him. Cruz stared back at it. Celia Cruz was telling him to kiss her. In the distance there was more fire.

The rifle stayed leveled at him, as if they were trying to scare him to death. Out of the dark interior, a voice sounded.

"This is a warning," it said.

That was all. The rifle was pulled backward into the Cherokee. The window went up and it sped away. No license plates, no lights, no nothing.

Cruz watched it disappear north on Potrero, staring after it even when he could no longer see it. In the distance, there was another burst of fire. Then he put it into drive and headed toward the Cantina. He heard shots on all sides now and he worried about being caught in the fire. In the dark sky a spray of tracer bullets appeared, burning phosphorescent red as they climbed and then disappeared into the night. What was happening made no sense. It was crazy, absolutely crazy.

Cruz turned onto Twenty-eighth Street. A woman with a baby wrapped up and clutched to her chest came running down the block, her mouth open in a scream. The street was full of patrol cars and two fire engines. Smoke was pouring from the Cantina, drifting in the headlights and swirling in the red rooflights of the cars. Cruz got out of his car. He saw windows blown out in other houses, the empty holes like blackened eyes. The whole front of the Cantina was gone. He heard children crying and dogs barking. More people were moving down the street away from the smoke. More weapons fire sounded far away.

He found Donnelly near a fire truck.

"What the hell's going on?" Cruz asked him.

"Somebody bombed it," Donnelly said, "and we have reports of shooting in about a half dozen other places. It looks
like they're finally going after each other."

He tapped Cruz on the chest.

"Your boy Hernandez was in on this one," he said. "The
night watchman said it was a guy in camouflage pants who
jumped out of a car, fired at the place and then threw the
bomb in. Watchman's on his way to the hospital now with a
wound in the leg."

Donnelly shook his head.

"These fuckin' people are crazy."

"Where else do you have shooting?" Cruz asked.

"Everywhere. Over near Castro, and on Dolores too. On
Twenty-fourth Street, there was a goddamn firefight."

Cruz ran to his car and headed for Twenty-fourth Street
and Dennis Miranda's house. He pulled onto the block a
minute later and saw what he had expected: Outside the apartment house were patrol cars and an ambulance. He looked
up and saw that the windows in the Miranda apartment had
been shot out. Again there were kids screaming.

Cruz ran through the lobby and took three stairs at a time.
The door of Apartment 2-B was standing open and was splintered with bullet holes. In the far wall were more bullet holes,
the gold-framed photographs were shot to hell and the floor
was covered with shattered plaster.

Cruz found Elaine Miranda in the living room holding her
screaming daughter to her chest, her own face marred by red
welts from crying. Dennis Miranda's grandfather stood guard
near a window just in cast they came back. In the bedroom,
there was blood on the floor. Dennis Miranda sat on the bed,
a paramedic bandaging his bloodied left arm.

The floor was strewn with shattered glass and broken plaster.

"What happened?" he asked Miranda.

The other man looked at him, eyes full of irony.

"Some friends paid us a visit," he said.

"Did you recognize any of them?"

Miranda shook his head.

"No, the Colonel didn't arrive in person, unfortunately."

Cruz mopped his neck and looked down through the shattered window to the street where the whirling red lights painted the houses as if they were on fire. He turned back to Miranda.

"Somebody bombed the Colonel's bar tonight," he said.

Miranda lifted his bandaged arm.

"It wasn't me. I was here being shot," he said. "And it wasn't anyone I know."

"Are you sure?"

"Yes, I'm sure," Miranda said.

Elaine Miranda had walked into the room, the baby over her shoulder.

"How about Elvira?" she asked. "Have you checked with her? Is she all right?"

It was enough to look at her face to know what she was afraid of.

Miranda got up, trailing bandage, went to the phone and dialed. He waited with the phone at his ear and waited some more.

"No answer," he said.

Cruz went out the door and headed down, taking stairs four at a time. He drove recklessly through the abandoned streets and skidded to a stop in front of the old ocher house. There were no patrol cars outside, but neighbors stood on porches across the street staring at the house. The windows in the top floor had been shot out.

Cruz took the front steps, found the door locked and kicked it in. He called her name and then ran up the stairs. In the little girl's room there was more broken glass and gutted plaster. He found her in her bedroom at the back of the house, sitting on the floor of her room with the little girl cradled in her arms asleep. She pulled the girl close to her and glared at him, as if should he get too close, she might go for him. In her eyes was an animal fear. He went easy.

"Are you all right?" he asked.

She stared at him a long time, eyes narrowed suspiciously, as if he were trying to trick her.

"Yes. We're all right," she said, her voice barely audible.

"Did you see who did this?"

She shook her head no.

He helped her up. She carried the sleeping child to the bed and tucked her in. Then he followed her into the girl's room, where she stood staring at the shattered windows.

"Do you still think my brother is the one who is dangerous?" she asked. "Do you still think he's the killer?"

Cruz looked through the shattered windows into the street.

"I don't know," he said. "What's going on here is crazy."

She held a broken leaf as if she were reading it like tea leaves or the palm of a hand.

"I told you it wasn't simple," she said. "I told you that in the beginning, but you wouldn't believe me. I said they were animals and they would make more blood flow. Violence is what they use to frighten, to stun the others of us so they can prey on us. We know these creatures and we know how these stories go."

In the next room the little girl whined, a frightened cry that escaped a nightmare.

"You better go see her," Cruz said. "I had to break the door downstairs, so I better stay down there and make sure you don't have any other visitors."

They stood at either side of the window, both their bodies weighed by the fatigue that sets in after fear. The child whimpered again.

"Be careful," Elvira Hernandez said, and then she went out.

Cruz went downstairs, closed the front door he had kicked

in, propped a chair under it, and pulled a stuffed chair out of the living room so it was right in front of it. He called Mission Station. They said the gunfire had ended. Patrols were still hunting, but there had been no arrests. The shooters had gone up in smoke. Cruz hung up, killed the light and sat down to spend the night. He slouched with his eyes closed and for a long time saw on the inside of his eyelids bursts of light and scared faces.

CHAPTER 17

At seven that morning Cruz let himself into the empty Homicide office. On his desk he found two messages related to the Soto case. Irv Hicks from Immigration had returned Cruz's call. The second memo was more interesting. It was from Father Bill Clarke, telling Cruz to see him after the funeral mass. "He says he has something important for you," it read. Cruz's bloodshot eyes squinted with interest.

He dialed Mission Station, found that Donnelly was still there and got him on the phone.

"Where are you?" Donnelly asked. He sounded tired and none too friendly. "The captain says he wants to have another little chat."

"I don't think I want to do that right now," Cruz said. "What happened last night? How many people hurt?"

"As far as we know, only two. The watchman and this guy Miranda on Twenty-fourth Street."

Cruz grimaced.

"They must be real good shots, these guys," he said. "They used enough bullets to wipe out Mission Station."

"But they didn't hit anybody else, at least as far as we know," Donnelly said. "We had two reports of bullets coming through people's ceilings. That's how bad they shoot. That and the two wounded. I don't understand it either."

"Did you catch any of these guys?"

"Nobody," Donnelly said. "We'd get a call on a shooting and by the time we got there everybody was gone. No men, no guns, no cars, no nothing. And nobody could tell what they looked like or where they went."

"They went up in smoke," Cruz said.

"What's that?"

"Nothing."

"The captain's calling in this guy Miranda, and Ortiz, too, the one who owns the Cantina," Donnelly said. "He says he wants to put them both in cells and keep them there."

"Tell him I think that's a good idea," Cruz said.

"But their lawyers won't like that," Donnelly said, "so instead he's going to tell them both to lay off and turn over the people responsible for last night or the patrol is going to get very unfriendly around here for everybody on both sides."

"Good luck," Cruz said.

"Where are you?" Donnelly insisted.

"I have a couple of leads I have to follow," Cruz said. "One of them may take me to Hernandez."

"You better hope it leads you to something," Donnelly said. "We have people packing their cars and leaving the barrio. We have others asking us to lock them up here so they'll be safe. And we got an interesting phone call last night."

"What's that?"

"About two in the morning, some guy calls here and says this was only the beginning. He didn't say what side he was on or give any other idea who he was, he just sounded ominous. But he told the desk man that the war had finally spread from Central America up to here and that there was going to be a lot more shooting soon. His exact words were, 'This is now a war zone.' That's what he said."

Cruz watched the sun exploding off the windows of the buildings and felt the mounting heat.

"What do you think of that?" Donnelly asked.

Cruz pressed his eyes closed tiredly and they came open slowly.

"Keep your head down," he said, and hung up.

He pulled up outside the church a few minutes before the beginning of the funeral mass. Either someone had asked for protection or the police were expecting big trouble. Out front were three patrol cars. At the main doors was a patrolman, and as he walked in Cruz saw another posted near a side exit, both with guns on their hips.

He dipped his fingers into the tepid holy water and blessed himself. In addition to the policemen, Cruz found the Pit Bull sitting in the last pew. He fixed Cruz with a stare that tried to be tough but was dulled by fatigue and stupidity and maybe the spaced-out aftermath of violence. Cruz wondered where the Pit Bull had been the night before, if he hadn't been out for a ride in a Cherokee van. Cruz genuflected and smiled at him. Then he walked up a side aisle.

The place was hot, like an oven just heating up. The casket sat before the altar covered in white flowers. The events of the night before had apparently made people wary. There were no more than a dozen souls there to bury Gloria Soto. Around them, the church looked big, empty and desolate.

All the way up front Cruz could see the Soto family, Gloria's mother, her grandfather, Victor Soto and his son Robert, this last one sitting ramrod stiff at the entrance to the pew. Three rows behind the Sotos sat Colonel Ortiz, and on either side of him, his watchdogs.

Cruz genuflected next to that same pew, excused himself to one of the sweating, glaring bodyguards, edged his way in and sat down next to Ortiz. The Colonel glanced at him with eyes that had dark lines under them. He didn't flash his killer smile.

Cruz hitched his pants and mopped his forehead and neck.

"Sorry about the damage to your place," he whispered. "Somebody really went after you."

Ortiz turned his body all the way around and looked at Cruz as if he were crazy.

"Somebody!" he said sarcastically. He shook his head in disbelief and pointed a finger somewhere outside the church.

"Go talk to those fucking guerrillas," he said in a gravelly, barely contained whisper. "Maybe they can tell you who threw the bomb."

The Colonel's whisper was too loud, and both Victor and Robert Soto turned around. Cruz nodded his condolences to them.

"I would talk to Miranda," he whispered to the Colonel, "but he got hit himself last night. You wouldn't know who tried to kill him, would you?"

Ortiz stared at the altar and shook his head.

"I was in my house last night," he said. "I was playing cards until one-thirty in the morning, when the police called to tell me about the bombing. I have witnesses."

"I figured you would," Cruz said. "But since it was your bar that got hit, I thought you might have a clue to who tried to get even."

"I have a lot of friends," Ortiz said. "Maybe some of them got angry because of what happened."

"I guess," Cruz said.

Ortiz sat stolidly, looking at the altar, and spoke like a high priest.

"If you use violence against another," he said, "you have to expect to become a target yourself. A person like Miranda, he knows that."

Cruz bobbed in agreement.

"I'm sure that's true," he said. "But the surprising thing is how quickly Miranda's enemies retaliated against him. Just minutes after the bomb went off, they were shooting at him, as if they knew it was going to happen."

"People were expecting trouble from those guerrillas," Ortiz said. "Those people have been on alert and I'm sure they decided that an immediate response would be the best lesson for Miranda and his friends."

"A rapid-strike force," Cruz said.

Ortiz looked tired, especially of Cruz.

"This is a political problem that you don't understand," Ortiz whispered. "You have the mind of a detective and you think in terms of crimes. But what has developed here is a political standoff. It goes back a long way and it involves everyone from our country. We believe in one way of life. They believe in another. There is no simple solution. If anything, I believe there will be more violence. I'm sorry to say that, but I know how these people operate."

Cruz pursed his lips and thought that over. It was the same message given to Mission Station by the ominous caller. All of a sudden the cold-blooded murder of a young woman was a political problem. And it was going to get worse.

"How about some guys in a red Cherokee van who don't know how to drive very well?" he asked. "Do you know them?"

Ortiz frowned at Cruz and shook his head.

Bill Clarke walked to the altar then in white vestments, trailed by two altar boys in white. Everyone stood. Bill Clarke began to say the funeral mass in his lousy Spanish. The Colonel and Cruz both listened in silence. The other mourners, lulled by the heat and maybe dulled by so many deaths over the years, chanted the responses lifelessly. Bill Clarke read the gospel, told everyone to sit and began his sermon with condolences and assurances that one does not suffer alone. Then he gave his sermon, which he made short and to the point, but which only made Cruz more uneasy.

"Gloria came from a country torn by war, a country where

many have died terrible deaths," Clarke said, eyes fixed sadly on the casket. "Others involved in that war have died in the heart and soul. They have committed terrible acts of violence and no longer recognize the suffering of others. They are unable to feel their common humanity with other men."

Cruz looked at the Colonel while Clarke spoke, but there was no change in his face.

"Many of Gloria's people have come here to this country and our city and they bring that war inside them," Clarke said. "Some are on one side, some on another. That much is inevitable. But they cannot continue to live that war here. It will bring only more death, more suffering."

The priest spoke, scanning the crowd, including the police at the doors, not allowing his gaze to fall on anyone in particular.

"Last night violence erupted here in this barrio in a way that has frightened many," he said. "The killing cannot go on. Let us pray for peace both in Gloria's country and in our own barrio. And let those who are troubled by the war they carry in their souls come to the church or to anyone who can help them and put an end to that pain and violence."

He blessed himself, went back to the altar then and continued with the mass. When it had finished, Victor and Robert Soto and two of the watchdogs carried the coffin slowly up the aisle into a waiting hearse. Several cars fell in behind it and the cortege drove off with the patrol cars bringing up the rear.

Cruz was standing on the steps of the church, watching, when he found Bill Clarke at his elbow.

"I saw before the mass you were talking to Joe Ortiz," the priest said. "Anything interesting?"

"He hasn't confessed any sins to me, if that's what you mean," Cruz said. "Not yet, at least, but I'm talking to him and his friends, like I promised."

"That might be some confession," Clarke said, watching the funeral cortege disappear down the street.

"I'm told you have something for me," Cruz said.

"I think so," Clarke said. Cruz followed the priest out of the sun and into the church vestry. Clarke pulled the vestment off over his head, revealing a white shirt underneath saturated by sweat.

"I received a call last night," he said folding the vestment. "It was a woman. She asked if my church might be willing to give sanctuary to a young Salvadoran man who is in this country illegally."

Clarke mopped his face.

"Did she mention Hernandez by name?" Cruz asked.

"No, not exactly," Clarke said, "but it was Hernandez she was talking about. I'm positive. I told her I would need more information and that I would want to meet him first. I asked if they were in the city. She said they were and I offered to go see him right then. She told me to hold on and she must have been conferring with him. She came back on and said that right then it was impossible."

"So I asked her if I could talk to him over the telephone. I heard her ask him that and he said no. I started getting suspicious then, so I asked her if he was in any kind of trouble. She said to me, very defensively, that he was not a criminal and that his life was in danger and that was why he had to be extremely careful. I started to tell her that maybe I could help, but I heard him speaking in Spanish, telling her to hang up. I tried to get her to stay on. I told her it wasn't necessary to tell me where he was, that they could come to the church and we could discuss the case here. I assured them I wouldn't call the police."

"And what did she say?"

"Nothing. The line went dead."

Cruz ran a hand through his thick hair.

"This woman, what did she sound like? Was she young? Old? Did she speak with an accent?"

"She didn't sound too old or too young," Clarke said. "And she didn't have any accent."

Cruz nodded.

"Stacy Stoner," he said.

The priest frowned.

"Could be, but I don't know," he said. "I've talked to Stacy on the phone, and it didn't sound like her. But I can't be sure."

Cruz squinted at him.

"If it wasn't Stacy, who else could it have been?"

Clarke shrugged.

Cruz frowned out into the glaring sunlight. The heat came off the pavement in waves and Cruz stared at it as if he were seeing a mirage. But it didn't materialize. He didn't see Hernandez, Stacy or anyone else. But it had to be Stacy.

"That's not much of a lead," Clarke said, "but maybe he'll come."

"And if he does?" Cruz asked. "Maybe he did kill that girl, Bill, and for sure he almost killed a cop."

The priest nodded tiredly.

"If he comes I'll try to get him to give himself up," he said. "That's all I can do is try."

Cruz handed the priest a business card.

"If they call again, give them my number," he said. Then he thanked the priest and went out into the sun again, like a man crossing a desert where the sand filled in all the footprints.

CHAPTER 18

An hour later, Cruz got his first break.

He was in his office, piecing together the interviews of the past two days into a report for Lieutenant Weintraub, when the telephone rang. It was Irv Hicks from Immigration.

"I think I have something for you," he said. Cruz scowled into the phone. That was what Bill Clarke had said and it had only added more questions to the case. He agreed to meet Hicks anyway, at noon at a doughnut shop on Mission.

The shop in question was a gathering place for illegal day laborers, and anybody who needed cheap hands could find enough men for a work crew sitting there over cold coffee any day of the week. That was no secret and every once in a while the INS raided the place and rounded up doughnut lovers. When Cruz walked in, Hicks was already there, sitting very much by himself. He was a big, red-haired white man in shirtsleeves and a tie, who even a blind man could tell was some kind of policeman. The place was usually crowded at midday, but now there was no one sitting on the red plastic stools to either side of Hicks and the last of the table customers, a couple of furtive Latin boys, were paying their check and beating a retreat.

"How's the most popular man in town?" Cruz said, slipping onto a stool.

Hicks chewed a cruller and shrugged. He took everything with a grain of salt these days. Once he had roamed all of Northern California detaining illegals, raiding sweatshops and restaurants in San Francisco and across the bay in Oakland, stalking the grape orchards and tomato farms in the valleys to the north and east, the artichoke and strawberry fields to the south. He had a reputation as a good officer, efficient and humane, but it was still a thankless job. The illegals hated him and so did the employers who were trying to get away with cheap labor. Nobody liked the "migra."

Then things got even worse for Hicks. When civilians started dying in large numbers in El Salvador and Guatemala, many California citizens, both Latin and not, decided they didn't like him either. They flexed political muscle and soon police departments in California were refusing to arrest Salvadoran and Guatemalan illegals, refusing to cooperate with the "migra" who would send the illegals back to their countries and maybe get them killed. Cities officially declared themselves safe ground for the refugees and soon everybody was treating Hicks as if he were the illegal. Now instead of casting nets for all the illegals, Hicks was primarily arresting and deporting refugees who were involved in criminal activities, and he was trying to bust coyote operations—in other words, real criminals. The denizens of the doughnut shop didn't know that. They simply smelled the "migra."

The black man behind the counter brought Cruz a coffee. All his customers had left, which was probably all right with him. Unemployed illegals weren't big tippers anyhow.

Cruz asked Hicks if he had any information on Saenz or Ortiz, and the other shook his head. He finished chewing his cruller and washed it down with coffee.

"What we have is a guy arrested by Narcotics for selling cocaine," Hicks said.

Cruz frowned.

"So what does that have to do with anything?"

Hicks shrugged.

"Maybe nothing," he said, and sipped his coffee. "But the guy said he made the money to buy the cocaine by bringing illegals up from the border. He told Narcotics he had information he was willing to swap about the operation and maybe the judge would go easy on him. This isn't his first drug arrest and he figures to do time."

"And he says he knows these guys I'm looking at?"

Hicks licked his finger, picked up the glazed sugar that had fallen to his napkin and licked it off. He shook his head.

"No, he didn't say that. His name's Monty. He's not the smartest guy in the world, but I guess he's a safe driver. He says he's been bringing loads of people up here the last month or so, two or three a week. He doesn't know anybody's name and different guys pay him. He said he'll take us to the drop house where he was leaving people. It's somewhere in the Mission and you told me you were looking for a place like that. Maybe this is it."

"Maybe," Cruz said, but he didn't sound excited. Drop houses, there had to be a few in the Mission.

Hicks paid the tab and left a buck for the counterman, and they went out to Hick's car. Sitting in the backseat of the car, wearing handcuffs, was Monty. Another white man in tie and shirtsleeves, with a blond crew-cut and a bull neck, sat behind the wheel and kept him company.

Cruz slipped into the backseat next to Monty. He was about thirty-five, skinny and wasted, probably from too much cocaine, with long greasy black hair, a pitted face and skittish eyes that, like Hicks had said, didn't look too smart. He smiled and said "hello" politely to Cruz.

"I understand you're going to take us to a house you know about, Monty," Cruz said. The car pulled away from the curb, heading south on Mission.

The other man nodded nervously.

"Maybe you guys can help me catch a break," he said.

"Maybe," Cruz said, "but I'm not from Immigration, Monty. I'm from Homicide."

Cruz had found that dropping the word "homicide" right away always put conversations with wise guys on a more serious level. You got their attention and avoided a lot of bullshit. Monty certainly took it seriously. His eyes opened wide, as if Cruz had suddenly swelled up in front of him.

"I don't got nothin' to do with no homicide," he said.

"Ever hear of a guy named Julio Saenz?" Cruz asked.

Monty looked at Hicks, who was riding shotgun. He was rattled.

"I don't got nothin' to do with killin' nobody, hey."

"Maybe you don't," Cruz said, "but one of the sheep who was smuggled up from down south was killed here over the weekend. Who's Julio Saenz?"

Monty shook his head in a way that shook his whole wasted body.

"I don't know."

But he did know something, you could see it in there waiting to be knocked loose.

"Where were you from Friday at sunset till Saturday dawn, Monty? That's when the girl was shot."

Monty tried to point out the window, but his hands were cuffed and he got tangled and more rattled.

"I was on a run to LA, picking up people," he said. "I couldn't 'a been here."

"Is that so?" Cruz said. "Who do you have for witnesses? The sheep? I don't think they'll want to testify, Monty. You ever own a .38-caliber pistol?"

"Listen, I never owned no gun." He reached for Hicks's shoulder, but Hicks shrugged him off. Monty pleaded with him. "This guy's trying to frame me with killin' somebody."

"The girl was alive when they found her," Cruz lied. "All

she said was a mule killed her. We figured it had to be you."

"She wasn't talkin' about me." He shook his head so much it looked like it might come off. "I don't know no girl who's dead."

"Julio Saenz said he made a run Friday night and it couldn't have been him who killed the girl," Cruz said.

Monty's wasted face got furious and he jabbed at his bony chest.

"Bullshit! Julio was here Friday. I made the run."

It came out of him before he could stop it. He winced with pain and watched Cruz as if he were hoping it had come out in some foreign language the policeman didn't understand.

"So Julio was in town Friday," Cruz said. "He's been lying to me."

Monty was sullen, staring out the window.

"I don't know where he was, because I was in LA," he said. He thought a moment. When Monty was thinking, you could tell. "I don't know where he was because I don't know him."

Cruz shrugged.

"Well, he certainly knows you, Monty," he said. "Well enough to try to pin a murder on you."

Cruz said nothing for a while as they continued south on Mission. He watched this last comment work its way through Monty's small brain, making his face twist angrily and his lips move.

"Yes, he's certainly playing you for a sucker," Cruz said.

"I was in LA," Monty said.

"Julio has the receipt from the motel he stayed at," Cruz said. "A place on Route 101."

"The Traveler's Hideaway," Monty said. He poked himself in the chest with his cuffed hands. "I stayed there. I got the receipt in Julio's name because he asked me to. He said he was foolin' around with some woman up here and his old lady was gettin' suspicious. He needed his name on the receipt so he could prove to her he been on a run."

Cruz listened and then shook his head sadly.

"I got bad news for ya, Monty," he said. "Julio doesn't have an old lady. The only girlfriend he had is now dead. Shot in the head with a .38. He's got a receipt and you don't. I think he set you up, Monty. I think he put your head right in the noose."

"You ask the desk clerk at the motel," Monty said excitedly. "I gave him money to put Julio's name on the bill, to say Julio was there, not me. That's the way Julio told me to do it because he stays there all the time and knows the guy. But you get that clerk to tell the truth and you'll find out."

Cruz nodded.

"You're not too smart, are you, Monty?"

Monty looked hurt.

"Maybe not," he said, "but I didn't kill nobody. That son of a bitch tried to set me up."

They moved slowly in traffic heading toward Geneva Avenue. Monty sat brooding, his lips moving, his hands scratching at each other. Finally he poked the driver in the back.

"Turn around," he said. "We gotta go back the other way."

Hicks turned and glared.

"The house I was takin' ya to, they don't use no more," Monty said. "I'll take you to the real house that motherfucker's using. Up on Bernal Heights."

Cruz remembered the hill Elaine Miranda had talked about, the house where Eric Hernandez had heard the gunshot. This address in Bernal Heights could be the winning number. He nodded to Hicks and the car swung around.

Ten minutes later, Monty led them onto one of the dirt roads that cut off the eastern base of Bernal Hill and overlook the interstate and farmer's market. It was a short stretch of country road in the middle of the city, a dead end that led nowhere, one you wouldn't drive on unless you lived there or you were lost in the maze of Bernal. Monty told them to stop and pointed down the street a few doors to a dark wooden house with an overgrown lawn and beat-up trellises that had vines crawling through them, covering the house's front porch and windows from view.

"That's it," he said. "That's where I dropped the people. I picked them up Friday night and dropped them here Saturday."

"Who's in there?" Cruz asked.

"There's no cars," Monty said. "That means it should only be the caretaker, the guy who's there all the time. He don't carry any gun."

"You're sure?"

"Yeah, I'm sure," Monty said. "And maybe a few sheep in there too. Sometimes they stay a day or two. Julio charges them a fortune and they got to get out soon."

"A phone in there?"

"No phone."

Cruz, Hicks and the bullnecked agent looked the place over and decided how to work it. First they put Monty in the front seat and handcuffed him to the steering wheel, making sure not to leave him the keys.

Hicks approached the front of the house, while Cruz and the other "migra" went quietly around the side to the weedy backyard and crouched on either side of the steps that led to the back door.

From there they listened as Hicks banged on the front door, heard a voice inside the house and then Hicks's answer. Fast footsteps, running footsteps, vibrated through the wooden floor and the back door flew open. A young man with a big brush mustache, jeans and a football jersey with "69" on it came rushing out, his eyes desperate for an escape route, as if he were a running back looking for a small hole to squeeze through and dreaming of long yardage. But the play didn't work. The bullnecked agent, who had probably been a defensive tackle in his day, cut him off, lowered his shoulder and stopped him cold at the foot of the stairs. When the shoulder hit number 69, the ribs cracked. The caretaker, wrapped in the big arms, hit the ground with a thud and stayed there, sucking for breath, tossing and whining with pain.

Cruz frisked him but found no gun. They got cuffs on him and Cruz went inside. He found Hicks in a side room facing down a half dozen illegals, men, women and a child, all of them dark and smooth-skinned and all of them with the same scared eyes, like deer frozen in the beam of headlights.

Hicks was telling them they shouldn't be afraid, but Cruz could tell they couldn't understand Hicks' bad Spanish and were only getting more scared. He reassured them and then asked one of the men when they had arrived at the house. He said Saturday morning and described a man much like Monty as the driver who had delivered them. No, he had never seen anyone who looked like Saenz or Ortiz.

Cruz drifted through the rooms. They were empty, except for reed mats, which were apparently used for sleeping. In the back, he found the caretaker's room, which had a dirty mattress on the floor, cigarette butts crumpled in an empty soup can and some unopened cans of food. On the floor next to the mattress were dark stains. Cruz crouched and scraped at the dried liquid and found under the scab that it was still damp. He touched his finger to his tongue and knew it was blood.

He found the caretaker, propped on the back stairs, grimacing and trying to hold his ribs with his cuffed hands. Cruz crouched in front of him.

"I'm going to sue you guys," he said between gasps of pain.

"Okay, you do that," Cruz said, "but first tell me whose blood that is in your room, amigo."

He scowled. "There ain't no blood in there."

"On the floor next to the mattress. Who was bleeding in there?"

The other man just shook his head and doubled over in pain. Cruz took out the photo of Gloria Soto and pushed the caretaker's head up so he could look at it. Right away, he could see recognition in the man's face.

"This is who did the bleeding," Cruz said. "Right in your room, didn't she? She's dead now."

The other man stared at the photo, grimacing and shaking his head.

"You killed her right here," Cruz said.

He frowned at Cruz.

"You're crazy," he gasped.

"Maybe I am," Cruz said, "but I also work for Homicide and sometimes I put people away for life."

Cruz took out his identification and the man read it, the pain in his face deepening. He was smarter than Monty; not only could he read, he knew enough to get clear fast when he heard the word "homicide."

"She was here, but she was alive," he said.

"When was that?"

"She was here lots of times," he said.

"With Julio?" Cruz asked. "This is where Julio used to screw her."

The man nodded, holding his gut.

"Very romantic," Cruz said. "When was the last time she was here, amigo?"

The man thought, rocking with pain.

"Friday night."

"What time Friday night?"

"Maybe midnight."

"With Julio?"

The man nodded and grimaced.

"Who else?" Cruz asked.

"Another guy, I don't know his name."

"The Colonel? Colonel Ortiz?"

The caretaker shook his head.

"I don't know no colonel. It was a young guy, short, with bad skin."

He was talking about the Pit Bull.

"The two of them came with her?" Cruz asked. "And when did they kill her?"

"I don't know nothin'," the caretaker said. "They gave me some money and told me to leave. Told me to get myself a few beers, not to come back until the bars closed. That's what I did. When I got back here, they were all gone."

"And there was blood on the floor."

"I figured maybe Julio and the other dude, they had a fight. I don't know."

"Did they have guns?"

"The short guy had a gun and I know Julio carried one sometimes."

"The girl? Did she seem scared?"

"That chick was always scared," he said. "She didn't seem any different."

"How about a guy in camouflage fatigues?" Cruz asked. "When you were leaving, did you see a guy like that hanging around?"

"I didn't see anybody else," he said.

"How about a yellow car, an old Chevy?"

He thought.

"When I was coming back up from the bar, just before two in the morning, a car came from down here," he said. "I think it was yellow. A man and a woman in it. Probably screwing down there at the end of the road."

He coughed and that made him double over with pain. Cruz left him like that, with the defensive tackle standing over him. Hicks and Cruz took the illegal people to the other car, where they definitely identified Monty as their mule. Hicks called on the radio for another "migra" car to help pick up the prisoners. Cruz thanked him, said to keep in touch and headed off walking toward Mission Street. He walked quickly, with a bounce in his step and a twisted smile on his lips.

CHAPTER 19

Cruz found his car and made his way to Mission Station. He walked into the day officer's cubbyhole, nodded to Donnelly, picked up the phone and got Sally Sessions, the secretary at Homicide. He told her to find the Homicide photographer and a forensics expert and send them to the address on the flank of Bernal Heights, the murder house. He described the room where he would find the dried blood.

"Tell the photographer it's a murder scene and we want every angle," he said. "Tell forensics I need blood samples and I want them compared with the blood of Gloria Soto, the girl we found dead on Twenty-first Street."

Donnelly had stopped writing his report and was all ears.

"Yes, that's right," Cruz said. "Right in that room, and I know who did her, too. Tell the people downstairs to update the bulletin on Julio Saenz. They already have the description. Tell them now he's a suspect in a homicide, the main suspect. He should be considered armed and dangerous. He drives a red Firebird. You can get the license information from Motor Vehicles. There's another guy involved, named Carlos Ramos. Get a bulletin out on him, also dangerous." He gave her a description of the Pit Bull, thanked her and hung up.

Now that he had Donnelly's attention, he filled him in on

everything that had happened with Monty and the caretaker and what he knew about the killing.

"I think your guys should stop looking for Eric Hernandez, at least for now, and make it Julio Saenz," he said. "Saenz is out there trying to get himself off the hook by gunning for Hernandez or maybe he's just running."

"Hernandez shot a police officer," Donnelly said. "That's still a crime around here."

"But if it isn't for homicide, maybe I can get him to turn himself in," Cruz said. "I think Stacy Stoner is out there with him or—" he thought "—looking for him too, and maybe she can get him to come in."

Donnelly made a face. "Stacy?"

"That's right," Cruz said. "It will be a lot safer for her and everybody else if we don't go after him."

Donnelly thought it over, and Cruz headed for the door.

"I'll leave you to tell the captain about this," Cruz said. "I don't want him to think I'm rubbing it in."

Cruz drove to Julio Saenz's house. Again there was no car outside. He rang the bell and spoke to the same old woman with the two gods hanging around her neck. She said she hadn't seen Saenz since Sunday when she had sent Cruz looking for him at the Cantina. She looked suspiciously at Cruz.

"I tell you where he is, and then I don't see him," she said. She had it backward: In her eyes it was Cruz who was the suspect. He didn't want to say that her Julio was a killer and was probably on the run, so he didn't say anything. He left his card again and asked her to call if she heard from him.

He drove around the block and stopped at the Cantina. The front was charred and boarded over and a sign said "Closed for Repairs, Will Reopen Soon." Cruz found the door open, went in and saw Confucius sweeping up broken glass in the barroom. The ceiling above the door was charred and the mirror behind the bar cracked.

"Seven years' bad luck," Cruz said, pointing at it. Confucius grimaced, as friendly as ever.

"Seen your friends Saenz and Ramos?" Cruz asked. "I'm looking for them."

The other man shook his head.

"I know," Cruz said. "You just work here."

He walked to the back and looked into the room marked "Office—Privado." The Colonel sat at a desk that was covered with stacks of money in various denominations. Next to the desk a floor safe stood open.

Ortiz didn't look up.

"Hello, Inspector," he said.

Cruz crossed to the desk and fingered a stack of bills.

"It's a good thing they didn't get in here, isn't it, Colonel?" he said. "It would have been very costly for you."

"They did enough," Ortiz said. He sat with the money splayed before him as if he were at the dinner table and were about to eat it. "How can I help you?"

On the right wall hung photographs. In one, Ortiz stood with a middle-aged woman Cruz assumed was his wife. The woman looked nervous. In another, Ortiz stood next to a large swordfish. He was smiling, showing he had more teeth than the fish.

"I'm still looking for Julio Saenz," Cruz said. "Except now I want him for homicide."

The word "homicide" didn't have the same effect on the Colonel it had on others. It was like water off a shark's back.

"He took Gloria Soto to a drop house in Bernal Heights Friday night," Cruz said. "He shot her there and then disposed of the body. We arrested a few people and they're talking. We're also dusting the place for fingerprints to see who else might have been there."

Cruz turned and watched the other man carefully, but Ortiz showed no concern. His eyes were as gray and as cold as the safe.

"I told you from the beginning that Saenz is a barracuda," he said. "It doesn't surprise me that he killed her."

"He had some help too," Cruz said. "That pit bull that follows you around everywhere. Ramos. He was with Saenz."

Ortiz thought that over, keeping his eyes on the man standing before him, as if Cruz were a small fish who was swimming too close.

"That one is not too smart, either," he said finally. "Who knows what he might do?"

"Do you know where I can find him?"

Ortiz told Cruz where the Pit Bull lived, an address on Dolores Street, and Cruz wrote it down.

"Anything I can do to help the law," Ortiz said.

Cruz nodded.

"You seem to be surrounded by small fish who have gotten themselves into big trouble, Colonel," Cruz said.

Ortiz watched Cruz intently.

"As a former police officer, I would still like to know the motive, Inspector."

Cruz picked up a packet of twenties, flipped it and caught it. Ortiz didn't watch the money, he watched Cruz's eyes.

"Money," Ortiz said.

"Smuggling people is big business," Cruz said. "Big enough to kill for."

"Is it? I don't know, I am in the restaurant business," Ortiz said.

Ortiz sized Cruz up again, as if seeing how the green color of money looked on him.

"People, you never know what they'll do for money. All kinds of people."

Then he looked down at the money sitting between them and then back at Cruz. Cruz met his gaze and smiled maliciously.

"Some people," Cruz said dryly. "What would you do for money, Colonel? Or what haven't you done for it? Maybe that's a better question."

Ortiz's eyes narrowed. Then the older man smiled and he began putting the money into a bank bag.

"Your theories have proven correct, Inspector," he said. "Everyone else was chasing the wrong man. But you knew where to put your nets. I congratulate you."

"It's not finished yet," Cruz said pointedly. "When we catch Saenz and Ramos, who knows what they'll tell us? It could lead to bigger fish."

Even then, Ortiz showed no concern. He closed the door to the safe, spun the dial and leaned back in his chair.

"The sea is very large and very deep, Inspector," he said. "We'll see what you catch."

Cruz glanced at the photograph of Ortiz standing next to the swordfish.

"Yes, we'll see," he said.

He left Ortiz sitting there, smiling his killer smile. He climbed into his car and drove to the address on Dolores, but didn't find the Pit Bull. He went back to his office, called Donnelly at Mission Station and gave him the address. Donnelly said his men would keep an eye on the place and on the Saenz house.

Cruz also called Stacy Stoner's office just in case, but was told that for the second day she hadn't shown up for work and hadn't called in. Cruz swore under his breath.

He had better luck with Elvira Hernandez, reaching her at the Pan-American Import-Export Company.

"I have some news for you," he said.

On the other end there was dead silence.

"No, we haven't found your brother," he said quickly. "In fact, I think I have good news for you. When can I see you?"

She wanted the news right then, but Cruz said no, he had to finish a report. She said she had to work late and Cruz told her he would be at a dance place off Mission after nine.

He hung up, ripped out the old report he had started earlier and began a new one, putting the pieces in a different order.

Cruz grabbed supper at a Mexican place on Mission, treating himself to fish à la Veracruzana, smothered in tomatoes, onions and olives, washing it down with two Dos Equis.

By nine he was on the street again. A few shadows moved along the sidewalks, but in general the streets were abandoned, as if the echo of last night's shooting had just died out. The restaurants were almost empty. Patrol cars navigated the streets alone, like alligators prowling narrow canals. Cruz saw some private security police standing guard outside businesses, guns on their hips. On the wall of a government office, someone had spray-painted "Death to the Guerrillas."

At the disco he ordered a rum and Coke and then another. The place was almost empty. On the dance floor, a Latino man who Cruz recognized as a pimp was dancing slowly with one of his girls. It was her night for a little personal attention, some TLC—tender loving care. But then it was back out on the street, war or no war.

It was almost ten when Elvira Hernandez came in, dressed in a wine-colored blouse and a black skirt slit up the side. Cruz signaled to her across the spotlighted dance floor. She ordered some sort of concoction with more than one liquor and Cruz asked for another rum.

Her eyes got right down to business.

Cruz sipped the last of his drink. He was feeling all right.

"I know who killed Gloria Soto," he said. "And I know it wasn't your brother."

Her reaction was slow, her gaze shifting back and forth from one of his eyes to another, as if she was looking for a lie, a trick.

"It was Saenz or Ramos or both of them," Cruz said. "They killed her in that house on the hill. Your brother told the Mirandas about it. We have a guy who puts them both at the house with Gloria at midnight Friday and we have blood on the floor. Neither of them is around. It looks as if they're running or maybe they're trying to find your brother to kill him and still try to pin it on him."

Her eyes were still fixed on him. They had grown, as if she were experiencing an apparition, but she wasn't sure it was for real. "I've told Mission Station to stop looking for your brother," Cruz said. "He's still in trouble, but at least it's not homicide. Given that those guys maybe were gunning for him, he can plead self-defense. I want you to get in touch with him. I want him to turn himself in."

That made her suspicious and defensive again. She smelled a rat.

"How do I know you're telling me the truth?" she insisted. "How do I know you aren't making it up and that you won't just grab him and accuse him of murder?"

"Because I'm telling you, that's why," Cruz said. "The important thing now is to get him out of danger, and Stacy too. I think she's still with him. We have to reduce the danger for everyone."

He let her search his eyes again. She did it a long time and then her gaze became sly.

"You have a very sincere look in your eyes," she said. "Does that mean you're lying? You told me people who look like that are always lying."

Cruz shrugged.

"Most of the time, not always."

The waiter brought the drinks. Cruz raised his glass.

"To the capture of the killers of Gloria Soto," he said.

"If you can find them after all this time wasted," she said. She lifted her glass and sipped.

"Have you been in touch with your brother in the last two days?" Cruz asked. "Can you get in touch with him soon?"

Again she was suspicious, thinking it over carefully before answering.

"Maybe," she said, "but I don't know what he'll think. All

I can tell him is to stay in one place and wait until you catch these animals. My brother is very careful. He is used to being hunted. That I believe you doesn't mean that he will trust you."

Cruz met her gaze.

"But you do believe me? You don't think any more that I'm a predator?"

She sipped her drink and stared at him intently, as if she were deciding the issue of Cruz once and for all. Natural enemy or unexpected ally? She watched him warily, as if he were a creature that might shed its skin and allow her to see what was underneath. But she needed to know right now if he was harmless or poisonous. How close could she get?

Cruz raised his eyebrows.

"Well?"

She took a drink of her concoction and her hard gaze softened.

"Why don't you ask me to dance?" she said.

There were a handful of couples on the floor, and Cruz nodded civilly to the pimp. He took her in his arms and they danced a samba. He felt as if he were slowly taming a wild animal, feeling the tension go out of her and her body become softer in his arms. They danced through sambas, into cumbias and merengues. All the time, she was looking far away as if she could see something happening in the street.

Now Celia Cruz was singing from somewhere in the jungle and the bird of love was calling to her with its strange and beautiful cry. Celia could feel it all through her and called back to it with her own love call.

With his feet he traced the complex designs and she followed him effortlessly, knowing every move he was going to make. He led her into a turn and she pulled closer, her cheek brushing his.

"I never thanked you for saving my brother the other night," she said, "when your friend wanted to shoot him down."

Cruz shrugged, in rhythm.

"I was just playing a hunch," he said. "A kind of instinct." He looked into her eyes. "Of course, you say I don't have any instincts."

She darted a glance at him out of the corners of her almond eyes and a smile curled a corner of her thin lips.

"Maybe you do have them," she said. "Some, at least."

"I inherited them from my mother," Cruz said. "She's a witch." He told her about his mother's consultations. "She makes contact with the dead, too, maybe that's why I'm a Homicide cop. I inherited that."

She thought that over as he twirled her away and then again brought her close.

"Being able to make contact with the dead, that must be very useful in your work," she said.

"It is. I also read minds."

Her eyebrows went up and she looked dubious.

"That's why you think you know it all," she said. He squinted at her. For a moment, with that look on her face and that tone in her voice, she reminded him exactly of Alice. It was something Alice had said to him in just that way and it shook him a bit. He gave Elvira a sidelong, suspicious look, then brought her close and went into a turn.

She said: "Also, for somebody who reads minds, it certainly takes you a long time to figure things out. It seems you don't read very well."

"Some days better than others," Cruz said. "When there are the right atmospheric conditions."

She nodded understanding.

"Some days you're cloudy," she said.

"Foggy," he said. "In San Francisco we get foggy."

"I would say so," she said.

They danced. The love bird was calling to Celia. Cooing with a Latin beat.

"It must make life very interesting, reading minds."

"Sometimes," he said. "It depends whose mind you're reading."

He held her close and they turned more slowly.

"Can you read what I'm thinking?" she asked.

Cruz held her at a distance and studied her eyes, their feet moving rhythmically in place.

"You're thinking about my instincts," he said.

Her eyebrows went up.

"That's absolutely right," she said. "I'm impressed."

Cruz pulled her close and led her into a complicated turn.

"What am I thinking about them?" she asked.

"You're thinking my instincts are much stronger than you believed," Cruz said. He pulled her very close and they moved slowly, sensuously.

"That's right also," she said. They stopped moving and only swayed. "I'm very impressed," she said.

A tone had entered the voice that he wasn't expecting at all. She had lifted her eyes at him and he looked into them a long time. They were the same eyes she had turned on him the first day, animal eyes with nothing in them to hide their intention. She didn't look away. "You have a very sincere look on your face," he said.

"Yes, I do," she said.

The bird called in the jungle and Celia sighed her answer.

"I spent last night at your place," he said. "Shall we spend tonight at mine?" He had told her that whenever someone looked deep into his eyes he knew they were lying. Now she did just that, her black gaze sinking into his suggestively, a sly smile curling her lips.

"No," she whispered.

CHAPTER 20

Cruz was flying over San Francisco when the city was shaken by an earthquake and started to crumble. From way above, he watched it fall silently. His plane landed in the middle of the ruins. Buildings were destroyed, but there was no sound, no sirens, no crying. Lying in the rubble he saw a friend of his who had moved away and no longer lived in San Francisco, but was now stretched amidst the ruins. It was as if not only the city had crumbled, but also its past. His friend looked more asleep than hurt, but when Cruz tried to wake him, he wouldn't answer. Now Cruz noticed how very pale the man was, and he got scared. The friend was dead. Nearby was another body partially covered by rubble, a woman with jet-black hair strewn over the crumbled stone. He moved toward her to see who it was, but suddenly he couldn't find her. He tried to figure out where he was in the city, but could not. Landmarks had fallen and their pieces had become mixed and undecipherable. All directions looked the same. The confusion was complete. Suddenly Cruz wasn't sure if it had been an earthquake that had destroyed the city or if a war was being fought. He listened. The silence was the kind that you heard after shooting. Now he was afraid he would be attacked and killed. He headed back through the ruined city, trying desperately to locate the plane and escape. On the way he saw another friend and went toward him, but when the man turned it was someone else completely. "I'm not 'So and So,' " he said angrily. Cruz miraculously found the other passengers, who were waiting for the airplane to take off again. It had turned cold suddenly, the way it did in San Francisco, and the passengers were changing clothes. Cruz put on new clothes also, but they were lighter clothes, not warmer clothes, and he remained cold. Then a loud bell sounded and everyone watched one another, too scared to move.

Cruz's eyes opened. He was staring through the open window, but for some reason the sky wasn't visible. For a moment he was gripped by the fear of the dream. He felt cold. He stared wide-eyed into the darkness. Then he saw the sky moving, drifting. While he'd been asleep, the fog had crept in quietly, as if it were sneaking up on him. It had closed in on the house and its cold breath had filled the room. Still it wasn't the cold that had woken him or an earthquake, but the sound of the telephone shrilling in the middle of the night.

Cruz turned on the light and rolled over to the side of the bed where she had been. The pillow still held the imprint of her cheek, but that side was already cold. Some time after midnight, he had felt a kiss on the forehead and a soft hand on his chest, then something whispered and half-understood about the babysitter. No, he didn't have to get out of bed, she would get herself home. Not to worry. She would be all right.

The clock said 4:11 and the phone shrilled. In the distance, a siren howled. Even before he picked it up, he was dead certain what had happened.

"Inspector Cruz. This is Mission Station."

"Yes?"

"I'm sorry to call you at this hour . . ."

"What is it?"

"A body, sir, a woman. On top of Bernal Hill."

Cruz said nothing.

"No identification, but in her pocket they found a card with your name on it, so the sergeant told me to . . ."

But Cruz was already out of bed, his still-naked body now enveloped in a chill that reached his bones.

He turned off Mission and as he climbed the hill the fog grew thicker and colder. He drove quickly, the tires squealing on the climbing curves, sliding dangerously on the street wet with mist. On the seat next to him sat his pistol in its holster. He wanted to use it. He wanted to have all of them in front of him and empty it, one after the other, in cold blood. He pictured it. The gun flared silently in his mind.

All around him, mist moved quickly. The sky was in motion, the houses and lightpoles caught in the moving fog were also drifting. Nothing was fixed to the ground. When he got to the parking lot at the top, the red rooflights were swirling, churning the fog so that it turned like the funnel of a tornado. Cruz got out of his car, stepping onto a cloud.

A patrolman walked toward him out of the mist, but his voice sounded as if it came from the fog itself.

"She's over here, Inspector." He led Cruz into nothing. "My partner had to take a leak, saw this thing wrapped up in black plastic, took a look and there she was."

He was cutting the mist with a beam from his flashlight as they went down the grass hill toward some blurred human forms. Other flashlight beams played over a dark package lying on the ground. The Homicide photographer was there, and his flash illuminated the scene for a moment and made black spots dance in Cruz's eyes.

Everybody said hello, all friendly, as if they were at a god-damn golf game and not a murder scene. A black cop named Robinson handed Cruz the card with his name on it.

"It was in her shirt pocket," he said. "The bullet just missed it. Got her right through the heart."

He flashed the light down on the woman's face. The ground moved under Cruz's feet. He saw the too pale, too long, very dead face of Stacy Stoner.

Cruz's hands clutched, trying to grab the mist to keep from being dragged away. He crouched next to the body and stared at it for a full minute, trying to settle himself, but it didn't work. Stacy's eyes had always been her beauty and her strength, but now they were open, fixed on the moving sky, and their gaze was out of control, unhinged. As if she couldn't understand why the sky was moving, why everything was being torn out of the ground.

"It looks like she's been dead a few days," Robinson said.

Cruz said nothing. He was looking at Stacy as if she were talking to him and he were listening.

Robinson crouched next to him.

"I figure she might have been lying right there a few days," he said. "This section is fenced off and nobody comes down this way."

Cruz was looking at his own business card now. Blood had soaked through Stacy's white blouse into the pockets and had colored the edges of the card. A novelty item for a Homicide cop. All it needed was the bullethole in the middle.

Robinson frowned at Cruz.

"We didn't touch anything," Robinson said. "We've been looking around for spent shells or the gun, but there's nothing."

But Cruz wasn't concerned with that either. He didn't examine the wound, check for footprints or worry about fingerprints on the plastic. When he stood up, he didn't say a word to anyone, but stalked back up the hill, jumped into his car and squealed the tires as he sped back down Bernal busting through the fog.

He got out of the car at the first pay phone on Mission, pulled out his notebook and dialed. It was 5:00 A.M. The telephone rang ten times and then her voice came on, groggy and whispery.

"It's me," he said.

"What is it?" In Elvira's voice was the beginning of fear.

He hesitated.

"Nothing. I was just making sure you were all right. Go back to sleep," he said and he hung up.

CHAPTER 21

At nine o'clock that morning Cruz was still driving the streets of the Mission, and on the seat next to him lay the gun. He hadn't slept, eaten, bathed or shaved and his eyes had glazed over into a sullen stare. He had fallen into the old pattern from his days working in patrol cars, crossing and methodically crisscrossing the streets of the Mission until he knew he had been down every last one. He paid no attention when the sun came up or when people started emerging from their houses onto the streets. He had eyes for only a certain few. As Elvira Hernandez would say, a certain species of animal. The monotonous rhythm of the patrolling brought him under a kind of control. The turmoil in his head had slowly been transformed into a brooding single-mindedness.

He pulled over to a pay phone, called the office and was told by Sally Sessions in a low voice, "Your butt's in trouble, honey.

"Captain Lara from Mission Station called this morning and left a message for the boss all about you," she said. "He had a lot to say and none of it was good. He says you're the one to blame for the death of this woman they found last night and that you're still out on some wild goose chase looking for somebody besides the killer. He says his men saw your car two nights ago parked all night outside the sister's place and he figures you have interests besides defending the public safety."

Cruz was staring at the wall of the phone booth, from which he learned that Michael loved Maria and Fran had done it with Scooter.

"Is that true, David, about the woman?"

Cruz rubbed a hand over his face.

"Is the lieutenant there?"

"No, the chief called him in," she said, "But before he left, he told me to find you."

"That's wonderful," Cruz said. "Just wonderful. Tell him I'm working and I'll be in later. Is there anything else?"

"Yes. That red Firebird you were looking for, they found it last night abandoned, parked in back of a gas station out on Bayshore. They're doing tests this morning because they found blood in the trunk. Also you should contact Hicks at Immigration. He called a while ago."

Cruz thanked her, hung up and stared out the smudged glass of the phone booth. He was picturing Stacy Stoner jackknifed in the trunk of the Firebird. He stayed that way several minutes, slumped in the booth like some drug casualty.

Then he called Hicks.

"Your information worked out for me yesterday," Cruz said. "Thanks."

"I'll use you as a reference," Hicks said dryly. "I think I have something else for you."

"What is it?"

"Maybe I have it wrong and it won't help you, but what was the name of the girl who was killed the other day, the one you found in the lot?"

"Soto," Cruz said. "Gloria Soto."

"That's what I thought."

"So?"

"Those illegals at the house yesterday, we got in touch with some of their relatives here in the city."

"Uh-huh."

"One of them told us that in order to get his family members brought up here, he paid money to a contact person in the Mission. He said he wanted to go to Central America to visit his relatives, but the guy told him 'Why not bring your family up here, get them out of harm's way once and for all.' So he did."

"And?"

"The guy he went to, who he paid the money, had the same name as the dead girl. What was it?"

"Soto."

"That's right. His name was Victor Soto, that's who the relative paid. A thousand dollars a person. Nice business."

Cruz found Robert Soto parked across from the Central America Travelrama, in uniform, keeping guard. He got out and gave Cruz his customary sharp salute.

"Is your father in there?" Cruz asked.

"Yes, he is, Inspector, safe and sound."

"And you're still keeping an eye out for Eric Hernandez?"

"That's right. That guerrilla will fall on this trail right here if he tries to get near him."

"That's funny," Cruz said. "There's a rumor going around that it's somebody else who's out gunning for your father. Some business partners of his."

He couldn't see the eyes behind the shades, but Robert Soto's momentary stillness was telltale. Then he smiled his incongruous smile.

"I don't know who you could mean," he said. "My father is always on the square."

"Uh-huh." Cruz scratched his cheek with one finger.

Patrolmen Rizzo and Melendez came up from behind Soto

on either side; Rizzo pinned the man's arms to his side while Melendez grabbed the gun. The dark glasses fell to the ground and the rent-a-cop looked at Cruz, his eyes fierce in his puffy face. He started to jabber at Cruz, but the two cops dragged him around the corner to the patrol car.

Cruz crossed the street, looked through the dusty window of the travel agency and saw Victor Soto hunched over his desk, as if the troubles of the whole world, every place you could fly to at least, were weighing on his shoulders. He rapped on the glass and when the man shuffled to the door, Cruz could see his eyes were redder and more wired than usual. He looked across the street and frowned at his son's empty car.

"I told your boy he could take a coffee break," Cruz said. "I'll take care of you."

Soto locked the door behind them.

"You look like you didn't sleep well last night, Mr. Soto," Cruz said, following the man back to his desk.

"I don't sleep well any night," Soto said. "So what is new?"

Cruz sat down across from the man and said absolutely nothing until the silence made Soto look up. Cruz was staring at him.

"What's new is that another woman has been murdered," Cruz said. "She happened to be a friend of mine. What's also new is that I know all about the little business you've been running out of here. And I think that's why your niece died and my friend was killed."

Soto's eyes had stopped moving, frozen with fear.

"I run a travel business," he said.

"Yes, I know," Cruz said. "I met some of your clients yesterday. Right now they're telling the Immigration Service about the personalized service you gave them. Not your ordinary tourist class, but a whole package: coyote, mule, and beautiful accommodations, sleeping on the floor of the drop house on Bernal Heights. Just one thousand dollars. It sounds wonderful. Where do I sign up to bring my relatives from Mexico?"

Soto lit a cigarette with his trembling yellow fingers.

"I don't know what you're talking about."

Cruz smiled.

"They were also telling the Immigration people about the wonderful people who served them along the way. Charming hosts like Julio Saenz and your friend Monty. Monty, now there's a guy with class."

"Smuggling people, that's Julio Saenz's business," Soto said. "I don't know anything about it."

"Yes, Julio was involved," Cruz said, "but his cut wasn't too big. After all, he's just a mule. He's not too smart, Julio. You also had to pay someone down in El Salvador to arrange things, but that didn't cost you too much, either. Local labor down there probably works cheap. The rest was all for you."

Soto's eyes looked as if they would pop out of his head and roll on the desk.

"I told you I have nothing to do with smuggling anything," he said.

"You didn't do any driving," Cruz said. "You're too nervous for that. But other skills were needed to make this business grow: marketing skills, selling technique. That's where you came in."

Soto stared straight ahead and Cruz knew he would try to cut his losses.

"People are afraid for their families," Soto said. "You don't know what can happen down there. They ask you for help."

Cruz squinted at Soto, calculating.

"What did you tell people, Soto? That their relatives would end up before death squads some day if they didn't get out quick? Is that what you said? Did you use the hard sell?"

Soto grew excited again.

"I had nothing to do with that," he yelled. "That was done down there. I don't know these thugs who went around scaring those people. I knew nothing about it until now."

Cruz looked incredulous.

"You mean someone actually was scaring these people down there so that they would want to leave the country and then you would help them leave? Is that it?"

"I didn't know that," Soto said. "I just knew I had to get my own family out. I went to them because I knew they smuggled people up here. After I paid them and Gloria and her mother arrived, they came to me again. They said it would be good if I worked with them. My customers who wanted to go down there and visit their relatives, I would tell them 'Why not bring your people to San Francisco.' If they wanted, they paid me and contact was made."

"And meanwhile your death-squad friends were scaring the hell out of people down there, putting their names on lists and getting them ready for you. Creating a demand for your product. Creating terror."

Soto was shaking his head.

"I didn't know that kind of thing was going on," Soto said. "I was just trying to help people."

"Yeah, at a thousand dollars a head," Cruz said.

"I didn't know."

"If you didn't know, who did know? Who was running it?" Who knew these death-squad people down there?"

Soto looked more scared than ever.

"It was your friend, the Colonel, wasn't it?" Cruz said.

Soto's face fell into his hands and Cruz leaned toward him.

"And your niece, Gloria, found out all about it from Saenz," Cruz said, "or from the Colonel himself. She said she saw something she shouldn't have seen and the Colonel was going to get her. It was Colonel Ortiz she saw. She saw him mixed up in all this, running it all. Then he killed her. And you helped him cover it up, the murder of your own niece."

Soto was shaking his head wildly now, as if he saw a demon coming for him.

"I don't know that he killed her. He swore to me he didn't."

"You got home that day from identifying the body and you didn't call a relative," Cruz said. "You called the Colonel. You knew he had killed her."

"He swore he didn't do it," Soto said. "He said it wasn't him and it wasn't Julio or any of their people. They told me at first they had to get rid of her because she knew too much and she was too crazy. She might say things. But I said 'no.' She was my own blood and I said they would have to kill me too and then the rest of my family. I told them I would make sure she didn't talk about it. They were afraid she would tell Eric Hernandez and his friends. I said I would tell her that if she talked to him I would send her back to our country and that would be enough to scare her."

"That was nice," Cruz said. "Back to where she had witnessed the massacre of Eric's family, where somebody would probably be waiting to kill her as well."

Soto looked helpless.

"I didn't know what to do," he said.

"You didn't know what to do, so you helped cover up her killing," Cruz said.

"No," Soto pleaded. "Joe Ortiz told me they took her there, but they didn't kill her. They let her go that night and told her to walk home and make sure to keep quiet or the death squads would get her. He said the next day, when I called him, it was the first he knew that she was dead."

"And you believed that?"

Soto's eyes were raw and he looked as if he might cry. He tried to nod yes, but his head fell into his hands and he cried.

"No, you didn't believe it," Cruz said. "You thought Ortiz

and his people had killed Gloria. You believed they might come after you, because you knew about it, and they would silence you the way they did Gloria. That's why you bought that gun and why your boy was posted outside with that .38. Because you were afraid the Colonel was going to come for you. To send his death squad after *you* this time."

Soto spoke through his hands.

"I had to do something," he said. "The business was going to hell. I had to do something. And once I got in, they wouldn't let me out."

Cruz watched the man's body shake with sobs. Then he signaled across the street to Rizzo, who came into the office.

"We're going to notify Immigration that Mr. Soto would like to make a confession," Cruz said to Rizzo. He turned to Soto, whose face was puffy with grief and, possibly, shame.

"The officer here will look after you until the Immigration men come," he said. "You don't have to worry anymore about the Colonel."

Cruz went out, got into his car and drove to the Cantina. The "Will Reopen" sign was still in place, but the door was locked and the building looked empty. Cruz drove then to the Prussia Street address he had for Joe Ortiz. He rang the bell and a dark-skinned Latin maid in a black uniform with a white lacy apron opened the door. Cruz asked for Ortiz and was told he was not at home. Through the open door, Cruz saw suitcases in the foyer. He eased his way past the maid.

In the expensively furnished living room he found the woman he had seen in the photograph in the Colonel's office, the one hanging right next to the swordfish. She was like the living room, also expensively furnished and with enough jewelry on her to start a pawn shop. She introduced herself as Mrs. Ortiz.

"I was looking for your husband," Cruz said.

"I'm sorry," she said in a heavy accent. "He left today on a business trip."

"Can you tell me where he was going?"

"He was going to New York City," she said, looking Cruz in the eye. Behind her, the maid made a face. She looked at Cruz and shook her head.

"Are you sure it wasn't south he was heading, Mrs. Ortiz? Maybe Los Angeles on his way to Mexico or maybe back to your country?"

The maid nodded her head yes.

"Oh, no," the Colonel's wife said, "Joe doesn't like Los Angeles. He likes New York. He never goes to Los Angeles."

"And what time did he leave San Francisco?"

"Oh, I don't know exactly," Mrs. Ortiz said. But the maid thought a moment and held up nine fingers.

Cruz nodded and asked if he might use the telephone. He got Irv Hicks on the line.

"Irv, a guy named Joe Ortiz left this morning for LA. He's the head of this coyote operation we visited yesterday. It was a real sweet business he had going, scaring the wits out of people down there and then charging them to bring them here. He and his buddies killed the Soto girl, so you better tell your guys to be careful. He left San Francisco International at nine this morning, probably trying to connect to further south. You should still be able to get him down there."

The Colonel's wife was glaring at him. Cruz gave Hicks the Prussia Street address.

"Mr. Ortiz's wife is here and will, I'm sure, be willing to cooperate. I'll leave an officer here to babysit her until you get here."

He hung up then, said good-bye to Mrs. Ortiz, kissed the maid's hand and left.

CHAPTER 22

The first news about Ortiz's attempted escape reached Cruz that evening. At a private airport outside LA, as they tried to hire a pilot and rent a small plane for a flight into Mexico, Ortiz and a man answering the description of the Pit Bull were spotted. A clerk delayed them and called Immigration officials, but Ortiz had grown suspicious, and as the officers approached the airport the two men jumped into their car and tried to get away. A shootout followed on the service road, the Immigration car was knocked out of commission and Ortiz and the Pit Bull escaped. Police from various departments combed Southern California hunting them.

In the middle of the night, they caught up with them. The call didn't come in to Homicide until ten the next morning.

"I have something for you," Hicks said. "Mr. Ortiz and Mr. Ramos."

"Where?"

"Right now they're in San Diego. Ortiz is in a cell and Ramos is in the hospital. He took a slug in the arm."

"What happened?"

"You're going to like this as much as I do," Hicks said. "The car was found just south of San Diego. We sent urgent bulletins to the border officials, so we knew they couldn't cross, at least not legally. We put 'copters in the air last night around midnight and they spotted them with searchlights. Ortiz and Ramos, with a coyote leading them, but this time trying to sneak back the other way. They were heading for a hole in the fence. We got them a couple of hundred yards from the border." Hicks chuckled. "I love that. The big coyote trying to sneak back the other way."

"So what happened?"

"Ortiz and the coyote threw their hands up right away, but this Ramos decided to take out his gun. They had to put a slug in him, but he'll be all right and he's been talking like a bird."

"What song is he singing?"

"That he's innocent, of course," Hicks said. "He says this other guy, Saenz, killed the Stoner woman because she knew about the operation and because she came to him and accused him of killing the Soto girl. That was Sunday night."

"That fucker," Cruz said.

"And Ramos admits he then killed this guy Saenz."

Cruz's brow stormed over.

"Saenz is dead?"

"That's right, since Monday afternoon, but Ramos swears he only killed him in self-defense. He says they had a meeting at the drop house, Ortiz got angry because of the killing of the Stoner woman, Saenz got paranoid, tried to pull a gun, and Ramos had to shoot him. That was Monday during the day. He told us where they dumped the body out in Marin. They took Saenz's car and then they dumped the car."

"Behind a gas station on Bayshore," Cruz said.

"That's right."

"How about Gloria Soto? Which one of them killed her?"

"He says he doesn't know anything about the killing of Gloria Soto."

Cruz made a face.

"Bull!"

"He says they took her to the drop house to scare her last Friday because she knew about the whole operation, the dirty work down there and up here. He says they kept her there until about one o'clock and then told her to beat it, without laying a finger on her. He said they all left there a few minutes later, him, Ortiz and Saenz, and they went to some guy's house and played poker all night. He said there were other people there, respectable citizens who can vouch for it.

"He said the last he saw her, she was alive, and he figures this Eric Hernandez must have been waiting for her at home and killed her out of jealousy."

"Unless he's lying through his teeth, which he probably is, or unless one of them caught up with her and killed her before she got home."

"Maybe," Hicks said. "I'm having Ortiz flown up here today, so you can ask him."

Hicks chuckled again.

"I wonder how much that coyote was charging them to take them back over. If he knew what they were running from, he could have made a fortune."

By the time Ortiz reached San Francisco, state police over in Marin had found Saenz's body and had sent Cruz a report. Cruz was still waiting for the results from ballistics and the blood samples.

Ortiz, his hands cuffed, sat in the Immigration offices with Cruz, Hicks, the bullnecked 'migra' and a stenographer. His gray suit was dusty and soiled. On his face, a stubble of beard had grown, a steel-gray color to match his eyes. On the wall before him, the president of the United States smiled. Ortiz didn't smile back.

Cruz sat in a swivel chair right in front of him.

"The sea is very wide and very deep, Colonel," he said, "but not deep enough."

Ortiz shook his head.

"I've done nothing illegal," he said. "You threw your net

and you caught the criminals, but me you have caught by mistake."

"So I should throw you back, Colonel? A big fish like you?" Cruz smiled and shook his head. Then he leaned toward Ortiz, so that his face was near the steel-gray stubble. "I think I'd rather have you stuffed and put you over my mantel, Colonel."

Ortiz showed his mouth full of teeth.

"I have done nothing illegal," he said.

"That's why you were trying to crawl through a hole into Mexico in the middle of the night."

"Ramos made me go with him," Ortiz said. "He had a gun and he threatened to shoot. He had killed Saenz. I found out about it only yesterday and he knew I would turn him in, so he took me."

Hicks coughed loudly and pounded his chest. Cruz shook his head.

"No, Colonel. You knew Saenz was dead Monday afternoon when we first talked. In fact, you had just come from the house on Bernal Heights where you saw him killed. Or rather, from having him killed. Then you came down and ate lunch. That's cold-blooded. When you and I talked, you were already saying Saenz had been a bad character, in the past tense, because you knew he was dead. Ramos says he killed him in self-defense, but when we talk to him a bit more, I'll bet he tells us he killed Saenz on orders from you."

"Why would I want to kill Saenz? What would be my motive?"

"Because Saenz was too stupid and too dangerous to keep alive. You knew he had killed Stacy Stoner. Eric told Stacy what he saw that night outside the drop house. Stacy went to Saenz and accused him. Saenz panicked and he killed her, wrapped her up and dumped her right up on the top of the hill. A guy who was trigger-happy and profoundly stupid was too dangerous to have around. So the Pit Bull put him away. Not in self-defense, like he says. We found the body and I

have the report. Saenz was shot with a .32, just like the gun
we took off the Pit Bull, and he was shot in the back three
times."

"He will blame me only to try to save himself and no one
will believe it," Ortiz said. "And I was not involved in any
illegal operation. It was I in the first place who told you that
Saenz was a mule."

"Yes, once you knew he was dead and that I could look for
him as long as I wanted and I wouldn't find him. That's why
you told me he was the smuggler. The Sotos were afraid the
whole thing would come down around them, so Robert Soto
agreed to lie to me about Saenz. To tell me that Saenz was
out gunning for Eric Hernandez when he knew Saenz was
dead. But Saenz didn't have the brains to run the operation
and he didn't have the contacts with the killers down there
who could scare people and bring you your customers. Your
marketing executive, Victor Soto, has told us all about it."

Ortiz's eyes glazed over.

"If we helped people come, it was for purely humanitarian
reasons," he said.

"Yes, and a thousand dollars a head," Cruz said. "It was
big money and that's why you got rid of Saenz and that's why
when I started sniffing around, you decided you had to put
me off the track and you staged that little war in the Mission."

"My place was blown up by those guerrillas, by those criminals," Ortiz said.

"You blew it up," Cruz said. "The guard will tell us that.
I'll bet on it. First you staged that scene at the funeral home,
accusing Miranda of planning to attack you. Then you blew
up your place and you sent your people to shoot up the barrio
because you wanted everyone to think it was because of politics Gloria Soto was killed. Some of the bullets came down
through people's roofs and when the police answered a call
of shooting no one was around because there never had been
a battle, just your boys making noise. Now we know it wasn't

politics, but greed that killed Gloria Soto. Your greed, Colonel."

Cruz leaned toward him again.

"You had Gloria Soto killed or killed her yourself," he said, "because she was going to strangle the goose that laid the golden eggs."

"I had nothing to do with that girl's death," Ortiz said.

"The day her body was found, Victor Soto called you up because he knew you had planned to kill her," Cruz said. "You lied to him and denied it."

"I didn't lie," Ortiz said. "I had nothing to do with her death. It was not me or anyone I know who killed that girl. I have killed no one. I made a solemn oath to her uncle that I would not let anyone harm her and as a gentleman I kept my word. You can give me a lie detector test, if you please, and you will see that I am telling the truth."

"If you didn't do it, then you had Saenz or the Pit Bull do it."

"It wasn't Saenz," Ortiz said. "Saenz wanted to kill her and he even arranged to give himself an alibi. In the end, Soto talked to me and I saved the girl. We took her to the house and scared her, but that was all. We told her to leave and she did, in good health. We all went to play cards at the house of a friend in Inglewood and many people can tell you we were there. It is just as I have told you all along, the girl was killed by the guerrilla."

There was rightousness in Ortiz's eyes, the look Cruz had seen before in criminals who were guilty of serious crimes, but became outraged when you accused them of somebody else's dirty work. The last refuge of the scoundrel.

Cruz looked at Hicks and Hicks raised his eyebrows. Cruz studied Ortiz.

"I killed no one," Ortiz said. "I left my country because I was tired of the killing."

"Uh-huh," Cruz said, and he got up. "Having people killed, Colonel, must get very tiring after a while."

Ortiz said nothing.

CHAPTER 23

The results from ballistics and from the lab came back the next morning, but by then Cruz already had a gut feeling what they would say and where it would leave him. None of the guns found belonging to Saenz, Ortiz and the Pit Bull was the gun used to kill Gloria Soto. The blood found in the drop house belonged to Saenz and not to Gloria Soto. Beyond that, the card game in Inglewood had been attended by some respectable people and the alibi for all three men stood up. On top of that, Ortiz took a lie detector test and it indicated he hadn't been involved in the killing.

In the end, Saenz had killed Stacy and now he was dead. Ortiz and the Pit Bull would be put away for killing Saenz. But Gloria Soto and her terrified eyes were still staring Cruz in the face.

He sat at his desk in the empty office and remembered other faces. Officer Klein, right after he was shot, his mouth open in a silent scream of pain. He saw Eric Hernandez standing in the photo, with the intense, deepset eyes, holding an M-16. And he brooded over Elvira Hernandez. He saw again the night they had danced together and what had come afterward, the way she had looked, the sounds she had made. He had never doubted then that it was real. What he kept seeing now wasn't that, but the look she had given him as they danced, as her voice dropped as she had let him know what she had in mind. He remembered the laughing eyes and the sly smile.

He drove to the Hernandez house. The car wasn't outside. Without bothering to knock, he walked right in. To Cruz, the place smelled of Elvira Hernandez, a strong air of vegetation trapped in the city. Playing with a doll in the junglish living room was the little girl who reminded him of the frightened Gloria Soto. She looked at him with those same big wary eyes.

Cruz controlled his temper.

"Where's your mother?" he asked softly.

The little girl shook her head.

"She's not here. She went out."

"Who's here taking care of you?"

"My grandmother," the girl said.

Cruz frowned. From the back of the house, the bird screeched. The girl's grandmother, the mother of Eric and Elvira Hernandez, was dead. Six months before and thousands of miles away, she had been gunned down by a death squad. When Stacy Stoner had described it, Cruz had pictured it as if he had seen it with his own eyes. But that was only what Eric and Elvira Hernandez had told everyone, and now maybe even that was a lie. Maybe everything from the beginning had been a lie made just for him, while her brother sank farther and farther away from him. Because, like she had told him with her eyes, you were true to your blood and not to strangers, to fools like him. Again he saw her, the laughing eyes and the sly smile.

"Where is she?" he asked. "Where's your grandmother?"

The girl pointed toward the back of the house. Cruz stalked out of the living room toward the kitchen. As he entered the doorway, he saw the woman from behind, working at the sink. She was holding a wooden spoon, stirring the contents of a large cast-iron pot. Above her, the green bananas had turned black. Gnats buzzed around them and an acid smell hung in the air. Cruz had seen her before. He recognized her right away by the black dress he had seen her wear at the funeral home and at Gloria Soto's funeral the next day. He had never talked to her, because he had never wanted to intrude on her grief. And he had convinced himself she would know nothing about the killing.

In the corner of the room, near where the bright red bird hung, the crazy old man was rocking in a chair. The bird squawked, but the man kept rocking, mouth open, eyes wild.

The little girl came up at his side.

"Is this your grandmother?" he asked.

She nodded happily.

Mrs. Maria Soto turned around and saw him, her eyes filled with surprise and alarm. They were the same eyes the little girl had, the same that Cruz had seen in Gloria Soto's face, and now that he was putting it together, the little girl's face was the same as that in the large photograph over the mantel in the Soto house. It wasn't Gloria Soto she looked like, but Ramon Soto. The woman standing before him was the mother of both Gloria and Ramon. Ramon, the dead brother who several years before had taken a machete in the back of the neck. That was the first killing and had started it all. After that death, Eric Hernandez, who had worked on the Soto plantation, had run away and become a guerrilla. It was clear to everyone that he had killed Ramon. Three years later, his family was massacred by a death squad because of his guerrilla activity. Hours after that, revenge was taken on Gloria's father, who had led the death squad to the house. He had been shot in the head. Gloria had run to San Francisco trying to survive, but she hadn't escaped. The killing had gone on. First Gloria herself, then Stacy Stoner, who had tried to help Gloria, and Julio Saenz, the mule who had preyed on her. And there might be more. Eric Hernandez was still on the loose and being hunted.

The woman before him had lost both her children and her husband and she had known all the others, every one of them. Cruz stared at her motionlessly as pieces moved in his brain and clicked into place. The woman was watching him, shaking her head slowly, already denying what couldn't be denied.

"This little girl is your granddaughter, Mrs. Soto," Cruz said. "Her mother is Elvira Hernandez and her father was your son, Ramon, who was killed."

The woman looked despondent. Then she spoke softly to the girl and told her to go back to her toys and everything would be all right. The little girl went out and they were alone with the crazy old man.

Cruz leaned against the refrigerator. He squinted at the woman as if deciphering the small print on a document.

"She's your granddaughter," he said, "but no one was supposed to know. Because her father was killed by Eric Hernandez, her own mother's brother. Is that it?"

The woman was transfixed. Her head was bobbing in a way that said both yes and no. Then she crossed to the table, lowered herself into a chair tiredly and let her head fall into her hands. Cruz leaned against the refrigerator, just as weary. It seemed to him that if he saw another person with his head in his hands he would just close his eyes, go to sleep, forget it all.

"You know these people, Mrs. Soto," Cruz said, "Your children Ramon and Gloria and the others whom you've known all their lives, Eric, Elvira, Dennis Miranda. Tell me what happened with them."

She was shaking her head, controlling tears.

"It didn't start with them. It wasn't the children's fault," she said. She looked up at the old man in the rocking chair, whose yellow teeth were bared in a growl. She motioned toward him. "It started with him. Long ago when he first started stealing land from people and making everyone despise him."

Her voice was not angry, but sad. The old man stared into nothing and rocked.

"How was that?" Cruz asked.

She looked into the past, shaking her head at what she saw.

"The big plantation the Soto family has today in El Salvador, they stole much of it from other people," she said. "Fifty, sixty years ago, the old man, he began making people sell their small pieces of land to him. He offered them almost nothing for the land, but if you refused, then certain friends of his in the army would come, accuse you of being a criminal or involved with subversive elements, and they burned everything down. He wasn't the only one to do that. Many of his friends made their plantations larger in that way. Stealing, so they could grow more cotton, more coffee, and sell it to the foreign buyers." She looked at him, begging for mercy with her eyes. "It was only after I married my husband that I learned about this and why the people hated them so much. The Hernandez family, Eric and Elvira's family, they lost their land that way too, and they had to work like peasants for him and his sons."

"And that's why Eric hated them and why he went after the Soto family," Cruz said.

She was staring into the past.

"My husband was the best of them. He at least tried to treat people decently. He didn't want them to kill Eric's family that day. He didn't know the mother and the children would get shot down." Tears rolled down her discolored brown cheek. She was shaking her head sadly at some ghost out of her past.

"But my son Ramon, he was more like his grandfather here. It wasn't his fault, it was the bad blood he inherited. He was my son, and I loved him, but he was mean. He wasn't good with people. Sometimes he told them that when he inherited the land he would return it to the families who had owned it. But he was only playing with them, torturing them. The people knew that. I was always worried that someday someone would get revenge."

"Did he mistreat Eric?" Cruz asked. "That's why Eric killed him? Or was it because of Elvira? Ramon made her pregnant and wouldn't admit it. Was that it?"

She shook her head and stared at the floor for a long time, as if trying to remember.

"I don't know who killed Gloria or who killed Ramon," she said finally. "My husband always said Eric killed my son and that's why he ran away. But Gloria, she told me that Eric didn't kill Ramon. The day Ramon was killed with the machete, Gloria was with Eric. They were together in secret. That's what she told me that first day. She swore to me on the cross. But later, after people knew Eric had run away and blamed him, Gloria told me to forget what she had said. That it was a lie, she wasn't with him. Still, I don't know what really happened and who killed Ramon."

"You think maybe she was telling you the truth the first time? That she was with him?"

The woman's head bobbed again, between yes and no. Cruz frowned.

"But why would she lie about it later? Why would she take his alibi away?"

The woman looked at him emptily, lost.

Cruz pushed his hand through his hair.

"And why would he run if he didn't kill Ramon? It makes no sense. Unless he was trying to protect somebody."

Cruz's face twisted in thought and his eyes moved as if he were scanning the scene of a crime for a clue he knew had to be there. When he looked at the woman again, she had begun to cry.

"Where was Elvira when Ramon died?" Cruz asked.

The woman looked at him mutely.

"Was she here or was she in El Salvador when Ramon died?" Cruz asked.

Her face was full of pain and the tears ran down the dark, creased skin. When she talked, she was like many relatives he had heard over the years, pleading their loved ones' innocence.

"Elvira, she was so sad when Ramon died, when she saw the body, her tears dried up," Maria Soto said, her fingers prodding her own swollen eyes. "She didn't talk. She didn't cry. She could only stare at him in her grief."

Cruz tilted his head and his gaze sharpened. Bad blood . . . Ramon . . . trying to protect somebody. No tears.

"So Elvira was there on the plantation when Ramon died?"

"Yes, she had come back, but . . ."

She was shaking her head at something invisible that was staring her in the face. That had stared her in the face for years. That Eric had not killed Ramon. It was the mother of her granddaughter who had done it. Elvira had murdered her son. Cruz watched her. She was trying to convince herself, but her eyes were ravaged with doubt and fear.

"It's true he treated her very bad," she said, pleading to Cruz. "Ramon, he was cruel to her. He was bad to her family." She shook her head desperately, her bloodshot eyes begging Cruz to believe her. "But he was the father of her baby. The father of her own child."

The little girl had come back into the kitchen. She stood for a moment watching the tears course down the face of her grandmother. The woman held out her arms and the girl went to her, disappearing in her brown embrace. The woman sobbed and the little girl shook with her grandmother's sobbing. Maria Soto looked at Cruz, her eyes glistening with tears.

"He was the father of her baby," she said again. "She couldn't have killed him."

In the corner, the old man rocked without pause. Right

near his ear, the bird screeched, but he didn't bat an eye.

Then the telephone rang. The woman, the girl wrapped in her arms, looked at it anxiously, as if it might blow up at any second. Cruz watched it ring a second time and then crossed, picked it up and listened.

At first there was nothing, but then he heard a woman's voice saying, "Hello." Cruz's brow furrowed. He had expected he might hear Elvira Hernandez on the other end. The voice he did hear sounded familiar, but it wasn't hers. In a moment, the woman said "Hello" again. Maria Soto and the girl watched him. The look on Cruz's face was that of a man who had lost his senses. The voice—no accent, American, thirtyish—asked, "Is anyone there?"

It was a voice Cruz recognized, the way one recognized a familiar gesture, or a perfume out of one's past.

"Yes," Cruz said. "Someone's here."

On the other end, there was a tense silence and then the voice asked suspiciously.

"Who is this?"

"Someone's here," Cruz said.

There was a gasp, excited talking, Eric Hernandez in the background asking, "Who is it?" and then the line went dead.

CHAPTER 24

Cruz didn't slow as he turned into the driveway of the yellow house with the peacock painted on the side. He hit the curb and fishtailed recklessly onto the lawn, his rear tires chewing up grass. The car came to rest half on the driveway, half off, pointed right at the house like a tank taking aim. As he jumped out of the car, he pulled his .357 Magnum. He took the stairs, tried the front door and, finding it locked, lifted his heel and kicked a spot right next to the door knob. The wood splintered, the door swung open and Cruz stepped in behind his gun.

It was pointed at her, sitting on a brocade sofa across from the window, a drink in her hand poised on the way to her mouth. A partly empty bottle stood nearby. She watched him without moving, her eyes shifting from the gun barrel to his face. Cruz saw a look he had seen before in homicide suspects who had been cornered. She had the look of someone counting her last moments. The gunsight stayed fixed on her for several seconds and then he lowered it and saw her breathe again. She sipped the drink and her gaze hardened.

"Is that the way you call on your lady friends these days?" she asked coolly. "No candy? No flowers?"

Cruz stepped by her, looking into the chandeliered dining room, the kitchen and bedrooms, but already he felt the emptiness of the place.

"Right to the bedroom. No fooling around," she called to him. "What is this world coming to?"

Cruz checked the upstairs room and then the downstairs, finding on the easel a portrait of himself on which someone had painted in black paint a set of horns, like the horns drawn in the dirt next to the dead body of Gloria Soto. Maybe Eric had drawn them, just as he had next to Gloria. Ramon might not have been his victim, but Gloria certainly was. He had killed her for betraying him, for rejecting him, for making him go crazy, for all the reasons that had caused Cruz to go hunting for him in the first place. It had all come full circle. Cruz cursed himself for his stupidity. Saenz hadn't done it. Ortiz hadn't done it. Ramon hadn't done it. There was no one else left. It had to be Eric. Cruz knocked the painting to the floor, went back up the stairs and stood before Alice, the pistol still dangling from his hand.

"Can I offer the gentleman caller some tea?" she asked.

He glared at her.

"Where did he go?"

She shook her head.

"It isn't correct to ask a lady about her other suitors."

Cruz loomed over her, his hand opening and closing on the grip of the gun.

"You're doing this to screw me," he said, "but you're going to screw yourself. This is serious."

She pursed her lips at the bitterness of the drink. She wasn't a good drinker and he could tell she was feeling it.

"It's not what I'm doing to you," she said calmly. "The question is what you're doing to him."

Cruz bobbed in front of her and she stared at the gun.

"Eric Hernandez killed a young woman," he said.

She shook her head brusquely, the way she always did, letting him know he was way off base.

"I hate to disagree with the gentleman caller, but he didn't kill anyone," she said. "He loved the girl. If you have any idea what that means anymore. It was those coyotes who did the killing."

"They killed Stacy Stoner and they killed one of their own, but they didn't kill Gloria Soto," Cruz said.

She sipped again, looked at him carefully and then patted the sofa.

"Why don't you sit down next to me?" she said. "There's no chaperone, but I'm sure I can trust you." She glanced at the gun. "You may try and kill me, but I'm sure you won't try anything really improper."

She raised her eyebrows seductively, but Cruz didn't sit.

"You've been harboring a killer," Cruz said. "Maybe you've even been sleeping with a killer."

"My Lord, that sounds exciting, doesn't it?" she asked. "But don't tell me you're jealous?"

Cruz made a face and she glared at him with the fire she got in her eyes when she was feeling righteous.

"Eric saw her killed in that house with his own eyes," she said. "He told me about it. Through the window, he watched one of them take the gun and put it up to her head and shoot. It all happened before he could move, before he could do anything to help her. He saw the shot and watched her fall. He followed them when they dumped the body, too, and saw she was dead. He told me about staring into her dead eyes, telling her how much he loved her. And the way he described it, I know he wasn't making it up. It was real as could be. During the last twenty-four hours, he told me about it over and over."

Cruz was shaking his head.

"He was lying to you," he said.

She smirked.

"Just because my husband lies to me, doesn't mean everybody does," she said. "I know when someone is lying to me."

"It didn't happen in that house," Cruz said. "The way it's built, raised up off the ground, there's no way someone outside could see through a window. If he saw it, it's because he pulled the trigger himself. He told you about it because he was feeling guilty for killing her."

She sipped her drink and looked away. Cruz loomed over her.

"He was waiting for her outside that house and he killed her," Cruz said. "He's not right in the head and he could be dangerous to someone else or maybe to himself. Maybe even to you."

She looked at him dispassionately.

"Are you sure you don't want some tea or a drink?" she said. "I hear you're drinking gin and tonics these days. I'm keeping tabs on you."

Cruz ran an anxious hand through his hair, barely keeping control.

"If he saw her killed, why didn't he tell the police?" he asked. "Why did he run?"

"Because you would have blamed him anyway, just as you're doing now," she said. "You were ready to go for the easy explanation. His sister told him that and she was right."

His eyes flashed with surprise and she noticed.

"Oh, yes, Elvira and I have gotten to be friends the last couple of days," she said. "We've talked quite a bit."

She gazed at him, calm and knowing.

"Is that right?"

"Yes, it is," she said. She sipped her drink.

In the distance a siren sounded. Cruz drifted around the room, his fingers kneading the grip of the gun. She watched him.

"You did all this just to get back at me," he said.

She thought about it.

"No, not completely," she said. "You weren't even the main reason I did it. I wanted to help him. He's a person with beliefs, with some faith. As you would say, he's a person with his head in the clouds. Just like me."

Her look grew cold and her eyes narrowed.

"Except my head isn't in the clouds anymore," she said. "I've come down to earth. I've been down to earth ever since you started screwing around on me. In fact, when you first started going out on me, I felt as if I was under the earth. I wanted to be dead and buried."

For long moments, they stared each other down while another siren sounded and then another.

"I'm sure that sounds overly dramatic to you," she said, looking away. "But it's true. For you, love is something that doesn't really exist. It isn't part of real life. It's only something that happens in the movies, and then only stupid movies. That's what I told Elvira."

Cruz frowned, and his wife turned her cold gaze on him again.

"I told her that you liked to make a movie out of it," she said. "Something that had a beginning and an end. That you liked clever dialogue, mischievous glances, you liked it to be a contest."

She paused and watched. His hand clutched and unclutched the handle of the gun. Then she looked whimsical again.

"You know, I've discovered I have a talent for the theater or the movies," she said. "Instead of a painter, I should have been a director. I told her how to act with you. I gave her the necessary motivation. I told her that in the short run she wouldn't have trouble keeping your interest. You would like the challenge of getting her into bed. That's what turns you on. That initial passion, being with someone who you don't know and who doesn't know you. It's only when somebody loves you, you can't take it. You're afraid of a woman who loves you because if you accept her love, then you can't go on thinking the world is cheap and vicious. You have to risk getting stabbed in the back. That's the way you see it. Anyway, that's what I told Elvira. And it worked, didn't it?"

Cruz's chest rose and fell with his breathing. She stared at him. In the distance there were more sirens sounding. Then she frowned and studied him as if she suddenly saw something in his face she hadn't seen before.

"Or did this one finally get to you, David?" Her eyes narrowed even more. "Gloria Soto's death and then Stacy Stoner getting killed, did it make a crack in your tough-guy act?" She studied him and Cruz stared her down. "I think it did," she said. "There's something in those eyes that's out of character. A new wrinkle. It looks like pain."

Cruz bobbed and turned away.

"You're screwed up," he said. But she wasn't listening.

"That's my luck," she said. "Just as I make my exit, you decide it's time to become a human being." She pressed her lips together and cocked her head as a thought occurred to her.

"Or maybe it was Elvira who got to you," she said. Her eyes were sad and wistful. "Maybe I was miscast. It wasn't a role for a white girl. It had to be somebody of your own blood to get into your system and to get you to care."

"You're very screwed up," Cruz said.

She nodded.

"Maybe," she said. "I have to admit I've developed a taste for vengeance." She looked away, considering something, and then back at him. "Of course, if I really wanted to get back at you, I would have slept with Eric. Or told you that I had. As your people say, I would have put the horns on you."

Cruz squinted at her coldly. He stayed that way a long time, as another siren sounded and then another. His eyes narrowed even farther, and he looked through her as if he were gazing at something small and far away. He squinted hard and finally brought it into focus. He looked at her.

"Did Eric tell you he was the one who drew the horns in the dirt next to Gloria's body?"

She didn't answer and watched him cautiously. His face was twisted with thought. Behind his eyes, connections were being made.

In the distance, there was a sputtering, like a short string of firecrackers. Another siren sounded and she followed it with concerned eyes. Cruz, too, was looking toward the noise. Then again the sputtering. She ran out the door after Cruz, but he was already in the car and the wheels were in reverse, flinging up lawn as if a bomb had gone off.

CHAPTER 25

When the time came to die, you had to have the dream clear in your mind. When the goddamn bullets were flying at you, you had to transform yourself into an idea. Then they could pass right through you and not hurt you. In the mountains that's what you told yourself when the soldiers had you trapped and it looked like you would die. Bullets didn't kill dreams. They didn't even scratch them. They only made them free to float in the air and be breathed in by others who would fight.

He had begun thinking that way the moment he had seen the police car stop and the two *guardia* get out with the guns on their hips. He had fired the M-16 right through the bag. The bullets had hit the car and the two *guardia* had gone flying for cover. In the street, the gunfire had echoed everywhere and people had run and screamed.

He'd dodged into the nearest house and the women and children there had gone running out, afraid. Now he was alone inside the house and the *guardia* was outside. They were preparing his death.

He went to the edge of the window and saw them moving behind the cars, preparing their attack. In the sky, a half block away, he could see the cross of the church drawn on the blue sky. He had almost reached it before the *policía* came at him.

Back home, he would have made it, but here he knew he would fail. This was their jungle.

He aimed the M-16 through the window but up at the sky, fired a burst and watched them scramble behind the cars like ants. He slid down the wall next to the window and waited for the return fire, but it didn't come. These *policía* were smart, they didn't waste bullets and they didn't give away their positions.

From his seat on the floor, all he could see out the window was the top of the church and the cross. In the end, it was like the priests said. You never died. There was no death. But you didn't go up to heaven like they said. You lived in people's minds. When people mentioned him later, his *compañeros* would say, "Eric Hernandez lives." Even though he was far from them and from the mountains, they would say that. For they were fighting for their own people and he was fighting for his. In the end, you fought for your own family, your own blood. You avenged them, for them you died. In the end, what was real was the anger you felt for what had happened to them.

From above him came a thumping sound and he knew the *policía* had fallen onto the roof of the house. He aimed the barrel of the M-16 up and fired a burst through the ceiling. Plaster fell, and splinters, and he heard scrambling up above. Then there was quiet. He kept the rifle pointed at the staircase, but no one appeared there. Not yet.

Outside, more sirens sounded. They were still arriving, preparing to come after him. He waited.

He was propped against the wall, and across the room a television was playing. He looked and saw a man and a woman embracing on the color screen. They were white people, expensively dressed, like in the movies. For a moment he felt his body. He felt his desire again. That was real too. Gloria had been real.

He looked away from the people on the television. What he wanted was for his body to disappear, to feel like air, to become the idea. To become an instant of history, like his *compañeros* said, a small piece in the machine of history.

Outside, he could hear the voices calling, the radios crackling, more sirens, and he wished, at least, it had come in the mountains, in his own jungle. There, after he died and the dream left his body, his *compañeros* would bury him right in the mountain and he would become part of it forever. That's what he was born for.

Suddenly there was silence outside, and just as in the mountains when the insects and birds fell quiet, he knew that was when they were coming.

CHAPTER 26

When Cruz got to the scene, he didn't see her.

What he saw was a whole block just off Twenty-fourth Street that had been transformed into a battleground.

The streets were cut off by patrol cars and he had to park at a distance. Coming toward him were residents who were being evacuated before the firefight broke out for real. He saw at least a dozen patrol cars, SWAT team vehicles and police ambulances. Cops were running to positions, wearing bullet-proof vests and helmets, holding shotguns, automatic weapons and tear gas rifles. On top of buildings all around, more men were perched holding sniper rifles with telescopic sights, all trained on a quiet white house in the center of the block. In the air over the next block, just behind the house, a police helicopter hovered. It was as if the United States Army had invaded the Mission to get Eric Hernandez. For one insane moment, Cruz envisioned the entire barrio going up in flames.

Just inside the police cordon, Cruz found Bill Clarke. He held a missal in his hands and was staring down the block as if looking at the scene of an accident and waiting his turn. He glanced up at Cruz, looking confused and angry.

"His sister came to see me," he said. "She told me she was going to bring him to the church. And then all of a sudden the shots rang out." He shook his head, annoyed. "He waited so long, why couldn't he wait a few minutes more? Why did he have to do something stupid and violent?"

"Where is she?"

The priest pointed toward several patrol cars parked in a driveway out of sight of the house and out of the sight of Eric Hernandez and his M-16. As Cruz approached the car, which was surrounded by cops, he heard her voice. It was an angry, tortured sound, crying and at the same time so hoarse it sounded like a growl. He found her locked in the backseat of a patrol car behind the metal grill, like a caged animal.

As soon as she saw him, she fixed on him with ravaged eyes in which he could see hope suddenly shine. She put her face up to the grill and her voice was a whisper and a low growl.

"They're going to kill him," she said. "Tell them he didn't kill anyone."

Cruz watched her as if she were really were a rare, talking animal.

"Didn't he?" Cruz asked.

She looked deep into his eyes. "He didn't kill anyone," she said. "Tell them it was me who killed Gloria. Tell them anything, but don't let them kill him."

Her eyes were filled with an animal grief.

It happened then. First there was a shout that made all the helmeted police stop and look at the quiet white house. Then from behind the house there was a sputter of fire, a pause and then a deafening fusillade that seemed as if it would tear the whole block from its foundations. It lasted possibly ten seconds and then it ended, leaving profound silence. The house still stood, as if by a miracle.

Cruz ran down the block, up the stairs, through the house, by the television which was still playing and into the backyard, where he found Eric Hernandez. Several helmeted police holding automatic weapons were standing around the body, which had fallen into a garden. Eric Hernandez was splayed face down, hands gripping the dirt like claws, trying to burrow into the earth.

A young cop said: "He walked out as if he'd just woken up and was looking at the day. Like nothing was wrong. I told him to drop the gun and he yelled something back at me. Something about dreaming. Maybe he said, 'You're dreaming.' I don't know. Then he started to shoot."

Medical personnel and police closed in on the body. Lara was there and Cruz could feel his eyes on him, but he edged away.

He went back to the police car. He slipped into the front seat and looked at her through the grill. Her fingertips were bloody where she had broken her nails clawing at it. Her dress was spotted with the blood and her face was swollen with anger and grief. But she was quiet, as if they had finally tamed her.

She looked at him sullenly.

"Let me go back to my child," she said. "They killed my brother and now she's all I have. I should be with her."

Cruz stared at her motionlessly for two minutes. Outside the car, policemen moved, loudspeakers crackled and sirens sounded. When he spoke at last, his voice was tired and matter-of-fact.

"Four years ago, you killed Ramon Soto," he said.

She frowned at him, but he shook her off tiredly and went on.

"You lived up here a long time and then one day you decided to go back. Maybe you went back to be with your family or to find your roots. I don't know. But what you found back there was Ramon Soto. You hadn't seen him in years. He was from a family that was the enemy, but he seemed different. He even used to talk about inheriting all the land someday and giving it back to the families who really owned it, including your family. He was good-looking, charming and educated, and after San Francisco every other man in that village must have seemed small-time and a bore. For all I know, you had been in love with him since before, just as Eric was with Gloria."

She watched him carefully, like a teacher listening to a student recite a poem, waiting for a mistake.

"Ramon made you pregnant," Cruz went on, "and when you let him know, he told you it was your tough luck. From what I hear he was a real son of a bitch. So maybe he even laughed at you and made you good and angry. After all, you were a peasant girl from a peasant family. You were helpless and you had no recourse. You were out in a field when he told you, no one else in sight. When he turned around, you grabbed a machete and buried it in his neck."

Her eyes narrowed, and her gaze was sharp and pitiless.

"Ramon Soto was the lowest of animals," she said. "He preyed on people's hopes and needs. He was worse than a snake. He belonged beneath the earth where he ended."

"Where you put him," Cruz said. She met his gaze without remorse. "But that happened down there and really isn't my case," Cruz said.

The radio in the patrol car crackled like the tension between them. Cruz gazed out the window.

"After you killed Ramon, you ran away and found your brother. He had sneaked off somewhere with Gloria. You told him what had happened and right then he decided to take the rap for you. Eric was always noble, always good. He ran away. He even told people he had killed Ramon because Ramon mistreated everyone. Gloria, meanwhile, had told everybody it couldn't have been Eric because she was with him when her brother was killed. But nobody believed her, because your brother was on the run and had joined the guerrillas and was even confessing to the killing. Gloria didn't know what was going on. She probably started losing her mind way back then."

Elvira Hernandez was staring out the window as if it were a window into the past.

"My brother was a hero," she said. "I told you that from the beginning. I also told you the Sotos were no good. I told you the truth from the beginning."

Cruz looked at her skeptically and glanced away.

"Gloria and Eric still saw each other sometimes when Eric came out of the mountains," he said, "but last year her father found out Gloria was going to meet him and he sent the death squad instead. You lost your family, and your hate for the Sotos grew even deeper, as deep as could be. As deep as anybody's hate could be. A couple of weeks later, Gloria Soto showed up here. You figured that, ultimately, it was because of Gloria that your family was dead. If Eric hadn't been involved with her, the rest of your family would still be alive. She was a foolish, half-crazy little girl."

"Gloria knew what she was doing," Elvira said icily. "She acted crazy, but she knew."

"Then Eric showed up and he was still in love with Gloria Soto," Cruz said, "but she wouldn't have anything to do with him. They'd convinced her he had killed both her brother and her father. She was with Eric when her brother was killed and knew it couldn't have been him. But she had become so unhinged she no longer knew what was real and what wasn't. But you did know. You knew that Gloria was driving your brother crazy. You tried to tell him Gloria and all the Sotos were no good, but he was still in love with her. He started acting more and more disturbed, dressing like a guerrilla, following her around. You knew if he got picked up he would be deported and end up back in the war down there."

She suppressed a laugh and shook her head at him.

"That shows how little you know about my country," she said. "If they deported him, a person with a guerrilla history, they would take him off the plane and shoot him right at the airport."

"Even worse," Cruz said. "That gave all the more reason to keep him out of trouble here. And Gloria Soto meant trouble. Then came Friday night. Saenz, Colonel Ortiz and the rest of the crew had decided to scare Gloria. They wanted to kill her, but Victor Soto wouldn't go along. Still, they didn't want her talking to Eric at all anymore."

Elvira Hernandez's head snapped up and her eyes flared.

"They were going to use her to kill him," she said. "They told her they wouldn't kill her, but they knew Eric was crazy for her and they were going to use her to trap him and kill him."

"Maybe," Cruz said. "Or Eric would commit suicide over her. Who knows? He was suffering enough. But that night he was following her and he was outside the drop house on Bernal Heights. When Ortiz and the others finally told Gloria to get lost, Eric was outside and picked her up. The caretaker coming back from a bar nearby saw the car go by and thought it was two lovers. But they weren't two lovers exactly. They were two kids, completely wigged out, trying to make sense of the world by looking at each other. Both of them had seen their lives shattered and when they tried to put them back together again, they came out all wrong. Each had reason to be afraid of the other, to be afraid of everything around them. That's why Gloria called Stacy Stoner's house. They needed help right away. But Stacy wasn't there. If she had been, Gloria wouldn't have died, at least not that night. They couldn't find Stacy. So Eric brought Gloria back to your house."

Her eyes narrowed now and he knew he was right.

"Eric was in pain. You saw it and felt it," Cruz said.

"He wanted to kill himself," she said. "For what? For nothing. For that stupid little girl."

"For a member of the Soto family," Cruz said. "That must have made you mad. Maybe he told you what he had heard outside the drop house. If he heard that, instead of killing her, they wanted to use her to kill him, that gave you all the more reason to get rid of her."

She was tensed but completely still, like a large cat sensing danger nearby.

"You killed Gloria that night in your own house. I send lab guys in there, I bet they find spots of blood you missed; maybe even the gun, hidden away," Cruz said. "You did it, because Eric was incapable of killing her. Just like you said the first time we talked, he would die before he would hurt her. But not you. You hated the Sotos with all your guts. You were natural enemies and sooner or later they would come for you too.

"You convinced him that night that Gloria would have let herself be used to kill him," Cruz said. "Or maybe he knew you were all he had left. But that night your brother decided it was him who had to run away. Again, you were the one who killed and he was the one who took the rap. He even went back to where you two had dumped the body and scratched the bull next to her body and drew attention to himself. He was the only one it could have been."

Cruz wiped the sweat from his face. She watched him with glistening eyes and said nothing.

"Then you started covering it all up," Cruz said. "You knew enough about what had happened at the drop house that you tried to lay it all off of Saenz and his friends. You were the one who pointed me toward them. You were the one who told me about Saenz for the first time and about Ortiz. But you were also trying to make me think you were covering up for your brother, that you were protecting him, because that's what I would expect you to do. When all along, it was him protecting his sister, just like the first time."

Cops were coming back from the house toward their cars, some with helmets off. Units were starting to pull away.

"And in the end you tried to tell these people it was you who killed Gloria Soto and nobody would believe you," Cruz said.

Elvira Hernandez, looking through the metal grill, didn't take her eyes off Cruz.

"Maybe they won't believe you, either," she said. "My brother is dead, so how can you know that's what happened?"

Cruz watched her.

"I know it's true because of my instincts," he said.

She looked deep into his eyes.

"My brother is dead," she said. "As far as they're concerned, the police have their justice. They don't want to believe me. You are the only one, just like always, who wants to believe something different."

She deepened her gaze, like tightening an embrace.

"Is it because you think I didn't really want you? That I only used you?" He looked at her now and she searched Cruz's eyes. "It wasn't that way. Before, I told you things, but that was only because my brother needed me. Without me, I don't know what he would have done. He's dead and now I have no reason to lie. And I wouldn't lie about something like this. Believe me." Her gaze delved into his eyes even farther. "Or are you afraid, the way you were with her?"

Cruz looked through the grill deep into her almond eyes for a long time. So long they both seemed to have stopped breathing. Then he ran his hand through his hair and shook his head wearily.

"That doesn't matter," he said. He shook his head slowly, without taking his eyes from hers. "Maybe, it's like a friend of mine says, you're one of the victims. Down there in that jungle your enemies hit you first. Sixty years ago they ripped off your family's land and that started it. Maybe people like Ortiz have the game fixed down there and they do what they want and get off clean. I don't know the place, but I've seen enough the last few days that I can believe it."

"That's the way it is," she said. "You know that. They left us with nothing except the rags on our backs and they made us work for them on land that really belonged to us. You expect us to go generation after generation abused by those animals and do nothing to avenge our blood."

He nodded absently.

"And if it was just animals like Saenz or Victor or Ramon Soto maybe Ortiz showing up dead, that would be something else too," he said. "They prey on people and when they get killed, cops up here might figure it was just some other animal who did the killing. It's part of nature. You look for the killers, but only among the other animals. If it was Ortiz or Saenz or Soto you killed, I probably would never have seen you."

"Is that what you wish, that you'd never met me?" she asked. She tilted her head and a sly smile crossed her lips. "I don't think so," she said.

Cruz thought about that under her intense gaze, and then she said to him: "We're the same, you and me. We understand each other. We live in the same kind of world and we both know what we have to do to survive."

Cruz studied her through the mesh and then nodded.

"I understand a few things about you," he said. "I understand how you killed her. At least, I think I do. I understand you were protecting your own when you put the gun to her head. I understand it was one of your instincts acting on you, to not let the Sotos get your brother. To help him survive, by killing her."

Cruz watched her through the mesh.

"But that's not the way it works here," he said. "This is a different jungle. Here you learn different instincts. Up here I can't let a girl like Gloria Soto get shot and let the killer walk." He slowly shook his head. "I can't do that. She wasn't a killer, she was a victim. And she didn't deserve that bullet in the head."

He squinted as if, from a distance, he were watching the shooting. She was perfectly still, rapt in disbelief.

"I can't," he said, looking into her eyes. "No matter what happened that night, I can't change my stripes or this place. Up here maybe there are people too who don't pay the way they should. But that's not the way it's supposed to be. As far as I'm concerned, in this jungle everybody pays," he said, his voice becoming deliberate. "You . . . me . . . everybody."

Behind him the radio issued a squawk and a metallic scratching. He watched through the grill as the hope slowly faded from her almond eyes. Then he took a deep breath, got up and went looking for Captain Lara.